"I WANT SOMETI

Sara looked where he pointed, to a patch of brilliant mauve in a sea of gently waving grass.

"They flower here every year. I keep it a secret because I don't want people trampling all over them."

"I'm glad you showed me," Sara said softly. "They're glorious."

Cal snapped off a single orchid and held it out to her so that she could see the complexity of the lipped, ragged petals. "This is for you," he said simply.

She stood still, scarcely breathing as he tucked the flower in the tangled curls above her ear. Then she lifted her face, watching the expression change in his eyes before he closed them and placed his lips gently on hers.

Suddenly the world became nothing but the touch of Cal's mouth and a delicious, sun-warmed happiness.

ABOUT THE AUTHOR

English by birth, Jocelyn Haley now has her roots firmly planted in the soil of Canada's Maritime provinces, where her seventh Superromance, *Drive the Night Away*, is set. A prolific author, Jocelyn has written numerous romances, as well as a mainstream novel.

Books by Jocelyn Haley

DREAM OF DARKNESS

HARLEQUIN SUPERROMANCE

11–LOVE WILD AND FREE
31–WINDS OF DESIRE
54–SERENADE FOR A LOST LOVE
88–CRY OF THE FALCON
122–SHADOWS IN THE SUN
217–A TIME TO LOVE

HARLEQUIN PRESENTS
writing as Sandra Field

905–ONE IN A MILLION
977–AN IDEAL MATCH

HARLEQUIN ROMANCE
writing as Sandra Field

2577–THE TIDES OF SUMMER

Jocelyn Haley
DRIVE THE NIGHT AWAY

Harlequin Books

TORONTO • NEW YORK • LONDON
AMSTERDAM • PARIS • SYDNEY • HAMBURG
STOCKHOLM • ATHENS • TOKYO • MILAN

Published April 1987

First printing February 1987

ISBN 0-373-70254-X

Printed in Canada

To read and drive the night away...

Chaucer
The Book of the Duchess (1369)

CHAPTER ONE

THE SUN WAS SETTING in stately, immodest splendor. Gradations of coral, fuchsia and purple hung over the lake and were faithfully reflected there in a melodramatic display that Sara regarded with as much satisfaction as if it had been arranged for her benefit alone. The line of trees on the far shore was as black and jagged as the teeth of a witch. The cackle of a loon echoed from a nearby cove.

Sara gave a pleasurable shiver. She loved the slow, mysterious summer evenings that so reluctantly relinquished their light. She loved the lake. She never felt as if she had arrived in Haliburton until she had perched herself on this weatherworn rock shaped like a bear and filled her nostrils with the miasma of spruce resin, mud and still brown water.

She had driven here from Halifax after a hasty and indigestible supper at a fast food place. The lease on her apartment would terminate at the end of the month, her furniture was in storage in Ally and Pete Naseby's basement, and her car was bulging with the rest of her belongings. She was in transit. Again.

She hugged her knees to her chin, deciding not to follow that train of thought, and instead allowed her mind to dwell contentedly on the welcome that would be awaiting her at Cornelia and Laird's. Cornelia was her elder sister, married to Laird Fraser and living in a comfortable two-story house overlooking the Coates River in the village of Haliburton, about five miles from the lake. Sara, who preferred to term herself in between jobs rather than unemployed, was to live with them for the summer. She squinted at her watch in the gloom. Cornelia would be expecting her. She'd better go.

Sara stood up, stretching the ache from her limbs. Since seven o'clock that morning she had packed books, clothes and dishes, lugged the loaded cartons down to her car, helped her friend Pete maneuver the heavier furniture into the truck, scrubbed floors, dusted drawers and cleaned windows. At the age of twenty-five she was an expert on the trials and tribulations of moving and had realized some time ago that practice did not lessen the accompanying stress. She was cherishing the hope that she might be able to stay in Haliburton in the autumn, having put her name in for substitute teaching several weeks ago; according to Laird her chances of winter employment were good. She very much wanted to stay in Haliburton, and not just to avoid the trauma of another move.

In the sky the fuchsia had faded to an inoffensive pink, the coral to a soft, limpid gold. Vowing that she would be swimming in the lake before the week was up, Sara turned her back on it and walked toward the car, her sneakers rattling the stones. Then they were crushing grass underfoot, and the thorns of the wild roses were snagging her jeans. Behind her the laughter of the loons wavered across the water. It was a sound Sara had known for many years, and she was long familiar with the sleek, tidily patterned black-and-white birds whose cry was like that of the insane. They were schizophrenic birds, she had long ago decided, masking their wails of unbearable loneliness under neat, efficient exteriors.

Shivering in earnest, for the air was chill now that the sun was down, Sara folded herself into her car and pushed the heaped-up clothes away from the handbrake. *Time to go to Cornelia's,* she told herself firmly. *Time for Cornelia's steady affectionate smile and Laird's deep laugh. Enough of the laughter of loons.*

She drove slowly along the dirt road, trying to avoid potholes. She already passed the north shore of the lake, cottage country, with yellow lights and strings of Chinese lanterns shining through the trees and radios blaring from wooden verandas. But this side was much more sparsely populated. The forest pressed to the ditches and the narrow ribbon of road bravely held it back. The first stars pierced the night sky like bullet holes. She wound up a hill, following the bend in the road, and suddenly slammed on her brakes.

In the white glare of the headlights the tableau was momentarily transfixed: a slender-legged doe, a spotted fawn and a dog, crouched, snarling.

The fawn was halfway down the ditch. The flanks of the doe were heaving, her brown fur patched and streaked with sweat. The dog was a German shepherd. A frayed piece of rope hung from its neck.

The dog made a sudden lunge toward the fawn. The doe snaked out its cloven hooves. Sara hauled on the hand brake and leaped from the car, her yell of outrage splitting the shadowed silence of the woods. She grabbed a rock from the side of the road and fired it at the dog. More by luck than judgment—for it was no accident that Sara had never been selected for the high school baseball team—the rock struck the dog on the hip. Its head swiveled, the lips drawn back, the pointed yellow teeth gleaming.

Sara stood her ground. "Shoo!" she said foolishly, her heartbeat almost drowning out the sound of her own voice. Then, more firmly she added, "Go away!" She reached for another rock.

But the dog had lost interest in her. Belly low to the ground, ears laid back, it began edging closer to the deer. The doe backed away, her hooves sending stones tumbling into the ditch in miniature landslides. The fawn had collapsed on its knees.

Sara's second rock went wide, clunking against the trunk of a tree. Frantically, her eyes searched the ground for a stick or a broken bough that she could use as a weapon. *Nothing.* She picked up another rock, a heavier one this time, weighing it in her palm, and heard from her car radio the incongruous, cascading rhythm of a harpsichord. It galvanized her to yell again, a yell with all the power of her lungs behind it.

The dog leaped for the doe's throat. Sara had the presence of mind to give another bloodcurdling screech as she flung herself forward, her fingers grabbing for the rope around the dog's neck. With the clarity of extreme fear she saw the matted fur on the deer's neck, the terrified, long-lashed eyes and the graceful curve of its ear; she also saw the knot in the rope and heard the snarl deep in the dog's throat. She grabbed the rope and with all her strength yanked backward on it.

Its breathing cut off, the dog fell on top of her. As her hip hit the dirt, the gravel bit into her flesh. She could smell the dog's fetid breath; its eye was red rimmed, the center as cold and yellow as a wolf's. She heard the dog snarl again. The gaping jaws struck at her throat.

She warded them off with one arm, beating at the black nose with her fist, and heard whimpering that she only later realized came from her and not the dog. She tried to roll over, to bury her face in her arms, felt claws ripping at her ribs and the stinking weight of the dog smothering her.

Then, suddenly, the weight was gone. Dimly, she heard a yelp of pain, then silence.

Her eyes had been squeezed tight shut. As she opened them, her body still cringing into the ground, a man's voice asked roughly, "You okay?"

Because he was between her and the car, his face was in shadow. In her overwrought state he looked huge, hovering over her like...like a vampire, Sara thought, wondering if she was going to faint, wondering if she had exchanged one danger for another, wondering how the dog had vanished so dramatically. Feeling her breath flutter in her throat like a trapped bird, she pushed herself upright. The two deer were still in the ditch, the doe with her head hanging and her sides trembling.

When Sara spoke, her voice sounded like that of a woman standing thirty feet away. "Are they all right?"

"Yeah. I'll turn off the headlights. They won't move as long as those are on."

"Shouldn't we see if the fawn is hurt?"

"No. You mustn't touch it. If you do, the mother will abandon it." He turned away from her, loped to the car and turned off the ignition and the lights. The scene was plunged into darkness and a thick silence.

Sara scrambled to her feet. She was trembling. "Where's the dog?"

"Don't move so fast—I don't want to scare the doe any more than she's already been scared."

"You didn't answer my question," Sara said, her voice quavering. "What happened to the dog? Did it run away?"

"The dog won't be going anywhere," the man said with a certain grim satisfaction.

"What do you mean?"

"Its neck's broken."

"*You* broke its neck?" Sara whispered, horrified.

"I pulled it off you and threw it over into the ditch. Just bad luck that it struck a rock."

"You're not the slightest bit sorry!"

"No, I'm not sorry." He advanced on her. "I already asked you . . . are you okay?"

He *was* huge. A good six inches taller than her own five-foot-ten and broad to boot. Sara took a step backward, wishing someone else would come along, and began sidling toward her car. "Yes, I'm fine," she said tremulously.

"Look, I didn't mean to kill the dog." His voice gentled. "And I'm not meaning to scare you now."

"I'm not scared," she lied.

"Sure you are, you've had a bad fright. Look, why don't you come to the house for a few minutes? I'll make you a cup of tea—or something stronger if you want it. I live just round the corner. I was out getting some wood when I heard you shout—and a lucky thing I did."

Sara turned away from him, fighting for control, and saw against a rough-edged boulder the dark shadow that was the dog's crumpled body. So the man had been telling the truth. The dog was dead. And he had killed it.

Behind her was only silence. She took several deep, slow breaths, her arms taut by her sides, and tried to think rationally about what had happened. The dog had been vicious. Unquestionably so. It had not been playing parlor games with the two deer, a nice little game of tag for fun. It had been stalking them to kill. And this man, whoever he was, had prevented that from happening, and in doing so had rescued her from a potentially very dangerous situation.

Slowly she turned around. She had stopped trembling, although she still felt distressingly light-headed. Holding out her hand, she said, her voice almost normal, "My name's Sara Deane. If your invitation's still open, I'd love a cup of tea."

The pressure of his hand was firm and brief. "Cal Mathieson. It's a three-minute walk. Want to leave your car here?"

"I guess so—there's so much stuff in it I wouldn't have room for a passenger. I'll just get my purse."

As she moved toward the car, the doe nudged the fawn to its feet. Sara stood still. The doe scrambled across the ditch and up the other side, the fawn trotting at her heels. With uncannily little sound the two animals disappeared into the trees.

"I'm glad they're safe," Sara said quietly.

"They wouldn't have been if you hadn't come along. I know that dog. It belonged to Percy Gillis. It was known as a deer killer. But I've never been able to catch it in the act."

"Oh." Sara shivered. "Then I suppose it is better off dead. And maybe I owe you an apology."

"A pack of dogs after a deer isn't a pretty sight. Happens around here more than it should."

Sara took her purse from the seat, locked the car and said uncertainly, "You won't just leave the dog there, though?"

"I'll give Percy a call from the house."

He led the way across the road, which continued its curve to the left. In a couple of minutes Sara saw the glow of lights among the trees. A wooden sign hung from a post by the side of the road. "Cal Mathieson," it announced. "Fine Furniture."

"I've heard about you!" Sara exclaimed. "You made a pine table and chairs for my sister."

"Who's your sister?"

The grass along the edge of the driveway was soft under her feet. "Cornelia Fraser."

"Mrs. Fraser's your sister? You don't look alike."

Cornelia was shorter than Sara, dark haired and placid by temperament, whereas Sara had a cluster of short, flaming red curls and frequently got into trouble because she acted first and thought afterward. "Cornelia says we should switch names. She looks more like a Sara and I should be called Cornelia," Sara explained.

Cornelia had talked quite a bit about Cal Mathieson, the big blond carpenter who lived alone in the saltbox house that had been left to him by Dougal Munroe, the cabinetmaker to whom Cal had been apprenticed. "He lives like a hermit," Cornelia had said of Cal. "Never dates, never gets drunk at the tavern, never goes hunting with the boys." She had run her finger over the smooth curve of a ladder-back chair thoughtfully. "But he certainly makes beautiful furniture."

Having now placed Cal, Sara had lost any qualms she might have entertained about following a strange man to his house after dark. Healthily curious, she let Cal usher her in the back door, which opened into the kitchen. As he flipped on the light and filled the kettle, she had her first good look at her rescuer.

She had already seen that he was tall and broad of shoulder. She now added to her description a thatch of untidy blond hair, guarded eyes as gray as summer storm clouds and a disconcertingly strong chin; she was not sure she would care to argue with the owner of that chin. He was wearing well-worn jeans, work boots and a checked shirt, and if he was flustered by the arrival of a strange young woman into a life that apparently did not include any young women, he did not show it.

He may not have shown it; but Cal was flustered. Customers occasionally came in the back way, and Peg Campbell, his secretary-cum-bookkeeper, made coffee in the kitchen twice a day, but young women with hair as vivid as flame and level gray-green eyes did not usually find their way into his kitchen. As her eyes moved from their scrutiny of his face to an equally frank scrutiny of the room, he saw that she had a generous mouth fashioned for laughter and a generous figure under faded jeans and a sloppy multicolored sweater. He liked her height; small women made him feel oversize and clumsy. He liked the slow dawning of her smile and the way the overhead light glanced from her cheekbones and caught sparks in her hair. He liked her silence; women who giggled and bridled and blushed tended to irritate him. He found himself waiting for her to speak with a pleasurable anticipation.

The room deeply satisfied Sara. All the modern conveniences were there, including a very expensive radio playing some excellent jazz. But it was the polished pine floor, hollowed in front of the brick fireplace, the worn stoop, the trestle table and matching pine hutch that held her attention. These were objects that had been used and cherished for many generations, that were settled and rooted in time and place.

Sara, who had never felt settled in her life, turned to Cal and said simply, "It's a beautiful room. And now do you mind if I sit down? I've got mud on my jeans, so I'll sit on the bench."

Wordlessly, he made the tea, took mugs from the cupboard and poured milk into a jug. All his movements were slow but somehow economical, so that he accomplished his purpose with a minimum of fuss. He filled a mug with tea and put it on the table in front of Sara. Even though the tea was hot, she took a big gulp, rinsing the sourness of fear from her mouth. "Tea always tastes better in Haliburton than it does in the city," she remarked. "Must be the water."

He held out the pottery jug. "Milk?"

"Thanks."

But as she reached for the jug, to her surprise he circled her left wrist in his hand and said, "Hey, what happened there? Your sweater's torn. And you're bleeding."

She looked at the jagged, bloodstained rip in her sweater and at her fingers, stained dark brown around the nails, pushing back her sleeve. There was an inch-long gash on her arm, from which the blood was oozing. "I didn't even feel it," she said. "Cal, I haven't thanked you for saving me from that dreadful dog. I don't know what would have happened if you hadn't come along."

"You were very brave to try and stop him."

"Brave—or incredibly foolish."

He grinned. "Maybe a bit of both. How long since you had a tetanus shot?"

"I have no idea."

"You'd better go to the hospital. You might need stitches, as well."

She looked down at the gash again. His hand was still resting on her flesh. Her pulses did not leap. She did not feel shaken by lust as she had the first time Joel had touched her. Her brow creased. This was a strange time to be thinking of Joel Crouse, her erstwhile friend and lover, the man she had been convinced she was in love with all last winter. She had broken up with him— not for the first time—three weeks ago and had not heard from him since. Her affair with Joel had been tumultuous and exciting; nothing like the peculiar sense of rightness she felt now, the sense of inevitability, as if she had been waiting for a long time for Cal's strong, tanned fingers to encircle her wrist. "It's silly," she said at random. "Now that I know the cut's there, it's starting to hurt. And my ribs are sore, too, where the dog dug his claws in." She finished gloomily, "I've only worn this sweater twice. It was on sale. Fifty percent off."

The sweater was wildly patterned in reds, oranges and pinks, all of which clashed with her hair. Cal stifled a smile. "Maybe you can mend it."

"I hate sewing. I had the distinction of being the only girl in junior high to flunk home economics two years in a row." She brightened. "But Cornelia might fix it for me. Cornelia's very clever with her hands. Do you really think I need to go to the hospital?"

"Yes."

The firm chin was very much in evidence. "I'd better phone my sister then and let her know why I'm so late."

"The phone's by the desk."

As Sara stood up, various parts of her anatomy protested the move. Wincing, she grumbled, "Rolling around on the ground with a dog is not good for you."

When Cornelia answered the phone she heard the simple announcement, "It's Sara. I'm late."

"I was beginning to worry."

"It's rather a long story, but I've been bitten by a dog, and I guess I should go to the hospital."

"Where are you?"

"I'm at Cal Mathieson's, he came to my rescue, and—"

"I'll be there as soon as I can get a sitter."

Cornelia was using what Sara called her "head nurse" voice, a voice her sibling used only rarely but always to great effect. "There's no need for that," Sara began. But she was speaking into an empty line; Cornelia had put down the phone. "Dammit," said Sara, and plunked down the receiver. "I'm twenty-five years old, and she still persists in treating me like a five-year-old. She'll be here in fifteen or twenty minutes."

"Then I'd better call Percy." Cal moved over to the phone and dialed a number. "Percy? Cal Mathieson. There's been an accident with your dog. I'm afraid it's dead." There was a loud string of profanity from Percy; perhaps fortunately, Sara could not distinguish all the words. Cal cut in neatly. "If you want to come to the house, I'll show you where the dog is," he said, and put down the receiver as Percy launched another string of curses. "Percy's the local dogcatcher, whose own dog always ran loose," he added to Sara. "He's also the bootlegger. Accounts for why he's tolerated round here."

"I'm pretty sure Laird pointed him out to me once. He used to work at the mill, then Laird had to fire him for drunkenness. The very next night all the tires on Laird's truck were slashed—but the culprit was never found.''

"That sounds like Percy, he'll never do anything to your face that he can do behind your back. How long have you been visiting Haliburton, Sara?''

"Seven or eight years." She added disingenuously, "It's funny we haven't met before.''

"We haven't. I'd have remembered you.''

His reply effectively reduced Sara to silence. She stared down at her hands, which seemed to have picked up a fair bit of dirt from the road, and wondered who would arrive first, Cornelia in a managerial mood or Percy in a vengeful one.

She was not long in finding out. A squeal of brakes in the driveway and a banging on the back door announced Percy. He burst in the door, ignored Sara and glared up at Cal with all the bravado of a man well steeped in gin; Sara could smell it on him, a palpable presence like that of a fourth person in the room. His first sentence, when stripped of various unprintable words, was a demand for the dog.

Cal took a step backward, presumably overwhelmed by the fumes of alchohol rather than by fear. "The dog's dead, Percy, I told you that. He was chasing two deer, a doe and a fawn. This young woman tried to stop him, and luckily I arrived in time to prevent her from being seriously hurt.''

Percy's raddled, red-veined cheeks shook like the wattles of a turkey. "Who killed the dog, that's what I wanna know.''

"I did. When I threw it into the ditch, it broke its neck against a rock. I didn't intend to kill it, but I'm not sorry it's dead. That dog killed more deer than any other dog in Haliburton; you know that as well as I do.''

''It's a goddamned lie!''

''It's the absolute truth.''

Percy seized the lapels of Cal's shirt; Sara, fascinated, thought he might burst with rage. ''I'll get you for this! Killing a poor defenceless dog, you rotten bastard, you...'' Sara covered her ears, rolling her eyes ceilingward as Percy assailed the morals of Cal and then of Cal's mother in prose that she hoped was as inaccurate as it was colorful.

But Cal had had enough. He detached Percy from his shirt by the simple expedient of lifting the other man off his feet. Then he said evenly, ''Watch your mouth, Percy, or I'll wash it out with soap—and don't think I wouldn't. That young woman's got to go to hospital because your dog bit her arm. Consider yourself lucky she's not laying charges. The dog's in the ditch just before you get to her car—and don't touch the car, do you hear me? Don't lay as much as the tip of your little finger on it.''

Percy spat in Cal's face.

Without taking his eyes from Percy, Cal said flatly, ''Open the door, Sara, will you?''

Giving the two men a wide berth, Sara did as he had asked. Cal dumped Percy on the outside step, shut the door in his face and swung round to the sink, where he turned on the tap full blast and doused his head in cold water. Then grabbing the towel, he scrubbed himself dry.

Out of some strange inner knowledge Sara said, ''Your mother's dead, isn't she?''

Cal turned away to hang up the towel. ''Yeah.''

"Percy didn't really mean what he said, Cal. He was just shooting off at the mouth."

"I am a bastard. My dad never did my mum the favor of marrying her."

His shirt was splashed with water and his hair was still wet; he was carefully avoiding her eyes. She said inadequately, "I'm sorry."

He shrugged. "They're both dead now, so I don't suppose it makes much difference."

From the tightness in his face she was sure it did still make a difference. For the second time since she had stepped into the kitchen, Sara could think of nothing to say. The truck had rattled past the house; to her infinite relief she now heard the smooth purr of a car motor. Cornelia. Quiet, sane, capable Cornelia, who always seemed to know what to do and say. Unlike Sara herself, who could be guaranteed to open her mouth and put both feet in at once. Whatever had possessed her to ask about Cal's mother?

A tap came at the back door. Cal unlatched it. "Hello, Cornelia."

"Cal." Cornelia gave him her slow, sweet smile and shook his hand. Then she looked across the room at her sister. "Sara dear, what have you been up to now?"

It was by no means the first time in the past twenty-five years that Cornelia had asked that question. Their father, who had died of a heart attack five years ago, had been an ambitious man whose steady rise through the ranks in the armed forces had necessitated moves from Nanaimo on the West Coast to Summerside on the east, including various points in between; throughout these disruptions in their childhood and adolescence the two girls had forged a close friendship, allies in a world where the only constant was change. Cornelia had married Laird Fraser eight years ago and had lived in the same house in Haliburton ever since, and it was this house as much as anywhere that represented home to Sara.

Now Sara crossed the room and threw her arms around her sister, resting her cheek on Cornelia's smooth, dark hair. "Hello, Lia," she mumbled. "Great to see you."

Cornelia returned the hug, then said, "I love your sweater. Now what's all this about a dog?"

Sara grimaced. "I was hoping you wouldn't ask. And the sweater needs mending."

"I should have known. Give."

Trying to tone down its evident melodrama, Sara relayed the story of the two deer and the dog and, as she finished, reluctantly pulled up her sleeve. "Cal says I should have a tetanus shot."

Cornelia gave the wound a professional look. "And at least two stitches, I'd say. Can you drive?"

"Oh, yes."

"Come along, then. You can follow me there."

"Very well," Sara said meekly. "Will you mend the sweater, Lia?"

"If you give the kids breakfast on my morning off."

"You drive a hard bargain."

"I know you can't tell one end of a needle from the other."

"What time are the kids waking up these days?"

"Oh, not before six," Cornelia said with irritating blandness.

"If only I didn't like the sweater so much."

"You'll certainly never get lost in the dark in it," Cornelia said agreeably. "I'm just going to give the hospital a call and tell them we're on our way."

Looking for sympathy, Sara glanced at Cal. But he was scowling so ferociously that when she spoke, her voice faltered. "We'll be gone in a minute, Cal. I'm sorry I've taken up so much of your time."

He said with blatant insincerity, "It doesn't matter."

As Cornelia put down the phone, Sara picked up her purse. "Thank you again, Cal," she said awkwardly. "I hope I'll see you again sometime."

He gave her a noncommittal smile and Cornelia a warmer one, and did not suggest another meeting. Sara gave the kitchen one last desperate look, wondering how she could be exiled from a place that felt so right, and allowed herself to be ushered out of the door. It closed behind them with a decisive, metallic click.

Said Sara, not bothering if Cal heard her or not, "He could hardly wait for me to be gone."

"Get in the car, love, and I'll drive you up the road to your car. I don't suppose you feel much like walking" was Cornelia's only reply.

When both car doors where shut, Cornelia added, "He's Haliburton's most eligible and most elusive bachelor, Sara. Evey marriageable female in twenty miles sooner or later throws herself at Cal Mathieson. I'm not even sure he notices."

"So I'm not to take it personally?"

"Not unless you're interested in lost causes."

"Does he hate eveyone or just women?" Sara asked flippantly.

But Cornelia gave her answer serious thought. "I don't think he hates anyone, Sara. He's just a loner. Self-sufficient, independent, intensely private. It's a tribute to his personality that although he's radically different from the rest of the villagers, he's also accepted by them…that's not easy, you know, in a small place. If I were you, I'd forget about him.''

Cornelia's advice was almost always sound. Sara sighed. ''I'll meet up with you at the hospital,'' she said, feeling resigned.

CHAPTER TWO

ONE HOUR, a tetanus shot and two stitches later, Sara was following Cornelia into the back door of her house. Laird was in the kitchen. "Just got back from my meeting," he said cheerfully, kissing his wife, then hugging Sara. "What's all this about a dog bite?"

Laird was ten years older than his wife. From his English mother he had inherited midnight-blue eyes and a strong sense of justice; from his Scottish father a stocky build, tightly curled brown hair and a set of firm Presbyterian principles that luckily did not exclude the imbibing of whisky. Sara was extremely fond of him.

She went through her story once again. Laird grinned at her. "Well, that's certainly a novel way to get to meet the misogynist of Haliburton."

"He's not a misogynist," Cornelia protested.

"No? He just doesn't like women," Laird rejoined. "Want a drink, Sara? Scotch or rum?"

"Best offer I've had all day. Scotch on the rocks," she replied promptly.

"I've got another offer for you. The principal of the school in Coates Mill wants to interview you the day after tomorrow. One of his teachers will be on maternity leave, so you could be working most of next winter."

"Laird, that's wonderful! I put my name in three or four months ago, but I never thought I'd get anything so soon."

"I told you the chances were good."

"I know you did. I guess I was scared to believe you." Sara dropped onto the nearest chair. "You have no idea what a relief that is. It's very upsetting to be unemployed. Not that I've got the job yet," she added hastily.

"I expect you will, if for no other reason than you're low on the pay scale."

"Two years' experience," Sara admitted. "Then I was laid off at the end of the probationary period because of cutbacks. An illustrious beginning to my teaching career."

"Let's drink to the interview," Cornelia suggested. "Merrill Webster is a pretty good principal; he'll recognize quality when he sees it."

Sara laughed. "You're so good for my ego!"

The whisky slipped smoothly down her throat, and her eyelids began to droop. She slept the clock round and woke up the next day with bruises scattered all over her body. In the sober light of day Sara decided she had done a very foolish thing to have tackled the dog; yet when she remembered the silent disappearance of the two deer into the woods, she could not feel sorry.

Her bruises were not helped when her nephew Malcolm arrived at ten-thirty to bounce on her bed. Towheaded Malcolm was four, and if one wished to be polite, one would call him an active child; Sara doubted that the word impossible would ever be part of his vocabulary. A few minutes later Caitlin slipped into the room and sat quietly on the edge of the bed, thin-faced, shyly smiling. Caitlin was six and the dreamer of the family. She and Malcolm understood each other not at all, tolerated each other most of the time and would stand firmly united in the face of a common threat.

"Gonna take us swimming?" Malcolm demanded.

"This afternoon," Sara said.

"At the lake?" Caitlin asked eagerly. "I love the lake. It's so beautiful—the wind makes little waves for the sun to dance on."

"I was there last night," Sara said. "The loons were laughing at the sunset."

She and Caitlin exchanged a look of perfect understanding. Said Malcolm, "Loons are birds—they can't laugh. When are you getting up, Aunt Sara?"

"As soon as you leave the room."

Sara had the attic room, with its slanting ceilings and picture window overlooking the river and the orchards, a view that had stayed the same for eight years and that she sincerely hoped would remain the same for the next eight. Laird had piled her belongings by the door. After getting out of bed, she began unpacking her clothes and hanging them in the closet, deciding that she'd wear her green-and-white silk print to the interview, hoping with all her heart that she'd get the chance to teach next autumn. Jobs were scarce; and she would love to spend the winter in Haliburton. She'd rent a place of her own, though; she couldn't impose on Laird and Cornelia for more than the summer. Envisaging a pretty little cottage by the river, she put the photograph of her mother on the dresser and some of her favorite books on the shelves. She'd have to get her stereo if she had a place of her own. And her cross-country skis and her skates. How wonderful to skate on the lake in February! Oh, Merrill Webster, please give me the job, she prayed silently.

MERRILL WEBSTER SEEMED entirely disposed to do so. He was a stout, jovial man, like a balding Santa Claus, yet with a native shrewdness underlying the twinkle in his eyes. He had already checked Sara's references; he took her on a whirlwind tour of the school and explained that she would be replacing Mrs. Brownleigh, who taught grade-nine English and whose pregnancies, because of spinal arthritis, debilitated her for the best part of a year. "She was determined to have a second child, though," Mr. Webster said briskly, galloping Sara past the cafeteria and the gymnasium. "Fine woman. Excellent teacher. You've always taught biology, Miss Deane?"

"Yes. If I were to get the position, I'd do a lot of preliminary reading this summer."

"That can easily be arranged. You might even want to visit Mrs. Brownleigh. Here's the secretary's office, copying equipment and so on. Staff room's next door."

Said Sara, stopping dead in her tracks, "You mean I've got the job?"

Already six or seven paces ahead of her, Mr. Webster threw back over his shoulder, "Of course. Starting in September and probably going until May at least. After that, we'll see. A couple of our teachers are near retirement."

Sara gave the principal's back view a dazzling smile and scurried after him. Five minutes later, having signed the necessary documents and fervently shaken Mr. Webster's hand, she was standing outside the school smiling at the robins who were quartering the lawn, she as much as they oblivious to the soft, drizzling rain. She wanted to sing and dance. She wanted to tell the robins of her incredible good fortune. Aware that Mr. Webster might be watching her, she instead climbed decorously into her car and drove to the town of Coates Mill.

Coates Mill had two banks, one supermarket, four churches and a real estate office. Sara parked in front of the supermarket, bought a large red watermelon for the children and the ingredients for a Caesar salad for the adults, and put the bags on the back seat of her car.

The real estate office was across the street. While she was waiting at the crosswalk she saw a man come out of the hardware store, a tall, broad-shouldered man with a flat package under his arm. Cal Mathieson. He looked just as she remembered him, big, slow moving, with an aura of self-sufficiency. She was, she realized, extremely happy to see him. She could tell him about her job. Hurrying across the street, she called, "Cal! Cal, guess what?"

He had put the package in the back of his pickup truck. Straightening, he turned to face her. His hair was curling slightly from the dampness, while his eyes held all the grayness of the rain. "Hello, Sara," he said.

Every marriageable woman in twenty miles throws herself at Cal Mathieson sooner or later. Recalling her sister's words, Sara came to a stop and said lamely, "I just got a job. For the winter."

"In Halifax?"

"No. At the consolidated school here. Teaching English."

Something flickered behind his eyes. "I see. That's good news."

His response could not be called anything other than lukewarm. She should have said goodbye and walked to the real estate office. "Why don't you join me for a coffee?" she suggested instead. "To celebrate."

"Peg'll be along in a few minutes."

"Peg?" Her voice was too sharp for her own liking. "Peg's my secretary."

"Oh. Leave her a note . . . she could join us."

He shifted restlessly. "I suppose she could wait. As long as we weren't too long."

Sara did not have red hair for nothing. "Cal, if you don't want to have a coffee with me, just say so!"

He gave her a long, considering look, then smiled. Was she exaggerating to think his smile was like the sun breaking through the mist? "Sara," he said, "I would like to have coffee with you."

The restaurant had barn-wood panels, wagon wheel lights and washrooms labeled Cowgirls and Cowboys. Sara had eaten there before and knew that the food, although unpretentious, was homecooked and tasted good. She hung her coat on the rack by the door, not unpleased that Cal should see her in a dress and high heels, smiled at the waitress, whose long skirts and mobcap were suggestive of a superior type of pioneer woman, and then glanced down at the menu. "They make wonderful pies here, do you think I should indulge myself?"

Cal did not even look at the menu. "Just coffee, please," he said to the waitress.

"Coffee and lemon meringue pie for me," Sara said. "Sure you won't join me, Cal?"

"No, thanks."

She sighed. "I wish I had your willpower. Cal, I'm so pleased about the job. I was laid off at the end of this term, you see. There's a two-year probationary period for city teachers, and because of budget cutbacks I was one of the ones to go. There's a chance I might even get on permanently here. I'm going to the real estate office to see if I can find a place to rent; I can't really stay at Cornelia's all winter."

"So you're an English teacher?"

"As of next September! I taught biology at Rockwood. But I got the curriculum from Mr. Webster, and I'll do a lot of reading over the summer. Lying in the sun. Tough, eh?"

Cal did not smile. In fact, he looked decidedly grim, Sara thought, mulling over the conversation in her mind to see what might have displeased him. "Do you take a vacation, Cal?"

"Oh, things usually slack off a bit in the summer."

"Do you like to travel?"

"No. I like being around home."

"I went to Britain last summer with two other teachers. After my mother died." For a moment her face clouded. "We were there three weeks and scarcely scratched the surface. I'd like to go back. Or go to Europe. Or Fiji. Or India. You name it, I'll go."

He stirred cream into his coffee and watched her take the first mouthful of pie. "How is it?"

Having dealt with her job and vacations and travel, were they now to discuss lemon meringue pie? Conversation with Cal Mathieson was an uphill battle, thought Sara. "What do you like to do in the summers, Cal?" she asked, ignoring his question. "Do you read much?"

He lifted his cup, drank and put it down before answering. "No, not really. I prefer listening to the radio. I work in the garden, swim, fix up the house, go to antique sales with Peg."

Peg again. Was Peg marriageable? Was he telling her obliquely that he was not free? Sara gave a false laugh. "I love auctions, but I always end up buying something I have absolutely no use for." She took another mouthful of pie, wishing she had not met Cal and been so brash as to insist he have coffee with her, deciding peevishly that the lemon filling was too sweet.

They talked about the weather at considerable length. Sara finished her piece of pie. They then discussed Laird's latest project, the reforestation of a large acreage south of Haliburton, and of the opposition of many of the locals who felt there were enough trees in Nova Scotia without planting more; Laird, Sara had often felt, was too progressive for the sleepy little town of Haliburton. From talk of Laird's problems, they moved to the confrontation between the lumbermen and the Haida Indians in British Columbia, a subject on which Cal was extremely knowledgeable.

Sara drained her coffee cup, declined the waitress's offer of a refill and wondered how something that felt so right could at the same time feel so much off key. To have Cal sitting across from her in a crowded restaurant seemed very natural; she found herself wanting to wrap her fingers around his wrist as she might have grasped the limb of a tree, to feel its reality, the flow and flexibility of life beneath the surface. But nothing Cal had said or done encouraged her to do so. His wrist was like a limb at the very top of the tree, far beyond her reach. To pursue its grasp would be, she thought with painful truth, courting danger. Trees grow tall. It is their nature.

When the waitress brought the bill, Sara reached for it before Cal could. "It was my idea," she said brightly. "Let me pay. After all, I did just about lasso you and haul you in here."

A glint of humor showed in his eye. "Sara, you're tall and I'm sure you're fit, but I don't think you could have hauled me in here if I hadn't wanted to come."

She had a sudden image of herself, redfaced and puffing, braced against the doorway of the restaurant while he bellowed and tugged against the rope like a steer at a rodeo. "I believe you're right," she said gravely, then heard her unruly tongue add, "You're a strange man, Cal. I don't think I've ever met anyone as self-contained as you. And that's on the basis of two short meetings. There, you see, you've retreated again—I saw it happen."

"You speak your mind."

"My worst failing."

"Most people don't."

"Oh, we all wear masks, don't we? We hide behind our occupations, behind conventions and manners and small talk. It always seems such a waste to me. A waste of valuable time. When my mother died—she was only fifty-two—I was left with the conviction that I mustn't waste whatever time I have, that life is to be lived as if each day is a valuable gift." Abruptly Sara stopped, a sheen of tears in her eyes, for she had loved her mother and had suffered with her through the ugly, inevitable stages of cancer.

Cal said quietly, "I feel the same way. But, unlike you, I like to be alone."

As if it were the most natural gesture in the world, she rested her fingers on his wrist. "Why, Cal?"

His eyes dropped. "We're different, Sara. I don't need people . . . but I think you do. And I'm sure you attract people because you're so warm and friendly. You're a beautiful woman."

Her throat felt tight. She realized, almost with fear, that none of Joel's extravagantly phrased compliments had touched her like Cal's simple statement of fact: *"you're a beautiful woman."* She swallowed hard and said, "Surely we all need people?" and saw him sit back in his seat as if to increase the distance between them, a tangible retreat.

"I've got to go," he said. "Peg'll be waiting."

Peg again. Sara opened her wallet to pay the bill, keeping her mouth firmly shut so that she would not tell him where Peg could go. She left the money on the table and eased out of her seat to get her coat. But Cal forestalled her; he could move very quickly for so large a man. He had taken her coat from the rack and was holding it out for her, and for a brief moment she saw his eyes travel the length of her body. Although the dress was a perfectly correct one for a job interview, it could not disguise the swell of her breasts or the smallness of her waist. Sara felt her cheeks grow warm and hurriedly turned her back, shrugging herself into the sleeves of the coat and belting it around her. Not looking back, she led the way out of the door.

The real estate office was beyond the hardware store. Cal and Sara walked along the sidewalk in silence, Cal presumably not feeling the need to talk, Sara unable to think of anything intelligent to say. It was almost a relief when a middle-aged woman burst out of the door of the dress shop next to the hardware store, stationed herself in front of them brandishing a large bag and said stridently, "Well, Cal Mathieson, where have *you* been? You've cost me money, I hope you realize. I'd never have bought that cute little suit in the window if you hadn't kept me waiting."

"You've been wanting to buy that suit for two weeks, now tell the truth," Cal drawled. "Peg, I'd like you to meet Sara Deane. Sara, Peg Campbell. She runs my business and tries her best to run me."

"I gave up on you years ago," Peg snorted. "You're worse than Dick. Dick's my husband," she explained to Sara. "Another of those men who never say a word but manage to get their own way all the time. Enough to drive you crazy. Don't know why I put up with either one of them. You're Cornelia Fraser's sister, aren't you?"

"Yes," said Sara, who was still wrestling with the implications of Peg's obvious unmarriageability. Gravity seemed to exert undue force on Peg, for her chin, breasts and belly drooped, and her ineptly dyed hair was tumbling from its pins. But her curiosity was like a laser beam, intense and precisely focused.

"I saw you a couple of years ago, and I said to my friend Amy, who's that now, and when she told me you were Cornelia's sister you could have knocked me over with a feather. No, I said, not Cornelia's sister, her so small and dark and you with all that red hair. Funny, isn't it, how people related can look so different. You could be Anne of Green Gables's sister, that's who you could be." And Peg laughed immoderately at her own joke.

It would take a substantial feather to knock over Peg Campbell, thought Sara. Perhaps Peg was one of the reasons Cal was so silent. Self-defence. Deciding to spare all of them further interrogation, she said, "You'll be seeing more of me. I'm substituting for Mrs. Brownleigh next year, so I'll be living in Haliburton."

"Well now, you don't say! Poor Marion Brown-leigh, what that woman doesn't go through to have a baby, makes you realize how lucky the rest of us are, doesn't it. I had my three just as easy as popping peas from a pod, and—"

"Peg," Cal said, "we've got to get back. I promised the MacKinleys that set of chairs by tomorrow."

"He knows I could stand here all day gossiping," Peg remarked to Sara, then addressed Cal. "Did you get the glass you needed?"

"It's in the truck."

"Three windows broken in the night," Peg said portentously. "And we all know who did it, don't we?"

Cal sighed. "Peg, you can't accuse someone without any evidence."

"Percy Gillis did it, that's who. You can't trust that man when he's into the booze, and Betty Marten saw him in town yesterday scarcely able to walk a straight line. Alcohol's the devil's brew, isn't it; I don't let my Dick touch a drop. He never has since the day he married me. All right, Cal, I'm coming, I'm coming. Nice to meet you, Miss Deane, I expect we'll see you again." And she gave Sara an arch smile laced with innuendo.

"Goodbye, Mrs. Campbell," Sara said faintly. "Goodbye, Cal."

Cal winked at her. She watched them walk toward the truck. To her surprise Peg got in the driver's seat, backed out of the parking lot very competently and drove off. Cal did not look back.

Sara walked past the hardware store to the real estate office, feeling as if she had been interviewed twice that morning. She only hoped that Dick Campbell could handle Peg as firmly as Cal could.

The young woman in the real estate office wore a tag fastened to her blouse that said, "Hello, my name is Dolores." She was on a first-name basis with Sara in two minutes, and soon Sara had several rental prospects. "There's a farmhouse two miles north of Coates Mill. You could fix it up any way you wanted. I'm sure the landlord would supply the paint," Dolores said briskly. "I have one side of a duplex in town, very central, although a little more expensive, of course. Then there's the Woodbury place on the lake road; they spend their summers there but they like to rent it during the winter."

"Near Middle Lake?"

"Very close. In fact, the lot, which is narrow but very deep, goes right back to the lakeshore. It's next door to the man who makes furniture . . . do you know that area, Sara?"

Sara felt a lump settle in the pit of her stomach. So the house next door to Cal was regularly for rent, and he had not seen fit to tell her so. "Yes," she said tonelessly. "I know the area. It's very beautiful there."

"The other choice is also in Haliburton, a self-contained flat in a family home. The proximity might be nice since you'll be living alone." Dolores made a show of consulting her watch. "Mr. Tomlin just stepped out for a minute. When he comes back I could show you the properties, if you're interested?"

"I'd appreciate that."

The farmhouse had a breathtaking view of the river and required far more basic repairs than a coat of paint, for the ceilings sagged, the walls bulged and the bathroom was a horror. The central location of the duplex meant it was right on the main street next door to the tavern, while the self-contained flat had walls like cardboard through which Sara could hear a baby wailing, a dog barking and two other children committing what sounded like ritual murder. She did not think her solitary state should necessitate that type of proximity. So she was left with the house next to Cal's.

It was a sizable cabin, yet winterized, with dependable plumbing, a small furnace and a wood stove in the living room. The walls did not bulge, nor were there neighbors in sight or earshot, let alone any taverns. There were trees, an amateurish flower garden and a narrow path that led to the lake. Sara signed the lease, which started in September, and went home.

THE NEXT DAY Cornelia, Sara and the children went to Halifax. Sara looked after the children while Cornelia did some serious shopping for clothes in the late-June sales whose signs had sprouted as ubiquitously as the flowers in the Public Gardens. They then went to a toy shop at Malcom's request and a bookshop at Caitlin's. While Caitlin browsed and Cornelia kept Malcolm amused, Sara wandered among the shelves, picking up one or two paperbacks that she thought would be useful next winter for her English class. A big display rack offered slashed prices on some coffee table books, one of which was on the construction of antique furniture. Sara picked the book up and leafed through it, liking the glossy photographs and the precisely drawn plans, which included measurements and instructions for everything from grandfather clocks to double-faced Sheraton desks with ponderous clawed feet. Cal would like this book. She was sure he would. It would make an appropriate thank-you gift for saving her from Percy's dog.

Cornelia had come up behind her. "I didn't know you were interested in antique furniture," she observed.

Sara closed the book and tried to look casual. "I'm not. I thought I might give it to Cal. He really did arrive just in the nick of time as far as that awful dog was concerned."

"Oh," said Cornelia in an elder-sister voice, "I see."

"Anyway, the price is right," Sara said defensively.

Luckily, Malcolm caused a distraction by toppling a pile of books to the floor. Sara fled to the cash register; small boys had their uses.

After lunch in a restaurant that specialized in calorie-laden desserts, they drove several miles out of town to the beach at Blandford, where gentle waves lapped on a long curve of white sand. As the children began to build a castle—a big heap of sand to Malcolm, to Caitlin a dwelling for princes and princesses—Cornelia and Sara stretched out on towels in the sun. "I feel full and fat and lazy," Sara grumbled. "I should never have eaten that dessert."

"Back to fresh fruit tomorrow. Do you miss the city, Sara?"

"Not often. Your place feels like home."

"What about Joel, do you miss him?"

"Sometimes, yes," Sara admitted. "Even though I wish I didn't."

"You were crazy about him for months, it's not surprising you miss him."

"Crazy is the right word. It was a crazy relationship. Up and down like a seesaw, never level or stable. Not like you and Laird. And yet I miss him. How's that for illogic?"

"What was the problem? I've never really understood."

Sara said simply, "It had gone sour, Lia. Too much fighting."

"And each time the breach got a little harder to repair?"

"That's right," Sara said, grateful for her sister's understanding. "I think about that relationship a lot—after all, we were together for nine months—and I always come to the conclusion that Joel wanted too much control. He's got a very domineering personality under all that charm, and he wants total, undivided attention all the time. At first I went along with him. It was soon after Mum died, and I was lonely and hurting, and it was wonderful to be swept off my feet. He sent me red roses and crazy cards and took me out for dinner and wrote poetry about my many charms... although I did object when he tried to call my hair auburn. I told him red rhymed with bed." She smiled reminiscently, watching Caitlin surround a tower with seashells. "But then he started getting jealous. He didn't like me to see my female friends, and watch out if I so much as looked at another man. Maybe only people who are insecure dominate, do you think that's true? He wouldn't give me any freedom, Lia, he always wanted to know where I was going and how long I'd be, until I couldn't stand it. So we'd have a fight. Then we'd make up and everything would be lovely for a while, but then it would start all over again. We had the last fight a couple of weeks before school ended, and I was so glad I was coming to Haliburton."

"I think you do have to be secure within yourself to allow another person freedom," Cornelia said thoughtfully. "And you also have to trust the other person."

"I guess that was it. I never felt he trusted me. But we did have a lot of fun together, and for a while I really was in love."

"Maybe you still are...just a tiny bit?" Cornelia suggested.

"I don't think so. Although if he were to walk up to us right now, I'd be pleased to see him." Sara poked at the sand. "I always used to think love was cut and dried. Either you were in love with someone or you weren't. Straightforward. No doubts. It isn't that simple, is it? Lots of gray areas in between...so maybe I am still a little in love with Joel."

"It was very natural that you fall for him—quite apart from him being extremely attractive. You were vulnerable after Mum died."

"Very. Lia, do you think they were happy? Mum and Dad, I mean."

Cornelia trickled sand between her fingers, the sea breeze stirring wisps of dark hair around her face. "I've wondered that myself. Possibly not. I don't remember Dad being around much, do you? If he wasn't flying, he was at the mess or playing squash or off with the boys somewhere. Macho stuff. I think the forces encouraged that. And Mum stayed home and coped with the two of us and the house and the car and the bills. Mind you, she was very loyal. I don't ever remember her criticizing Dad. But I don't remember them having much fun together either, do you? They seemed to give or go to an awful lot of parties because it was expected of them, because Colonel so-and-so would be there or General somebody-or-other. Not because they wanted to."

"She never spoke about Dad. Not even when she was so ill. And I never had the nerve to ask."

"They were hard, those last few months, weren't they? The chemotherapy and all its horrible side effects. The way she lost weight and got so weak…it was wonderful for her that you were there, Sara. But it certainly meant you bore the brunt of it."

"You had the children and Laird. You couldn't come into the city every day."

"I know I couldn't. At least rationally I know I couldn't." Cornelia traced a careful pattern in the sand with her forefinger. "But I still feel guilty about it, as though I let both of you down."

Sara took her sister's hand. "Mum understood, she'd raised two children herself. She was always glad to see you whenever you could come, but she never complained when you couldn't."

Two tears dripped onto the back of Sara's hand. "I still miss her a lot. Do you?" Cornelia asked softly.

"Of course I do. You know, Lia, I suppose this will sound sentimental, but if I had to choose a word to describe Mum, I'd say she was gallant. She did what had to be done, she never asked for pity and she could almost always produce a joke."

"But she kept her emotions well hidden. You never really knew what she was thinking."

Sara said gently, "You can be a bit like that yourself. Mum's been dead over a year, and this is the first I've heard that you feel guilty."

"I know." Cornelia gave her sister a watery smile. "One of the reasons I married Laird is because he won't allow me to keep everything locked up inside."

Sara sneaked a look at the children, who were happily sloshing pails of water into the moat around the castle. "I get the feeling Cal could be a lot like you. You told me he was a loner, and very self-sufficient. I think you were absolutely right."

Cornelia hesitated. "You seem very taken with him."

"He feels right," Sara blurted. "And don't ask me to explain that, because I can't." Scowling, she then proceeded to try and explain it. "Joel was romance. Red roses, pounding hearts, high-pitched emotions, fantastic sex. I don't feel that way with Cal. I just feel comfortable. As if in some strange way he fits with me—or could, if he'd let himself." Her brow wrinkled in intense thought. "Joel sometimes reminds me of Dad. He's very ambitious for one thing, and he's self-centered in somewhat the same way Dad was. His agenda comes first and the rest of the world can fit in with it. I'd never want to marry a man like Dad; you'd always feel you were third or fourth on the list."

"Laird is the opposite of Dad," Cornelia said with a wry smile.

"So he is," Sara said slowly. "I don't think Cal's much like Dad, either. Freud says we either marry a carbon copy of our father or else his exact opposite...I do hate it when psychologists predict our behavior!"

"So are you thinking of marrying Cal?" Cornelia asked innocently.

Sara pulled a face. "Of course not! I've had exactly two conversations with the man. But I had to buy that book, Cornelia. I needed the excuse to see him again."

"I have a chair that needs repairing, you can take that, too," Cornelia said comfortingly.

"Do you think I'm crazy? I'm certainly fickle, I suppose. Three weeks ago I was fighting with Joel."

"I'm afraid you'll get hurt, that's what worries me."

Prophetic words, Sara was to think later. Yet not even the fear of being hurt could have kept her from visiting Cal the following week.

CHAPTER THREE

SARA VISITED CAL in the morning, a few days after she had bought the book. The July sunlight was playing hide-and-seek among the rustling leaves of the poplars, and the birds were in full voice. She felt happy and very nervous.

When she pulled into the driveway, Cal's truck was parked by the barn, which had double doors and a neatly lettered sign announcing the entrance to the workshop. Partly as a delaying tactic, partly because she had not yet seen his property in daylight, she took a few minutes to look around.

The frame house was a classic saltbox, two stories in the front, one behind. It was painted a soft gray, with an antique-blue door, whose brass fittings reflected the brightness of the sun. Old-fashioned rosebushes and hollyhocks nodded against the walls. There was a small orchard behind the house, the trees tidily pruned, while a sweetly scented honeysuckle rambled up the south wall of the barn. Time had been spent on the property, and love. With an ache in her heart Sara knew what it was to envy another person his possessions.

She had seen enough. She took Cornelia's mahogany chair out of the back seat of her car, tucked the book under her arm and marched toward the barn, a determined figure in her white denim pants and orange shirt. But the double doors were locked, so she had to enter via the side door, which was labeled office. The office was a sizable room, bright and well-organized. Unfortunately, it contained Peg.

"Miss Deane! Or do you mind if I call you Sara? I said we'd be seeing each other again, didn't I?" Peg patted her jumbled curls and favored Sara with a red-lipsticked, suggestive smirk.

Sara's parents had believed in good manners, her father for strategic reasons, her mother because they showed respect for others. So Sara said cordially, "Good morning, Peg. How lucky you are to have such a wonderful view of the garden! Is Cal here? Cornelia asked me to bring this chair in." Sara felt she was only adjusting the truth a little.

"He's in the shop. Works real hard he does, no matter if it's in sun or rain. But he leaves every scrap of paperwork to me, says his business is wood, not paper. All the ordering and the bills and the inquiries— keeps me busy I can tell you."

"I'm sure it does," Sara said politely. "Shall I go through?"

"You go ahead, I'm sure he'll be right pleased to see you." Peg smirked again.

Her lips compressed, Sara carried Cornelia's chair through the inner door and closed it firmly behind her. The barn was cool and cavernous and very quiet; there was no sign of Cal. She put the chair down and walked across the smooth board floor, breathing deeply of the mingled scents of sawdust and stain, her eyes following the massive beams to the peaked roof. Hand tools were arrayed in neat rows along the walls; big power tools whose function she could only guess stood about the floor like guests at a rather stolid party. Then a door creaked behind her and Cal came in. He was balancing a couple of boards against his leather apron; when he saw her, he stood still. Not a flicker of expression crossed his face.

She suddenly wished she had not come, that she had never seen the book on antique furniture. Cal did not need a present from her. Or her presence, she thought with a kind of desperate humor, knowing she could not share the pun with him. He did not even look as if he remembered who she was. "Hello, Cal," she said awkwardly. "Cornelia has an antique chair that needs repairing, so I brought it over."

"I've got quite a backlog at the moment. It'd be a month before I could get it back to her."

"There's no hurry."

He came nearer, putting the boards on the scarred surface of a workbench. "I'll get Peg to check the schedule."

"That wood's a pretty color," Sara ventured.

"Mahogany. I order it from Ontario."

"You mean Peg orders it from Ontario," she said wryly.

He smiled. Not widely, but at least it was a smile. His hands were smoothing the surface of the mahogany as a lover might caress the body of his beloved. Emboldened, Sara came closer. "What will you make from it?"

Warmth crept into his voice. "A tilt table. A mate to the one in the corner."

"Show me," she said.

The table was circular with a scalloped, raised edge and a softly glowing surface as smooth as glass. Cal talked of laminations, band saws and bits; of filler and sandpaper and varnish. He showed her the hand-carved legs and his set of carving tools. "Dougal made them years ago out of an old harrow disc," he said. "I apprenticed with Dougal Munroe when I turned sixteen. This was his property. He left it to me when he died. I owe everything I've got to Dougal."

It was the longest speech he had made about his background. "When did he die, Cal?"

"Three years ago, when I was twenty-two. Dropped dead of a heart attack with a hammer in his hand. Just the way he would have wanted to go."

Her face shadowed. "He was lucky."

Cal hesitated. "How did your mother die, Sara?"

"Cancer. She was sick for over a year."

He rested his hand on her shoulder, his eyes clear and unguarded. "That must have been hard on you. And when they're gone, it leaves you lonely, doesn't it?"

So Cal was sometimes lonely. "Yes, it does. You were fond of Dougal, Cal?"

His arm dropped to his side. "He was like a father to me," he said roughly. "A crabby old Scotsman who'd have his hand cut off before he'd admit to emotion, but who taught me all he knew and left me his house and his tools and his land. Yeah, you could say I was fond of him."

"No wonder you were lonely when he died. Because at least I have Cornelia and Laird and the children."

If this was an oblique attempt to find out more about Cal's family, it failed. He said brusquely, "That night your sister came here to get you, you looked nice together, the two of you. Look, before I start gluing this wood I'm going to make some tea at the house. Why don't you join me? You'd better show me the chair first, though."

Laird had bought the chair at an auction. Swiftly Cal ran his fingers over it, talking more to himself than to

Sara. "I'll have to splice the wood in the back and glue the joints. A new dovetail here, see how it's broken? No problem."

"I'm impressed. I'd have thrown the chair on the junk heap."

He looked shocked. "This is in good shape. You should see some of the stuff I get. It's a part of my job I like, taking something old that's been ill-used and bringing it back to beauty and usefulness. Just as satisfying as making something new."

He led her out through the back door. A flock of tiny birds flew away from a feeder hanging from a maple tree. The sun struck warm on Sara's face. With the book tucked casually under her arm she followed Cal into the kitchen. The room was just as she had remembered it and seemed to welcome her as a friend would. While Cal made the tea, she brought up the subject of Cornelia again, chattering on about the effects on her father's ambition on their upbringing, with the resulting closeness to her sister. "Maybe it helps that we're different in so many ways. For instance, the reason she wants that chair mended is so she can make a needlepoint seat for it. I'm useless at needlework or anything to do with my hands." She gave him an engaging smile. "I'd be hopeless at your job. Probably saw off my fingers on the first day."

"I've taken a few pieces out of myself over the years." He spread his hands on the table; there were small white scars on his fingers.

Panic-stricken, Sara realized how badly she wanted those fingers to touch her with affection, to acknowledge the strange sense of belonging that she herself felt. Greatly daring, she ran her nail along a narrow white line at the angle of his thumb. "What happened there?"

"I was learning to use a backsaw. The air was blue that day... Dougal didn't have much patience with incompetence, and I'd bled all over a good pine board." Abruptly he covered her hand with his own and looked straight into her eyes. "It's funny, I've talked more to you today about Dougal than I've talked to anyone else in months."

His hand was warm on hers; she could feel the calluses on his palm. "Why, Cal?" she whispered.

"Dunno...maybe because I like you. It was a damn fool thing you did to tackle that dog, but it was brave, too. And at least you cared enough to try. Most people would have kept going."

"I like you, too."

"That's the other thing. You say what's on your mind."

Deciding there could not be a more opportune time to give him the book, Sara said with an endearing touch of shyness, "I bought you a present to thank you for rescuing me from the dog," and pushed the parcel across the table.

Cal said nothing. As if the temperature had suddenly dropped, his features hardened and drew in upon themselves. His movements slow, even reluctant, he drew the package closer and tore at its brown wrapping. When the book was revealed, he stared at it in silence without attempting to open it, his eyes like chips of stone.

Appalled by his reaction, not understanding it in the least, Sara said, "What's wrong? You haven't even opened it."

With insulting speed he riffled through the pages, then clapped the covers shut with a sound like a gunshot. Sara jumped. "Cal, what have I done wrong? Is the book too elementary? Have I insulted you? I didn't mean to. I thought some of the furniture in it was beautiful, that you might enjoy browsing through it."

With exaggerated care he put the book down, squaring it with the corner of the table. The pulse at the base of his throat was pounding as if he had been running. She sensed in him a leashed violence, all the more frightening for being so tightly checked. "I've got to get back to work," he said.

"Please tell me what's wrong," she begged.

He did not look up. "Nothing's wrong," he said flatly. "It's a great book."

He was lying to her, blatantly lying. And she had no idea why. She only knew that the serenity of the kitchen had vanished. She pushed back her chair. She had to leave before she burst into tears or picked up the book and cracked him on the head with it. "Don't let me hold you up," she said with a sarcasm rendered less than convincing by the quaver in her voice. "Thank you for the tea."

Mother dear, you'd be proud of me—good manners to the last, she thought, and stubbed her toe on the step because she wasn't watching where she was going. Instantly, her good manners abandoned her. Sara slammed the back door with a most satisfactory thud. Only after she had done so did she realize that Peg at her desk had a perfect view of the back door and would no doubt extract the maximum amount of drama from such an exit. *Let Cal explain,* she decided meanly, got in her car, slammed its door, as well, and reversed in front of the barn with scant regard for the well-being of the clutch.

At the end of the driveway she had to stop because a truck was barreling along the road toward her, a red-and-white truck scabbed with rust, one headlight empty as an eye socket, the windshield veined with cracks. The driver was peering through the glass at her.

In a squeal of brakes the truck juddered to a halt. When the man clambered out, Sara was not particularly surprised to see that it was Percy. A session with Percy seemed a fitting end to a disastrous morning.

Her window was already rolled down. As Percy thrust his face at her, she backed away from his breath and said with cold precision, "Good morning, Mr. Gillis."

"Don't gimme none of your lip. If Percy's good enough for the rest of the world, it's good enough for you."

He inserted his face still farther in the window. Hair grew in clumps in his ears like last summer's grass; he needed, among other things, a shave. Sara glowered at him. "I am not in the mood to trade insults with you," she said tightly.

"I ain't forgotten what you done to my dog."

"Your dog bit me!" She pulled up her sleeve. She had had the stitches taken out a couple of days ago. "There's the scar."

"If you'd let him be, nuthin' would've happened. If you're gonna be around Haliburton for long, you'd better learn to keep your nose outa other people's business, you hear me?"

"It would be difficult not to," she retorted, her cheeks bright pink with temper. "I'm not the slightest bit sorry I tried to stop your dog, Percy Gillis. He would have killed those deer if I hadn't. And now I would appreciate it if you would remove yourself. Because if you don't I'll shut the window in your face."

Percy leered. The effect was quite horrible, reminding Sara of the gargoyles she had seen last summer on an ancient church in Sussex; Percy could have been the model for them.

"Sassy little bitch, ain't ya? I like a gal that's got a bit of spunk."

"Out!" Sara yelled.

Percy blinked and withdrew. Sara whipped around the back of his truck, where the license plate dangled dispiritedly from a piece of wire, and took the curve in the road at reckless speed.

But by the time she had reached the paved road and the little cluster of buildings that was the village of Haliburton, she had both slowed down and cooled down, anger replaced by the slow seep of depression, the episode with Percy superseded by memories of her abortive visit with Cal. If she had ever had any rapport with the opposite sex, she was rapidly losing it, she thought miserably. First Joel, now Cal. She'd better devote herself to her sister's family and to good works. She'd certainly better forget the blond-haired carpenter with the big, gentle hands. A challenge was one thing, masochism another.

When Sara slammed the back door on her way out, Cal was still sitting at the kitchen table. He flinched from the noise. Moving like an old man, he got up from the table and picked up the book that she had given him. He crossed the hall to the living room, which was at the front of the house, and through one of its square-paned windows watched her drive as far

as the end of the road and then engage in discussion
with Percy. He did not think he needed to go to Sara's
rescue this time. She was perfectly capable of handling Percy, a conclusion that was upheld when Percy
removed his head from Sara's window with considerable haste. Absently running his finger along the spine
of the book, a faint smile touching his lips if not his
eyes, Cal wondered what she had said to oust Percy.

Sara took off in a shower of small stones. Percy got
back in his truck and, after a couple of false starts,
followed her at a more moderate speed.

Cal began turning the pages of the book, slowing
when he came to a grandfather clock, a mahogany
dining table, an open-shelved dresser. Their propor-
tions delighted him. He glanced at the scaled-down
plans, then at the small-printed pages of instructions.
Briefly he closed his eyes. The sound of his own
breathing was harsh in his ears.

In a gesture savage in its intensity, he threw the book
at the far wall. The spine snapped. The book thudded
to the floor, its white pages billowing like sails in the
wind.

Cal covered his face with his hands.

CORNELIA WAS IN THE KITCHEN baking cookies when
Sara got home. Malcolm was rolling a small gray ball
of dough up and down the counter, a process he called
helping, while Caitlin was tucked up on a red cushion
in the window seat, her nose in a book, oblivious to
everything going on around her. Cornelia took one
look at Sara's face and said, "Have a cookie. And why
don't you put on some coffee?"

"I had tea at Cal's."

Malcolm was now molding the dough around the corner of the counter, humming tunelessly to himself, and Caitlin turned a page. Cornelia pressed a row of cookies flat with a fork and said, "It didn't go well?"

"No. I shouldn't have gone."

"Put on some coffee, Sara. I need one, even if you don't."

The strong scent of the coffee beans, the whirl of the grinder and the hiss of steam from the kettle were somehow comforting. Sara passed Cornelia a mug of coffee and poured herself some, helping herself to a cookie that was still warm from the oven.

"What went wrong?" Cornelia asked.

Sara bit into the cookie, remembering in minute detail Cal's inexplicable, icy withdrawal after she had given him the book, and said, "I don't really want to talk about it, Lia—I just shouldn't have gone, that's all. I shouldn't have taken him a present."

"Is there anything I can do to help?"

"Not a darn thing. Except pick up the chair when it's ready. I'm not going near there again."

"He can mend it, can he?"

"Oh, yes. He's busy, so it'll take about a month."

"A lot can happen in a month."

"Nothing's going to happen, Lia," Sara announced, meaning every word she said. "Because I'm not going near Cal Mathieson ever again!"

The day passed. Cornelia was on the afternoon shift at the hospital where she worked as a nurse, so Sara looked after the children, prepared supper and got them to bed. She then played three games of cribbage with Laird, losing all three because her mind was not on what she was doing, and went to bed herself. She fell asleep instantly, but at four o'clock in the morning was wide awake. She punched her pillow, had a drink of water, read for a while, then shut her eyes tightly and tried to ignore the first tentative notes of a robin from the big oak tree beside the house. Finally, at five, she got up and went to stand by the window.

A soft white mist had wrapped itself around the elms along the river. The leaves of the oak tree were gilded with early morning light and the grass was wet with dew. Everything looked clean and fresh, unsullied by the doubts and disappointments of the day. Impulsively Sara went to her drawer and pulled on her swimsuit, putting on jeans and a sweatshirt over it. She'd go to the lake and sit by the shore and listen to the birds. At this hour of the day she'd have the place to herself. She and the loons.

Sara crept downstairs, left a note for Cornelia and put her car in neutral to coast down the driveway so the sound of the engine would not wake the children. As she passed through the deserted village she felt better than she had since the previous morning, so much so that she even drove past Cal's house without giving it more than a cursory look.

As she had anticipated, she had the lake to herself. She even looked in vain for the black-billed loons. The sun was creeping into a cloudless sky, turning the lake into a mirror in which the reflected trees were as still as their counterparts on the land. Her towel looped around her neck, Sara began to walk along the shore, balancing on the rocks, breathing deeply of the night-cooled air. She saw water striders, tadpoles and reed-like plants with white, translucent petals; a swamp sparrow darted among the bushes, and ahead of her a rusty blackbird waddled along the shore. She walked slowly, rubbing a bay leaf between her fingers, smiling into the shiny black eye of a chickadee on a pine branch over her head, watching for the path into the woods on her left that would lead to the house she had rented for the winter. It was a pity the house was next door to Cal's. But by September she would have forgotten about Cal; a brief, unsatisfactory episode, a dead-end street in the journey of life.

Very poetically put, Sara, she told herself with a grin. *You'll do well teaching English.*

She climbed over the rounded boulders of a promontory, enjoying the stretch of her muscles and congratulating herself that she had not stayed in bed to toss and turn. Then, as she ducked under an alder, she suddenly froze to stillness as an animal freezes at the scent of danger. From the cove on the far side of the promontory she heard the splash of water. There was not a breath of wind, and she had not seen any sign of a boat. Was it a moose?

Very excited, for she had never seen a moose in the wild, Sara crept over the next few rocks, taking care not to disturb the underbrush. Crouched low, she peered through the screen of tamarack and alders.

The unknown swimmer was not a moose. It was a man. A man with slicked-back blond hair and broad shoulders. Cal. The last person in the world she wanted to see.

CHAPTER FOUR

HURRIEDLY SARA RETREATED a couple of steps, still bent low. But her sneaker dislodged some rocks, sending them tumbling into the water with an inordinate amount of noise.

"Hello!" Cal called. "Someone there?"

Sara scowled at the spreading ripples on the water. Her sense of solitude, of having the lake to herself, was gone. She could stay hidden and hurry back to her car without having a swim. Or she could join him.

The splashing was coming closer and added to it was the huff of breathing. She did not want to be discovered crouching ignominiously among the rocks, like a female Peeping Tom. Slowly she stood up and once again clambered across the boulders. Her red hair shone in the sun like a beacon.

"Sara!" Cal said. "Where did you come from?"

She grabbed a spruce bough for balance. The cove was deeply indented, edged with gray sand and a grove of silver-trunked birches. Cal was farther away than she had thought, for his voice had carried across the water. He was churning toward her in an unstylish but very effective crawl. No wonder she had heard splashing, she thought with a twinge of amusement. And then he stopped at least thirty feet away from her and said, treading water, a strange note in his voice, "I wasn't expecting to see anyone."

"Neither was I," she replied, not sounding overly friendly.

"I swim every morning."

"At five-thirty?"

"It's the only time of the day I can count on having the place to myself."

Sara sounded definitely hostile now. "I'm sorry I spoiled it for you. I'm going, anyway."

"Sara, don't—"

"Don't what?"

"Don't leave," he said lamely. "It's a beautiful day... we shouldn't be angry with one another."

Her fingers relaxed their hold on the bough, because she knew exactly what he meant. "I planned to go for a swim, too," she said tentatively.

He looked disconcerted. "Oh. But you haven't got a swimsuit."

"I'm wearing it." Relenting, she gave him a generous smile. "You're right, it is too nice a day to be trading insults. Why don't I join you? Is the water cold?" She draped her towel across the nearest bush and knelt to untie her sneakers, not really expecting an answer, purposely disregarding how ridiculously happy she felt to have met Cal this way. Maybe, she thought, pulling her sweater over her head, you shouldn't say things like *I never want to see Cal Mathieson again,* even if you did only say them to your sister. It was tempting fate.

Her jeans joined her sweater on the bush. Her swimsuit was a severely styled emerald-green maillot that did full justice to the curves of her figure. Feeling absurdly shy, she began to slither down the rocks.

In a strangled voice Cal said, "You're going to have to turn your back, Sara, while I swim to shore and put my shorts on."

One foot extended into the water, her arms braced against the rocks, she gaped at him. Then, as his meaning registered, she threw back her head and laughed, a joyous peal that echoed across the lake. "Cal Mathieson! You're skinny-dipping."

He grinned, his teeth a white gleam in his tanned face. "You got it. I told you I wasn't expecting to see anyone. Turn your back, Sara."

She slid down into the water, wincing from its chill searching of her flesh. "Oh, no," she said demurely. "I think I'll come after you."

He was laughing and backing away from her at the same time. "That swimsuit looks like business. Don't tell me you used to be an Olympic swimmer."

"Not quite." She took a couple of strokes toward him. "But I won the two-hundred- and three-hundred-meter freestyle at the Nova Scotia Open eight years ago, and I was on the university swim team for three years. I've been a speed swimmer since I was seven, Cal."

"Just my luck...surely you learned to tread water in all those years?"

"Not as much fun as racing. Or chasing." She took two more strokes.

"If you're that good you can swim across the lake while I get my shorts."

"But I like the cove," she said soulfully. "It's so beautiful."

He took another backward stroke, churning up the water around his face so that he sputtered. "Then I've got a suggestion. Go back to the rocks and leave your swimsuit there. Then we'll be equal.''

"I don't think much of that idea.''

"I thought women wanted equality these days.''

"I'm not sure your suggestion is what they have in mind.''

She had been edging toward him with underwater finning motions of her arms and was close enough to see the drops of water dribbling from his hair and the laughter in his face. He looked young and carefree; with a pang she remembered the control he normally clamped on his features, the barrier he kept between himself and the rest of the world that made him look both older and much less approachable. She wanted to keep him laughing. She had the feeling there had been too little laughter in his life.

He floundered backward again. "I could yell for help.''

"No one would hear you.''

"I could surrender.''

"Give up? Oh Cal, you disappoint me.''

"Or I could go on the attack.'' In his own unique variation of the breaststroke he lunged toward her, waves rippling in pools from his body.

She gave a breathless laugh, instinctively backing away. "Cal—''

"You're giving up? Oh Sara, you disappoint me.''

She was giggling helplessly. There were only about fifteen feet between them, so that she could see the wavering outline of his torso through the water. "I'll race you to the shore and then I'll turn my back,'' she suggested, and crossed her hands in front of her body in the approximate vicinity of her heart. "Promise.''

He took a single, purposeful stroke nearer. "Can I trust you?"

Mischief gleamed in her eye. "Life is full of risk, Cal."

"So it is. Risk for both of us, perhaps?"

The gap between them had shrunk to five feet. Determinedly keeping her eyes trained on his face, Sara gasped, "Am I the one who should be calling for help?"

"Do you want to?"

"That's a totally unfair question!"

"Good. I'd have hated it if you'd said yes."

Three feet, two feet, one foot. With a wet finger Cal traced the angle of her jaw. "How did this happen, Sara Deane? You and I alone here...."

His lashes, darker than his hair, were stuck together in wet little spikes. She discovered that she wanted to kiss him. Quite badly. "Fate," she said.

"After yesterday, I figured I'd never see you again."

"That was a fair assumption," she replied warmly. "I had no idea I'd meet you here this morning."

"Or you wouldn't have come?" He added clumsily, "I knew I hurt you yesterday. I'm sorry."

His apology was unquestionably sincere. "Yes, you did. But I hurt you, too, didn't I? I didn't mean to, Cal. And I still have no idea why."

"I know you don't." His smile returned, deflecting any further questions. He tugged at one of her curls. "How about that race? Or are you scared I'll win?"

She almost asked, what race? so bemused was she by his closeness, by the knowledge that he was naked and very beautiful to her. She stammered, "I...I'll give you a head start."

"No way."

"Okay. Go!"

She buried her face in the water and kicked out strongly, not looking to see if he was beside her. Using every bit of her energy and expertise she streaked toward the shore. Sublimation, the Freudians would call this, she thought, and saw beneath her the blurred outline of rocks on a sandy bottom. She swam until she could touch the bottom, then stood up in a flurry of water, her breasts and shoulders touched by the sun.

Cal was several feet behind her, trundling along in a way he could probably keep up for hours. He stopped a safe distance away from her and straightened, the water running in rivulets down his chest. "You're a good swimmer."

"All the bases where my dad was stationed had pools. I was lucky. Why don't I get your shorts for you?" She waded ashore, picked up the blue swimming shorts lying on the sand beside a pair of deck shoes and turned back to the lake. The sun was full in her eyes, outlining the man's body, throwing his elongated shadow over the gently swaying water so that he looked larger than life, a surrealistic denizen of a dream world. Her footsteps slowed. Was she dreaming? Had she fallen back to sleep in the attic room at Cornelia's, and was now dreaming this meeting in the serenity of dawn? Was he real? Was she?

The dry sand slid between her toes and a small stone dug into her heel. The man called, prosaically, "Come on, Sara, I'm getting cold standing here." She gave her head a little shake and paddled into the water.

Cal took the shorts from her, she turned her back and a few moments later he said, "Let's swim some more, shall we? Sara, are you all right?"

She was close enough that she was in his shadow, so she could see his face. She gave him a small, strained smile. "I'm fine."

He made a movement toward her, then shook his head in bewilderment as if he had walked into a brick wall. "You change me," he said roughly. "I don't behave like myself when I'm around you."

She said in a low voice, "I had the sensation a minute ago that I was dreaming. That none of this is real."

"It's no dream." With something of the same roughness he clamped his hand on her shoulder. "And you're all too real. Sara..." He drew her toward him, and she obeyed as bonelessly as a rag doll. When he bent his head, she raised her own, her lips eager, her hands already sliding up his hair-roughened chest. But at the last moment he drew back.

Under her palms she felt the tension in his body, and saw in his eyes a confused mixture of desire, resentment and fear. *Fear.* Cal Mathieson was afraid of her.

He stepped back from her so abruptly that the water swirled about their hips. When he spoke she sensed he was trying desperately to sound matter-of-fact, even though his chest was rising and falling and his eyes were still dark with hostility. "You're like a witch with your red hair," he said. "You've put a spell on me."

If he was trying to be funny, the joke fell flat. "Don't be silly. I'm just an ordinary person."

"Not to me you're not."

Her lashes flickered. "Don't hate me," she whispered.

He let out his pent-up breath in a long sigh. "I don't hate you, Sara. But you scare me. Yeah, you sure scare me."

"I don't mean to."

"I never said you did."

She wiped at the water trickling into her eyes and shook out her curls so that droplets flew in all directions, like jewels in the sunlight. "I detest this conversation!" she said vigorously. "Neither one of us is saying what we really mean, are we, Cal?"

His smile was wry. "Reckon not."

"So why are we wasting time by talking?"

His eyes narrowed. "What else do you have in mind?"

"Swimming," Sara retorted. "Nothing but swimming!"

"Okay then, let's swim. No more races, though. I don't stand a chance with you."

She had the feeling that at last he had spoken the literal truth. *I don't stand a chance with you. You could,* she thought. *Because despite the fact that you're as full of quills as a porcupine, I like you, Cal Mathieson. And explain that to me if you can. Because I can't.*

She said nothing of this, partly because she did not think he wanted to hear it, partly because she did not want to add herself to the list of all those other young women who had tried to lure Cal into intimacy. "We could dive for rocks," she suggested.

"I'm a much better swimmer underwater," Cal said. "It's probably because when I was learning how to swim I spent a lot more time under the water than on top."

Her laugh sounded relaxed and normal. "We might find an oyster with a pearl in it."

"Or a leech."

She shuddered. "That's when you'll really see how fast I can swim."

He grinned. "Last one in's a rotten egg."

It was an incantation from childhood, bringing back memories of thrashing bodies and shrieks that split the summer air. But before Sara could move, Cal had arched his body and plunged beneath the surface of the lake in an eruption of spray and hissing air bubbles. She filled her lungs with air and dived in after him, and in the next few minutes discovered that Cal's natural element was indeed beneath the water. He could stay under far longer than she, and his big body in the murky green depths had grace and power, as though he were freer, more truly himself, than he could ever be in the air.

They played for half an hour, ending in an underwater chase that Cal won as decisively as Sara had won the earlier race. When his head finally broke the surface, he let out an exultant whoop at the top of his lungs. The crows cawed in derision from the birch trees and Sara began to laugh. "I'm truly humbled!" she called. "I quit."

"Get your clothes and walk round the shore. We could have breakfast at my place."

She gave him a radiant, wet-faced smile and swam toward the rock where she had left her clothing. She felt very happy, very much an integral part of water, air, rock and sun. She and Cal were like two creatures of the wilderness, she thought, and as such were in perfect harmony. It was only in conversation that they stumbled; words became barriers, fences, thorned hedges impossible to penetrate.

She hauled herself up on the rock, leaving tracks for the sun to dry, and slipped behind the trees to change into her jeans and sweater. As she trekked along the shoreline toward the cove, pushing aside branches, her ears sifting through the myriad bird calls for those she recognized, she wondered what it would be like to eat breakfast with Cal. Breakfast was a very intimate meal. Would there be intimacy between them, or only the renewed strain of ambivalence and things unsaid?

Wearing deck shoes and an old gray T-shirt along with his wet shorts, Cal was waiting for her on the beach. The lake was as calm as if they had never cavorted in its depths, as if they had never existed, Sara thought with a frisson along her spine. She said, forgetting her resolution to keep words to a minimum, "Someone could come along here in five minutes and never know we'd been here."

"That's the way it should be. We should leave the wilderness unmarked by our passing."

Because he spoke seriously and without affectation she heard herself say, "Is life the same, do you suppose? Do we pass through and leave no real mark?" She scuffed at the sand with her feet. "What is there to show that my mother lived? Some needlework, a few photographs and letters. That's not much."

"She lives in your memory. Yours and your sister's."

"And is that all?"

Cal twisted the towel that was draped around his neck, his face very thoughtful. Then he said deliberately, "Every piece of furniture I make is a memorial to Dougal."

"So my mother lives in my actions as much as in my memory—is that what you mean?"

"Reckon so."

Her throat felt tight. "Was Dougal the only person in your life to show you kindness?"

Cal snapped the towel at a nearby rock with a crack like a whip. "Don't you start feeling sorry for me."

It was an answer of sorts: all that she was going to get. "You don't pity those whom you like," Sara said soberly. Then, attuned to him as she was, she added, "And that's enough talk about the meaning of life for one morning. How about breakfast?"

She had read him right, for there was relief in his smile. "I make the best scrambled eggs in Hants County. Not to mention my omelets."

"And I'm a mean hand with a toaster."

"Better than with a needle?"

"Much better," she said firmly. "Cornelia says I learned to cook because I like to eat. You can always depend on sisters for the unvarnished truth."

"Let's go, then," Cal said.

He led the way along the narrow strip of sand to a winding pathway edged with bracken and the feathery green of tamaracks, whose roots projected from the black, peaty soil like knuckles from a hand. Fractured by the trees, the sun lay in splinters on the fronds of ferns and the leathery leaves of Labrador tea.

After three or four minutes they came to a fork in the path. Cal looked back at Sara. "You in a hurry?"

She shook her head, knowing she would be content to spend the whole day with him. He paused briefly, almost as if making a calculation in his head. Then he said, "I want to show you something."

They took the right-hand fork in the trail. As it gradually sloped downward, the underbrush changed to alders, scrub spruce and yellow-flowered cinque-foil, with the whine of mosquitoes a counterpoint to the delirious songs of birds. The ground grew soggy.

The path opened on a marsh, its acid-green grass whispering to itself. Dragonflies hovered over the grass.

Against the pale sky swallows darted in an intricate, never-colliding dance.

Cal edged to the left over the wet clumps of grass, which sucked greedily at his shoes. Sara followed, swinging at the cloud of blackflies and mosquitoes that circled around her head. Eat or be eaten might be the rule of nature, but she had no wish to furnish a meal for a ravenous insect. However, when she swatted a mosquito on her wrist, it left a circle of blood. Her blood. *This had better be good, Cal Mathieson,* she thought darkly, and felt the muddy water of the swamp seep through her sneakers.

A few minutes later Cal stopped, then sank down on his heels; he appeared oblivious to the mosquitoes. "There," he said.

Sara squelched up behind him. The bog opened into a field enclosed by tamaracks. A profusion of mauve flowers spiked the gently waving grass, a clear note of color in a world of varying greens.

Sara forgot the hungry mosquitoes. She murmured, "How beautiful...they're a variety of orchid, aren't they? I've never seen so many before."

"They flower here every year. I keep it a secret because I don't want people trampling all over them."

"I'm glad you showed me," Sara said softly. "They're such a glorious color."

He snapped off a single spike and stood up, holding it out to her so that she could see the complexity of the lipped, ragged petals. "This one's for you," he said.

Their hands brushed as she took it from him. Joel had always given her expensive presents, hothouse roses and heavy gold jewelry, conventional presents such as are valued by worldly people. Cal, however, had brought her to a place both private and precious to him and shared its beauty with her, a beauty symbolized by the sheath of tiny purple blossoms in her hand. Cal's seemed like the perfect gift; Joel's gifts had always carried a subtle message of indebtedness. "Thank you, Cal," she said simply. Her face, raised to his, was without artifice.

With an awkwardness that touched her, for he was a man skilled with his hands, he took the blossom from her and tucked it in the tangled curls above her ear. She stood still, scarcely breathing, and heard him say, "There. I think that'll stay, although your hair's not really long enough. Hold still, Sara, there's a blackfly on your neck."

So much for romance, thought Sara. Nothing like the great Canadian outdoors for keeping your feet firmly on the ground. Or in the swamp, as the case might be. Cal's fingers pressed against her skin, then he was wiping them on his shorts. "One down, a hundred to go," he said lightly.

His face was close to hers, so close that she could see the change of expression in his eyes and knew what he was about to do. Feeling as if she were in a dream where a too-sudden movement would waken them both, startling them like the deer, Sara lifted her face and closed her eyes and felt his mouth move gently against hers. The world became nothing but the touch of a man's mouth and a delicious, sun-warmed happiness.

It was a kiss beautiful in its simplicity. Yet all kisses must end, and this one was no exception. Cal stepped back from her, his feet sinking in the mud. "I've been wanting to do that since the first night I met you. Even if I shouldn't have done it."

Sara smiled faintly. "I wasn't exactly fighting you off."

"You won't have to. It won't happen again."

The smile left her face. She felt like a child slapped for something she had not realized was a misdeed. "We did nothing wrong, Cal."

"I shouldn't have done it," he repeated stubbornly.

She said in frustration, "You open a door and then you close it in my face."

His expression was very different from that of the man who had tucked the flower into her hair. "I won't be opening any doors for you, Sara."

"Because they're locked," she said intuitively. "And you've thrown away the key. Cal, why have you done that?"

A swarm of blackflies was circling his head. He thrashed out at them in a gesture both violent and impotent and said coldly, "That's not your business."

"Fine," she said irritably. "I'm being eaten alive. Let's get out of here."

He pivoted as rapidly as a man can whose feet are inches deep in mud. Without speaking to each other, they traversed the wet grass and reentered the coolness of the forest. They were marching through the copse of alders when Sara suddenly grabbed his arm. "Look," she whispered, crouching down. "Through the bushes . . . it's a yellowthroat."

A tiny yellow bird, black-masked, was flitting among the interwoven branches. Cal knelt beside her, his movements slow so as not to startle the bird. But when it came within ten feet of them it flicked its tail and darted out of sight; they could hear the burr of air in its feathers like the sound of a tiny engine.

Sara had forgotten she was supposed to be angry with Cal. She sat back on her heels and said with great satisfaction, "That's one of my favorite birds. Have you ever heard it sing? It goes *witchity witchity witchity witch*."

Her imitation was not a good one. Cal tipped back his head, pursed his lips and, in a high-pitched whistle, produced a far more convincing imitation of the song of a yellowthroat. Convincing enough for the bird itself; deep in the alders the yellowthroat answered him.

Sara glowered at him. "Do a white-throated sparrow."

He produced the clear, plaintive notes of the sparrow, then imitated the sibilant call of a chickadee, the scolding of a blue jay and the gossipy burble of a bobolink.

Trying not to laugh, Sara said severely, "Do you ever have flocks of females following you around the woods?"

"Only the feathered kind."

"That's the kind I meant, Cal Mathieson!"

"Oh. Sorry," he said meekly, not looking at all meek.

She loved it when the somber gray of his eyes was lit by laughter. "I bet you know a lot about the outdoors."

"I know a lot about the habits of birds and plants, but I'm not so good at giving them their fancy Latin names," he said easily, then cocked his head. "There goes the yellowthroat again."

"I'm not going to answer. Ouch, my knees are getting stiff." As she tried to straighten, she snagged her sweater on a branch. "Oh no, have I torn it? I can't ask Cornelia to mend another sweater so soon!"

"Hold still." As Cal reached over to free her, his hand inadvertently touched the softness of her breast under the loose sweater. He must have seen her instinctive shiver of response. He said roughly, "Oh God, Sara . . ." and pulled her toward him.

It was a kiss very different from their first—hungry, deep, almost desperate in its intensity. And when he eventually drew back, each was trembling. Even Cal's voice was not quite steady. "Ten minutes ago I said that would never happen."

"Yesterday morning I'd decided I never wanted to see you again," Sara responded, just as shakily.

He made a valiant effort to collect himself. "Maybe we should go home and do something ordinary like scramble eggs."

"And burn toast." Spontaneously she laid her palm against his cheek. "You're a nice man, Cal."

"Nice?" he said quizzically.

"It is a misused word, isn't it?" She frowned. "It's funny, I hardly know you at all but I feel as though I could depend on you. That you'd be there if you were needed."

"Dougal used to say the same thing," Cal said dryly.

"Dougal knew you a lot better than I."

"Dougal and you are as different as chalk from cheese," said Cal in a tone of voice that indicated the discussion was closed. "C'mon, breakfast."

But they did not hurry through the sun-dappled woods, for there was something about the early morning peace that precluded hurry. They saw a pair of rabbits and a flock of tiny kinglets; they heard the *rat-tat-tat* of a woodpecker's beak against a dead tree; they chewed spruce gum. Although Sara had lost all track of time, Cal had not. As they emerged into the clearing behind the barn, where firewood was neatly stacked, he said, "Peg doesn't arrive until nine. So we've got lots of time for breakfast. But you might want to be gone by then, otherwise she'll figure you were here all night and she'll make sure everyone in Haliburton hears about it, too."

Sara remembered Peg's arch, bright-eyed smile and knew he was right. "My car's parked at the lake. Maybe you could run me over there after breakfast."

Cal said stiffly, "I don't drive."

"What do you mean?"

"I never drive the truck. I don't have a license."

"Why ever not?"

His eyes were clouded again in the way she had come to dread. "Years ago I was responsible for an accident," he said, his voice devoid of emotion. "I decided I'd never get behind the wheel again, and I've stuck with that. Peg drives the truck for me."

"I noticed she did the day at the hardware store, but I didn't think anything of it. Cal, you're a grown man now, shouldn't you stop punishing yourself?"

"Lay off, Sara."

She bit her lip. Although she wanted to know more about the accident that had marked him so lastingly, she was sure it would be useless to ask. Another closed door. Another set of quills. "Do you object to breaking eggs for omelets?" she said crossly. "Just thought I'd ask since I seem to get in trouble no matter what I say."

He answered with commendable patience, "I decided long ago there are some things it's not worth talking about . . . they're better forgotten."

"But they're not forgotten!"

"They would be if people like you would let them be."

"You're going about it entirely the wrong way. Read any basic psychology book and you'll see what I mean."

"Sara," Cal said tightly, "do you or do you not want breakfast?"

She countered with a question of her own. "Why do we fight so much?"

"Dougal always said I was stubborn as a knot in a piece of oak. And I wouldn't say you give up easy, Sara. Must be all that red hair."

Gravely she held out her hand. "Truce? Let's scramble the eggs and not each other."

"Best idea you've had yet," he replied, and ducked as she swung at him. So they were laughing when they went into the kitchen.

Cal's scrambled eggs were light and fluffy, flavored with herbs that he grew in the garden. Sara did not burn the toast. They ate on the back porch, drank scalding coffee and talked about wildlife and bird feeders. They were relaxed. They were comfortable with each other. Sara could quite easily have routed Peg to Outer Mongolia.

At twenty to nine she stretched and said lazily, "I suppose I'd better go if I want to keep my morals intact in the eyes of Haliburton."

"I'm sorry I can't drive you."

"I'll walk along the road, it's only a couple of miles . . . may I use the bathroom, Cal?"

"Through the hall and up the stairs, first door on your left."

"Thanks."

The stairs had carved oak banisters and a circular window of stained glass casting shadows of ruby and purple on the smooth gold boards. The woodwork in the bathroom was exquisite. But the room needed plants and ruffled white curtains, Sara decided critically. A woman's touch.

If she had had the nerve she would have sneaked along the hallway to find Cal's room; as it was, she contented herself with peering into the living room at the foot of the stairs, where an old grandfather clock presided, peacefully ticking away the minutes and hours. Cornelia would have given a month's salary for the pair of love seats flanking the brick fireplace, not to mention the pine corner cupboard. Then Sara's eyes were caught by an object on the floor against the far wall. She frowned in puzzlement. It was a book. A book with a glossy cover and splayed white pages. The book she had given Cal.

Someone had thrown the book against the wall.

From one moment to the next the peaceful, sunlit room had become the stuff of nightmares, the ticking of the clock like the ticking of a bomb that would maim and kill. Very slowly Sara crossed the room, wanting to flee into the sunshine and forget what she had seen, knowing she could not, that she was pulled to the book as an addict is drawn to the drug that will destroy him.

She knelt on the polished pine floor. Her supposition had been correct. The book had been thrown against the wall, thrown with such force that the spine was broken and the pages were hanging free like white, fallen petals. Sickened, she gathered the book up as if it were a weeping child, got to her feet and left the room. In the hall the old-fashioned mirror threw back a reflection of her fixed stare and pale cheeks.

She found Cal still sitting in the sun, his legs up on the railing, his eyes shut. He looked ordinary, peaceful, relaxed. Yet because it must have been he who had thrown the book against the wall, he, too, had shifted from reality to nightmare. He had shown her a field of flowers and kissed her with heart-stopping tenderness; at the same time he had destroyed the gift she had given him. She said in a voice she would never have recognized as her own, "Cal, why did you do this?" and held out the ruined book.

He opened his eyes, a smile on his lips. Then he saw her strained white face and the book in her hands and his smile vanished. As ice coats a pond in the early days of winter his features congealed, all expression gone.

"I forgot about it," he said. "I meant to hide it."

"Why, Cal? Why did you do it?"

Slowly he got to his feet. "I can't answer that, Sara."

"Can't or won't?" She let the book fall on the table, as if she could not bear to touch it for a moment longer. "You didn't just drop it. By accident. Anyone could have done that. You threw it. You had to have thrown it to have done so much damage." She let all the pain show in her face. "I thought you liked me."

The words were torn from him. "I do."

"Oh, sure you do! So much so that you destroyed the present I gave you." She blinked furiously, determined not to cry in front of him. "I don't understand you, Cal. You're like a split personality, warm and gentle one minute, full of rage and destruction the next...you meant to kill that dog the night we met, you broke its neck on purpose."

She had cracked the ice. "I did not!"

"Is that why you live alone? Because you can't be trusted, because you've got a violent temper that you can't control? How did the car accident happen, Cal? Come on, tell me—did you deliberately cause it?''

"If you believe that of me, then you'll believe anything!''

She leaned forward, gripping the edge of the table with clenched fists. "What am I supposed to believe? We judge people by their actions, what else can we do?''

"There's an old saying that you don't judge a man until you've walked a mile in his moccasins.''

Her shoulders sagged; she felt suddenly exhausted. "But you won't allow me to walk in your moccasins. You keep too much hidden.'' Blindly she looked around. "I've got to get out of here, I can't take any more of this. Where's my swimsuit?''

He picked up the rolled, damp towel from the bench and as he passed it to her, rested his hand briefly on hers. "I'm sorry you found the book, Sara. I should have hidden it.''

"I'm sorry I found it, too. But I'm even more sorry you ruined it.''

As if she had not spoken, he went on heavily, "I knew when I kissed you, it was wrong. That I shouldn't have. I wish to God things could have been different— but they are what they are. You'd better not come here again.''

She gazed at his hand, seeing the thin white scar along his thumb, knowing that his soul was scarred far more deeply than his hands, knowing also that she could not heal him. He would not allow her to. "I won't come here again," she said. "I can't. Goodbye, Cal." Without meeting his eyes she pulled her hand free, took her towel and ran down the porch steps, then along the path to the driveway. She was nearly to the road when she heard a car approaching. *Peg,* she thought, her heart sinking. She could not face Peg.

Like a frightened rabbit, she scurried into the undergrowth and ducked behind some bushes. The car engine grew louder. She closed her eyes and heard the car pass, heard it come to a halt near the barn. Peg's shrill voice called, "Morning, Cal! Enjoying the sun, eh?"

Sara covered her ears so she would not hear Cal's reply. The engine was shut off. The car door squealed open.

She could not see the barn or the car. She started worming her way through the tangled vines toward the road. When she reached it, she jumped across the ditch, trying hard not to remember the doe and fawn, and began walking along the shoulder in the direction of the lake. She walked very fast, finding relief in action, and deliberately did not allow herself to think about Cal or the book or the way he had kissed her. She could control her thoughts, but she could not control the sting of unshed tears or the dull ache lodged in the region of her heart. For more than a book had been destroyed. Much more.

She was somehow surprised that her car was exactly where she had left it and that the lake was still serenely basking in the sun. She drove home to Cornelia's, where more by good luck than planning, Laird had already left for the mill and the children were out playing. Cornelia was in the kitchen drinking coffee and reading the paper. "Got your note," she said lazily. "Did you have a good swim? You look like a drunken Hawaiian."

"Hawaiian? Why?"

"The flower over your ear."

Sara reached up and pulled the orchid from her hair. The stem was bent and the petals bruised and crumpled. She sat down on the nearest chair and burst into tears.

"Sara! What's the matter?"

Sara felt her sister's arms go around her. She grabbed them and held on tight, and cried all the harder.

Cornelia, wise in the ways of her younger sister, waited until the sobs had died to sniffles, shoved a box of Kleenex in Sara's lap and said firmly, "Tell me what happened."

Hiccuping a little, Sara did so, including in her narrative the two kisses and the ruined book. "I think he's a psychopath," she finished wildly, dredging up terms from her undergraduate psychology courses. "Or a sociopath. Or a schizophrenic."

"Nonsense. Cal Mathieson is none of those things."

"You didn't see that book."

"There must be a reason. Something to do with Dougal, maybe. Cal's a good person, Sara."

Sara sniffed. "It's immaterial whether he is or not. I won't be seeing him again."

"That's what you said yesterday," Cornelia commented.

"I mean it today!"

"Haliburton's too small a place to decide you're going to ignore one of its inhabitants."

"Oh, stop being so reasonable, Lia! If I do see him, I don't have to talk to him. What shift are you on today?"

After glancing at her sister's flushed and tear-swollen face, Cornelia accepted the change of subject. A few moments later Malcolm came in crying, because he had skinned his knee, and Cal was not mentioned again.

CHAPTER FIVE

SARA DID NOT SEE CAL for more than two weeks, although she still could not think of him without a sharp pang of disappointment—at least disappointment is what she called the unpleasant emotion in her breast. She kept herself busy reading for her English courses, looking after Malcolm and Caitlin and working on her suntan, the latter never an easy matter for she was fair-skinned and burned easily. She was lying on a towel on the grass one morning listening to the radio when the news came on. The announcer was her friend Pete Naseby, husband of her good friend Ally. Sara sat up, noticing absently that pieces of grass were sticking to the suntan lotion on her legs. She needed a visit with Ally, she thought impulsively. Ally always cheered her up.

She hurried into the kitchen and rang the number for Ally's house, the same house where her furniture was stored for the summer. On the second ring Ally said, "Hello?"

"It's Sara. I need a visit to the big city. Are you free for lunch?"

"Sure! What time?"

Sara looked at the clock over the sink. "Twelve-thirty?"

"I'll make a reservation at Alfred's. Their salads are out of this world. Meet you there?"

"Wonderful." Sara scurried upstairs to tell Cornelia her plan and to get dressed.

She chose a gathered yellow skirt with a blouse brilliantly patterned in red and yellow, for many years ago she had stopped restricting herself to the safe autumnal colors that went with her hair. Her high-heeled sandals were distinctly shabby; she'd buy a new pair, she decided with a thrill of anticipation. Shopping was a wonderful diversion when your life was devoid of dates.

Ally and she had been classmates three years ago and friends ever since, even though they made an unlikely looking pair, Ally being blond and petite. She was already seated in the restaurant when Sara arrived. After they had hugged each other affectionately, Sara very quickly decided on a crabmeat and avocado salad and then said feelingly, "Great to be in the city again!"

"All that country air getting to you?"

"A bit, I guess. But I have a job, Ally—teaching English of all things. I may need help!"

Ally was a reading specialist. Beginning their salads, they talked shop for a while. Then Ally said casually, "Are you seeing Joel today?"

"No. I haven't heard from him in weeks."

"So it's really over this time?"

"I guess so. I drove past his apartment building but his car was gone. He may even be away for the summer. Anyway, he's probably met someone else."

"You don't sound too pleased by the prospect," Ally remarked, buttering a piece of herb bread.

"It's none of my business, really. But I miss him sometimes, and I wonder if he misses me."

"He did keep you rather under wraps, Sara," Ally said gently.

Joel had not appreciated the amount of time Sara had spent with Ally and Pete; it had been one of the issues he and Sara had fought over. "I know. And I know it would never work...."

"No other prospects? No handsome dairy farmers or sexy lumbermen?"

"Nary a one." The story of her brief, confusing relationship with Cal seemed too complicated to share, even with Ally. Besides, it was over before it had really begun, so there was no point in talking about it.

Ally looked calculating. "Maybe Pete knows someone at the radio station."

"I can't drive thirty miles for a date."

"Then you'd better get interested in Holsteins."

"Yes, ma'am! In the meantime I'm going shopping for some new shoes. Red ones."

Ally chuckled. "Not purple?"

"My tastes are very conservative," Sara said decorously.

"Sure—the basic primary colors. There are sales in all the shoe stores—can I come with you?"

SARA LEFT THE CITY midafternoon, having bought two pairs of sandals. She noticed on her way out that Joel's car was still not in the lot. Cornelia loved her new shoes, and Sara settled back into the slow peaceful summer routine. The July days passed, one by one, until late one afternoon a week or so after her shopping expedition, Sara had an unexpected visitor.

She and Cornelia had just finished making a batch of apple pies for a church bake sale when they heard a car roar up the driveway and come to a halt at the back door. A minute or two later Malcolm burst in the door. "Mum, guess what!" he cried, jumping up and down in excitement. "There's a guy outside with a red car just like my model. He says I can go for a drive in it. Can I, Mum? Can I?"

A man had followed Malcolm into the kitchen, a handsome, black-haired man. Sara blinked. It was Joel, her former boyfriend, teacher of mathematics at Rockwood Junior High, lover of fast cars and of malleable women.

"Well," said Sara, "fancy seeing you here."

As confidently as if he owned the house, Joel crossed the kitchen and kissed Sara firmly on the mouth. "I just happened to be passing," he said, "and thought I'd drop in."

"Haliburton is not a place one just happens to be passing, Joel," she responded amiably. But there was a gleam in her eye, for she had forgotten how good-looking Joel was with his crisp black curls, sea-blue eyes and athlete's body, all packaged with a charm which he knew how to use to maximum effect.

He took a spotless handkerchief out of his pocket and rubbed her left cheek. "Flour," he said. "You look terribly domesticated, Sara. Wouldn't you like me to take you out for dinner?"

She would. But she did not want to give in too easily. "There's only one restaurant in the area, and it's the kind of place where you have supper, not dinner."

"We could go to Halifax."

She smiled at him guilelessly. "But then you'd have to drive me all the way home."

If Joel had had plans for her to stay at his apartment, he kept them to himself. "What's the food like in this restaurant?"

"Down home, country cooking."

"What I don't do for you."

Malcolm could not contain himself any longer. "Can I go for a drive, Mum?"

Cornelia, who had met Joel before, fixed him with a gimlet stare and said, "Yes. As long as Joel stays under the speed limit."

"Yes, ma'am. I'll take him for a drive, Sara, while you get ready."

Sara looked down at her shorts and blouse, neither of which was unmarked by the apple pies. "I can take a hint."

He kissed her again, a not unpleasurable occurrence, and departed with Malcolm. Cornelia said calmly, "You can have some of my Oscar de la Renta bath oil. Do you think he wants you back, Sara?"

"I don't know."

"Would you go back?"

"I might," Sara said with a touch of defiance. Her ego had been badly enough bruised by Cal that Joel looked doubly attractive. Better the devil you know than the one you don't, she thought darkly, and ran upstairs to turn on the bath water.

She was wearing her prettiest sundress and her new red shoes when Joel and Malcolm returned, and knew she looked her best. Joel may have agreed. At any rate, after he had skillfully reversed out of the driveway, he said, "Sara, I want you back."

She smothered a smile; Cornelia would be amused. And how like Joel not to ask how she was or if she was dating anyone else. "Did you drive all the way up here to tell me that?" she temporized.

"I hate the telephone, you know that. I miss you, Sara. A lot more than I thought I would. And I've changed. I'm sure I can allow you more freedom now."

His use of the word allow did not thrill her. "I'll be living here next winter, Joel, because I'll be teaching from September until May. An English teacher at the junior high is on maternity leave."

For a moment he looked less than pleased. "I thought you'd be moving back to Halifax in the fall. Are you going to live with Cornelia all winter?"

"No, I'll have my own place."

He brightened. "Then I can stay over. Or you can come to Halifax on weekends."

He appeared to be taking her consent for granted. "Well, we can think about it," she said noncommittally, then added as his face fell, "I am pleased to see you, Joel."

She was telling the truth. But would she have been as pleased had she been dating Cal? She did not think so. Furthermore, she had the uneasy feeling people could not reactivate the past; a dead relationship was a dead relationship.

They had to park some distance from the restaurant. As Joel got out of the car he took a paper bag from the pouch in the door. "I bought you a present," he said. "Well, two presents, actually."

A very beautiful gold chain bracelet was taped to the cover of a book. Sara would have preferred the book alone. "Joel, you really shouldn't have," she protested.

He kissed her on the tip of the nose. "Yes, I should. It's my way of saying I'm sorry, Sara, and that I've erased jealousy and possessiveness from my vocabulary."

She could remember flinging those words at him during their last fight, and obviously he had remembered them, too. As he fastened the chain around her wrist, she wondered a little wildly if there was anything symbolic in his action.

The book was *The Alley Cat*. "I've heard about this," she said appreciatively, glad to talk about something other than the bracelet. She glanced through some of the reviews in the front.

"It's extremely funny in places. Here, let me read you one of my favorite paragraphs."

They were wandering down the sidewalk, Joel reading aloud in a dramatic baritone, Sara chuckling because the book was indeed very funny, when a shrill voice said, "Sara Deane! Aren't you the naughty one! Another young man!"

Peg Campbell, in a flowered dress that emphasized all the defects of her figure, was stationed in front of them roguishly shaking her finger. Said Sara, without enthusiasm, "Hello, Peg."

"Aren't you going to introduce me to your friend?"

Briefly Sara contemplated saying no. But before she could say anything, Joel had stretched out his hand with a smile calculated to dazzle any member of the opposite sex, let alone one as susceptible as Peg, and said, "I'm Joel Crouse. Has Sara been stepping out on me again?"

As Sara's cheeks grew pink with temper, Peg's eyes nearly popped out of her head. She tossed her limp gray curls. "I must admit I had hopes for a nice little romance between Sara and my boss," she replied, her breasts rising and falling in a sigh of ponderous dimensions. "But it's not to be, I can tell—you're ahead of the game, young man!" She leaned forward and added with a confidential air ruined by her piercing voice, "She's a lovely girl, isn't she? But you don't need me to tell you that!"

Sara winced. The only thing that could possibly make this scene worse would be the arrival of Cal. She said in her best schoolteacher's manner and with complete untruth, "Nice seeing you, Peg. But we must be going or we'll be late for dinner." She tucked her arm in Joel's and gave it an authoritative tug, and saw Cal coming down the sidewalk toward them.

He was carrying a bag of groceries, and she saw from his expression that had he been able to avoid her, he would have. But Peg had seen him, too. "Come and meet Sara's friend," she cried. "You're out of the running, Cal!"

Not for the first time in her life Sara wished the ground would open and swallow her. She said weakly, "Hello, Cal. I'd like you to meet a friend of mine, Joel Crouse from Halifax. Joel, this is Cal Mathieson."

Cal shifted the bag of groceries to his left arm and the two men shook hands. Neither one smiled. Peg was watching with such avid interest that Sara heard herself gabble, "How are you, Cal? Joel's given me this wonderful book. Have you heard about it? It's very funny. I'll lend it to you when I'm through, if you like. They've made a movie and a TV series out of it, how's that for a Canadian success story?"

Cal said coldly, "I never read novels. Are you ready, Peg? We've got to get the stuff from the station before it closes."

"And we mustn't make Sara and Joel late for dinner, must we?" Peg said coyly. "Have a good time, you two, and don't do anything I wouldn't do."

Sara's instinctive reply to this would have been censored for obscenity. She forced herself to smile, wondering if it was Peg's example that had discouraged Cal from matrimony. It was a reasonable assumption.

"Goodbye, Peg, Cal. Come along, Joel." She pulled at his arm as if he were Malcolm.

The restaurant was six doors down. They were seated across from each other in a booth and had been handed menus before either of them spoke.

"I think I'll have—" Sara began.

"Who was that guy?" Joel demanded.

"I met him purely by accident and we have never had a single proper date, and why am I explaining all this to you anyway?"

"That woman sure didn't give the impression that the two of you had never had a date."

"If you're feeling charitable you could call Peg a romantic, if you're not, then she's a born trouble-maker. Take your choice," Sara said shortly.

"You're very upset over someone you claim you scarcely know."

"Oh, shut up, Joel!" Sara exploded, then hurriedly rearranged her face for the benefit of the waitress. "Could you give us a couple more minutes, please? We haven't really had time to look at the menu yet."

"What does he do? Where does he live?"

"He makes very beautiful furniture, and he lives by himself on the lake road. Joel, do you realize we're having another fight?"

Assuming an air of dignity, Joel replied, "I was merely asking for an explanation."

"If you trusted me, you wouldn't have to." Which was, she realized miserably, another line she had already used with Joel.

He ran his finger around his collar and said with a manful attempt to be casual, "Do you recommend the steak?"

"The beef is pretty dependable here, and their home fries are wonderful. They do very good fish and chips, as well, nice light batter."

The waitress brought each of them a drink; and the food was excellent. By the time they had finished eating, Sara's ruffled feathers had subsided and Joel had apparently forgotten Cal and Peg. At some length he described the summer-school session he had attended and a couple of movies he had seen lately. He was an entertaining conversationalist, and when he unobtrusively led the discussion back to plays and movies they had seen together, Sara felt the pull of nostalgia, as perhaps he had intended she should. When he suggested they drive out to the lake to watch the sunset, she was perfectly agreeable. Her mistake was in pointing out the house she would be renting the following winter, because as they proceeded around the next turn Joel saw Cal's wooden sign on the post at the end of his driveway. "That's the same guy, isn't it?" he said sharply.

"It is, yes. But you can't even see one house from the other."

"So he'll be your next-door neighbor all winter."

Irked, she spoke the literal—and still painful—truth. "Cal Mathieson is not interested in a relationship with me."

"But you're interested in him."

"No, I'm not! What would be the point?"

Joel looked over at her. "*I'm* interested in a relationship with you. I still love you, Sara."

She hesitated, playing with the folds in her dress. "I honestly don't know how I feel about you, Joel. Can we just leave it at that for now?"

"Sure we can. I'm not worried, Sara, we had too much going for us to let it drop...we must be nearly at the lake, are we?"

For Sara the lake at sunset was so evocative of her arrival in Haliburton and her first dramatic meeting with Cal that for once the call of the loons and the encircling, protective trees did not bring her any peace. As her shoes crunched in the tiny stones at the water's edge, she found herself wishing it was Cal walking beside her rather than Joel, yet knowing at the same time how impossible that was. Joel was the one who wanted her. Not Cal. She should be happy to have Joel's company...shouldn't she? They had, after all, been lovers for months. Only last week she had driven past his apartment building and wondered where he was. And with whom.

Nevertheless, she was relieved when Joel turned back to the car without having made any more overt moves than an arm around her shoulders; and Joel was the type of man who would consider it obligatory to put his arm around a pretty woman under the summer stars. As they climbed back in the car and headed in the direction of Haliburton, she knew how glad she would be to get home to Cornelia's. Although ambivalence was not a comfortable frame of mind, she did not want to make any decisions about Joel tonight.

Because she was feeling a little smug that she had at least decided that much, she was doubly disconcerted when Joel suddenly swung the car to the left up a narrow dirt trail about half a mile from the lake. "Where are we going?" she demanded.

"You remember this road, Sara. We went up here once before."

She did remember. It had been a sunny day last spring, and had been one of the last times they had made love. "Joel, I want to go home."

"Relax, Sara, this is for old time's sake. After all, I can't very well invite myself to stay overnight at Cornelia's, can I?"

He parked by the open field, the headlights swinging over the tall grass and the wildflowers. Then he reached over, deftly took Sara in his arms and began kissing her.

Sara tried to respond. She tried very hard. As Joel's lips moved against hers and his hands rhythmically stroked her shoulders, she made herself remember all the good times they had shared, in bed and out, all the fun and the laughter on the cold winter evenings in the city. She willed her lips to return his kiss and her body to come alive, and knew she had failed when he murmured against her mouth, "Relax, sweetheart, you're as tense as a spring. It's me, Joel, remember? And I love you."

His words brought panic, not comfort, claustrophobia rather than freedom; so strongly that Sara knew she could not make love to Joel. She had moved on...had she outgrown him? She would like to remain his friend. But not his lover.

It was not the most opportune time to arrive at such a conclusion. *Handle this in a dignified way, Sara,* she told herself. *You're a big girl now. You don't have to kiss anyone you don't want to.*

She got her head free between kisses and said clearly, "Joel, please don't do this. I..." But she should have remembered how strong Joel was. He crushed her against his chest, which in the confines of the car was a less than comfortable position, and silenced her with another passionate kiss.

Sara gurgled in her throat, banged her fists on his chest and kicked out at him with her new red shoes. The final move was the successful one, for she hacked his shin decisively enough that he stopped kissing her. "Sara, don't be ridiculous, you don't have to play the outraged virgin with me. Come on, darling, let's take the blanket and go and lie in the grass."

So Joel had planned this, even down to having a blanket in the back seat. "Joel, I'm sorry, but I don't want to make love to you. I can't!" Sara said emphatically.

He ignored the emotion in her voice. "It'll be fine, Sara. You're just nervous because it's been such a long time."

She said with frantic truth, "We can't put the clock back."

"We're not putting it back. We're putting it forward to the future. A future we'll both share," he said with insufferable self-confidence, and kissed her again.

Sara was beginning to be frightened. The field of wildflowers was a long way from habitation, and Joel had never been overly amenable to reason. She felt the thrust of his tongue in her mouth and the dig of his fingers in her back, and panicked. She had one hand free. She lashed out at him in the dark, missed him altogether, and caught her wrist on the metal bar of the headrest. "Ouch!" she sputtered. "Dammit, Joel Crouse, let go of me!" Grabbing her purse from the seat, she thrust it at his nose.

He backed away. "You're overreacting," he said with a noticeable effort at restraint.

"No, I'm not! I said I didn't want to kiss you and I meant it."

"For God's sake, calm down. You're acting as if we've never made love before."

"I can't help that!" She fumbled for the door handle with one hand, her other ineffectively trying to pull her skirt down around her knees.

"Were are you going?"

As he grabbed at her bare arm, his nails grazing her skin, she felt her control snap. "I never want to see you again!" she hissed. "Go away, get lost, and don't come back."

Joel had never been renowned for an even temper. "You agreed to go to the lake. What was I supposed to think?"

Sara propelled herself out of the car, banged the door shut to spare herself the trouble of a reply and glared out over the field, where the daisies shone like earthbound stars. But Joel rolled down the window. "This is your last chance, Sara," he snarled. "Get in the car and I'll drive you home."

"Or smother me in revolting kisses. No, thank you!"

"Oh, go to hell!" Joel exclaimed with more vigor than originality. He threw the car into gear and rocketed down the track, stones flying out from the tires like bullets sprayed from a machine gun. She heard each aggressive gear change until the sound of the engine faded in the distance. She was left in the velvet silence of a summer night.

She bent and picked a daisy, shredding its petals one by one and letting them fall at her feet. Had she been leading Joel on? She had toyed with the idea of renewing their relationship... and she should have remembered this deserted field and Joel's strong libidinous instincts. *You're an idiot, Sara,* she scolded herself. *You're at least partly responsible for getting yourself into this mess. Now get yourself out. A five-mile walk will do it.*

Sara could easily have walked five miles with sneakers on her feet and a sweater around her shoulders against the evening chill. But she was wearing her new red shoes, pretty, narrow-strapped sandals with dainty heels, which were not intended for long walks on gravel roads. She was hobbling after half a mile, had blisters by a mile and, when she tried walking barefoot, cut her toe on a piece of glass. She put her sandals on again. Had Joel driven up the road she would have risked her virtue and gotten in the car. But she knew Joel too well to expect that he would come back to get her. Joel could be even more stubborn than she. He was probably halfway to Halifax by now.

She was in genuine pain by the time she reached the lacquered sign at the end of Cal's driveway. The barn was in darkness, and only a faint glow of light came from the living room windows. She had two choices. Walk three more miles to the village, by which time she might be crippled for life, or knock on Cal's door and phone Cornelia.

She had a third choice. Sit down in the ditch and cry.

Very carefully she removed her sandals. Then she padded up the narrow strip of grass along the driveway, leaves rustling against her bare arm. The grass felt cool and soft under her aching soles. If Cal was home, she thought dreamily, she'd ask him for a cup of tea. Her mother had been a great believer in the recuperative powers of a cup of tea....

Five feet ahead of her a black shape emerged from the bushes. Sara screamed with all the force of her lungs.

"Who—my God, Sara!"

Cal's voice. Cal's arms going around her. Cal's mouth kissing hers as if he were a starving man confronted with a banquet. Sara closed her eyes, dropped her sandals, put her arms around his neck and discovered why she had not wanted to kiss Joel.

She learned a lot about Cal in those few seconds: that he could be generous, ardent, yet curiously humble, that he could combine passion with immense sensitivity. When they finally broke free of each other, a small voice whispered in her brain, *You're in love with this man.*

No, I'm not. I scarcely know him.

Doesn't matter. You know he's right for you.

Kissing under the stars is not a reliable way to pick a mate....

Suddenly afraid that she might have spoken the words aloud, Sara stammered, "I'm sorry I screamed."

"I thought you were Percy. Three more windows were broken last night, so I figured I'd keep an eye out for him." Cal's callused palms stroked the slope of her shoulders. "But you're definitely not Percy."

She was recovering her wits. "I'm not flattered that you should mistake the two of us."

He laughed softly. "What are you doing here, Sara?"

With secret delight she leaned against him. "It's a long story," she mumbled, luxuriating in the warmth of his skin under her cheek.

"If you keep that up, I'll start kissing you again," he said huskily.

Light-headed with love and the pain of her lacerated feet, she murmured, "Promise?"

This time as they kissed, Cal's hands moved from her shoulders to explore the smooth, bare planes of her back. Then they fell to her waist, pulling her fiercely toward him.

He wants me, she thought giddily; his body was giving her the message unequivocally. And in a dizzying surge of desire she knew she wanted him just as badly.

Again it was he who ended the embrace. "Sara, we mustn't continue," he said incoherently. "We can't do this. It's no good...."

Even in the darkness she could see the struggle in his face, a struggle that verged on torment. "Don't look like that, Cal," she whispered. "I wouldn't hurt you for the world."

His voice was hoarse. "You hurt me just by existing."

She searched his face for clues to his meaning and found none. Wanting only to smooth the strain from his features, she said with attempted lightness, "Will you do me a favor—let me sit down in your kitchen while you make me a cup of tea?"

Insensibly he relaxed. Matching her tone, he said, "Sure. On the condition you'll tell me what you were doing creeping up my driveway at ten o'clock at night."

"I wasn't planning to break your windows, you can take that on trust."

She leaned down to pick up her shoes, followed Cal along the driveway and tiptoed over the coarse gravel toward the back door. In the kitchen he pulled out a chair for her. She sat down and let out her breath in a long sigh. As he filled the kettle at the sink, she surreptitiously inspected her feet, which were in worse shape than she had suspected. She tucked them under the chair well out of sight.

Cal turned the stove on, then said calmly, "I'll get you a sweater, you're cold."

The sweater was far too large for her and rough against her skin, but elusively it smelled of his body. She snuggled into it and said, "I'm feeling better already...I should call Cornelia."

"Cornelia can wait. You've got a long story to tell me."

"I was hoping you'd forgotten."

He warmed the teapot and added some herb tea. "No, I hadn't forgotten."

Deciding to give him the condensed version, Sara said very rapidly, "After dinner Joel drove me out to the lake so we could see the sunset. But instead of taking me home afterward he went up a side road and...and tried to make love to me and when I wouldn't he drove off and left me."

Her cheeks were pink. Cal poured boiling water into the teapot and said, "Have you known him long?"

Not long but well. Sara blushed a deeper shade of pink and said overloudly, "We were lovers for nine months. But we're not anymore."

"So why did you turn into my driveway? Figured you'd go from him to me?"

"No!"

She was scarlet-faced now. "Why, Sara?" Cal persisted, his gray eyes giving nothing away.

"Because my feet hurt," she said. "That's the only reason. I didn't think I could walk three more miles."

"So that's why you had your shoes off. Show me your feet."

She tucked them a little further under the chair. "They're okay," she said. "But I'm sure ready for that tea."

He crossed the room and knelt by her chair. "Show me."

He was close enough that she could have stroked his thick, corn-colored hair. "They're a mess," she admitted. "Don't embarrass me by making me show you. If I hadn't been so stubborn, I could have driven home with Joel."

"I'm glad you were stubborn," he said gently. "And you don't ever have to be embarrassed with me, Sara."

She was deeply touched, for she sensed the truth in his words. He was telling her she could be herself with him. No false fronts, no games. Very slowly, because the movement hurt, she stretched out her ankles.

The cut on her toe, although shallow, had bled very messily; her heels and one instep were marred by raw, red blisters, while dirt from the road was ground into her skin. She said meekly, "I told you they were a mess."

He looked up at her. "It's a good thing your friend Joel's not here now. I'd like to kill the bastard."

Rather to her dismay, because she would have called herself a civilized young woman, Sara felt a thrill of primitive pleasure travel along her spine. "Wouldn't be worth it," she said with mock severity. "Jail wouldn't suit you at all. You like your freedom too much."

"How did he think you were going to get home?"

"I don't expect he thought about it at all."

"Damn good thing you're through with him—you deserve better than that."

She wrinkled her nose at him. "I surely, at the very least, deserve a cup of tea."

For a moment she thought he was going to kiss her again and was conscious of disappointment when he got to his feet instead. He poured the spiced orange tea into mugs and cut her a slab of porridge bread, which he slathered with butter and homemade jam. Then he immersed her feet in a basin of hot water cloudy with antiseptic. The first twenty seconds were the worst; Sara chewed hard on the bread and tried to think higher thoughts, and Cal, after one look at her face, busied himself cutting more bread and phoning Cornelia.

After a few minutes he lifted her feet from the water and carefully dried them on a clean white towel. His hands were exquisitely gentle. Sara thought of the beautiful furniture and the ruined book and wondered if she would ever understand the paradoxes in this laconic, intensely private man whose choice was to live alone but whose loneliness smote her heart.

Her feet were against his jean-clad thigh. She watched as with one finger he slowly traced the blue veins in her instep and felt the ache of desire stir deep within her. She had a desire to know his body, certainly. But greater than that was a desire to break the barriers around his soul, to bathe it in the life-sustaining waters of love. "Cal," she said softly, resting one hand on his firm shoulder, "why did you touch me like that?"

For once his face was unguarded. "Because you're beautiful, and I want you," he said with a simplicity that disarmed her.

She had no idea what she would have replied, nor, if they had been left alone, what would have happened next. But a car turned into the driveway, its tires crunching in the gravel. Cal lifted her feet from his leg to the floor, picked up the basin and walked over to the sink. Sara drained the last of the tea from her mug.

It was not Cornelia. It was Laird, looking pugnacious. He shook Cal's hand and frowned at his sister-in-law. "Where's Joel?" he demanded.

Laird at times could sound very parental, and this was one of those times. Sara said flippantly, "He and I parted company when I declined to participate in a necking session."

"I never did like him, Sara, too much charm and not enough substance."

"I hate to admit it, but I think you're right."

"Of course I'm right. But there was no sense telling you that six months ago, you wouldn't have listened. We all have to make our own mistakes."

"Right again," she said gloomily. "But do you have to discuss my abysmal lack of judgment in front of Cal?"

Laird looked from one to the other of them, his stocky body dwarfed by Cal's greater height. "Dare I ask how she turned up here?"

"She walked," said Cal.

"Smartest thing she did all evening by the sound of it. Ready to go, sis?"

Cal spoke for her. "I'll carry her out to the car. Her feet are sore."

Sara stood up and said warmly, "Oh no, you won't!"

He advanced on her, grinning. "Oh yes, I will. Bring her shoes and purse, Laird, will you?"

Sara grabbed for her purse. "You stay out of this, Laird!"

"I have every intention of doing so."

"Cal, I walked two miles to get here, I can walk fifty feet to the car—"

Cal's hands were on her elbows, his eyes sparked with devilment. "But I'd like to carry you. Gives me a chance to prove my manhood."

She could think of other ways he could do that. Her lips mutinously set, she said, "I'm too heavy."

He flexed his muscles. "Makes it a challenge."

It was difficult to resist the twinkle in his eye. "We're making a spectacle of ourselves."

"Laird's going to hold the door for us, aren't you, Laird?" Moving very quickly for so big a man, Cal suddenly scooped her up in his arms. "There. That's not so bad, is it?"

It was exceedingly pleasant. "You should be beating your chest and emitting war whoops," Sara said pettishly.

"If I beat my chest I'll drop you. Hold the door, Laird."

Sara was almost sorry it was only fifty feet to the car. Carefully Cal lowered her into the passenger seat, took her purse and shoes from Laird and put them on her lap, then wiped imaginary sweat from his forehead. "You're right," he said, "you are heavy."

"It was all that porridge bread." Abruptly she sobered. "Thanks, Cal. You were a friend in need tonight."

"Pleasure," he said. "Look after those feet. Laird, I'll see you around." And with that, he closed the car door.

Sara had hoped he would at least kiss her cheek. She was silent until Laird had driven to the outskirts of Haliburton, then she said in a small voice, "I'm sorry I dragged you out late at night like this, Laird."

"Put it down to a learning experience," he said easily. "And let me tell you something. I've lived in Haliburton as long as Cal Mathieson, and I've never seen him look at a woman the way he looks at you."

"Oh." Sara felt the heat creep up her cheeks, and said not another word for the rest of the journey home. Cornelia scolded her roundly, treated her blisters and packed her off to bed.

CHAPTER SIX

IT RAINED THE NEXT DAY. Cornelia was on day shift, so Sara looked after the children, hobbling around the house in heelless slippers. Malcolm's friend Tony had come over and the two boys had noisily taken over the rec room to play spaceships; Caitlin's friend Jessie was to arrive after lunch, so Caitlin was curled up in the window seat reading. Sara had the radio on, and was thinking about Cal and making a stew for supper when the telephone gave Cornelia's double ring. Maybe it would be Cal, calling to see how she was. Sara hurried to the phone, banged her sore toe on a chair leg and picked up the receiver, her face screwed up with pain. "Hello," she said.

"Hello, darling."

"I am not your darling, Joel Crouse!"

"Look, I don't blame you for being annoyed with me. I shouldn't have driven off like that, but I'd so wanted to make love to you, Sara, you have no idea how beautiful you looked among all the wildflowers—"

"Joel, this is a party line. At least three other people could pick up the phone any minute."

He said irritably, "I don't know why you want to bury yourself in the country where you can't even talk on the phone in privacy."

"Because I have a job here, that's why."

"Sara, I didn't call to discuss party lines. I wanted to apologize!"

"Fine. You've apologized."

"You're still angry with me."

"I certainly am."

"Come on, Sara," he coaxed, "I've said I'm sorry."

Sara frowned at the far wall, knowing she had to verbalize what was now clear in her mind: for Joel himself had cured her of her ambivalence. Joel, and her inner knowledge of how she felt when she was with Cal. Hoping that Caitlin was absorbed in her book and that old Mrs. Murtridge, who lived down the road and who loved a good gossip, was not listening in, Sara said more calmly, "Joel, I know we've been through this before, but this time we really are finished. I don't want to go out with you anymore. Please don't phone here again."

"You're being very childish. Not to say unforgiving."

She bit back several retorts. "We had some lovely times, and you were good for me after Mum died. Let's not ruin those memories by ending up angry with each other."

"I'm not angry," he said with patent untruth. "But I do think you're making a bad mistake, Sara."

"The mistake would be to perpetuate scenes like last night's," she replied with as much patience as she could muster.

"I've explained why that happened. It wouldn't happen again, I promise. Listen, why don't you hop in your car and we'll go down to the South Shore and poke around all the antique shops, you know how you enjoy doing that."

"I can't, I'm looking after the children. Anyway, I'm trying to tell you we're finished."

"Then at least come into town this evening, and we'll have a proper dinner."

"No!" she said forcefully. "Joel, I've got to go, the stew's going to burn. Enjoy the rest of the summer, won't you? Bye." Very carefully she replaced the receiver.

From the window seat Caitlin said, "The stew isn't even on the stove, Aunt Sara. Was that the man in the red car?"

Sara gave a guilty start. "Yes. I told him a white lie because I didn't want to talk to him any longer."

"Good. I didn't like him very much."

"Why not?"

"He talked to me like I was a baby," Caitlin said scornfully. "Or only four years old like Malcolm. I'm six. Aren't you going to go out with him anymore?"

"No, I'm not."

Caitlin closed her book. "He was very handsome," she said judiciously. "Kind of like the frog prince after he stopped being a frog. But handsome is as handsome does, that's what Jessie's mother says."

Jessie's father was an exceptionally homely man. Sara hid her smile and addressed herself to the stew.

As she did the household chores and monitored the children's activities, Sara found herself profoundly relieved that she had finally settled the matter of Joel. His visit would have been worth it for that alone, but what he had done, of course, was bring her in contact with Cal again. With an ease that was telling, she slipped from thoughts of Joel to thoughts of Cal, trying to understand her reaction to the big, slow-spoken carpenter. Somehow on the basis of their few chance meetings she was convinced he needed her. He had, for reasons she did not know, locked himself away from the normalities of family and friends, of marriage and children. But Laird was a perceptive observer, and if Laird said she represented something special to Cal she was prepared to believe him. Perhaps Cal did share her feelings of rightness but was afraid to verbalize them or to act upon them. Certainly she had the power to hurt him; his tormented face in the darkness of his driveway was proof of that. Did that also mean she might have the power to help him?

She was afraid to use the word love for the peculiar combination of comfort, contentment and sexuality she felt when she was with him. She had thought the palpitating excitement of her relationship with Joel had been love. But she had been wrong. So was the quieter, deeper current of feeling with Cal to be called love? Joel was like a tumbling stream, the rush of rapids; Cal the river itself, slow-moving to the sea.

She was too unsure of any of her conclusions to share them with Cornelia. But when Laird suggested they all go to the dairy bar for ice cream after the stew, she declined, and when they had left, she looked up Cal's number in the phone book. Aware that her heart was beating uncomfortably fast, she dialed the seven digits.

He answered on the third ring. "Mathieson's Furniture."

She had not expected this crisp, businesslike response. She said uncertainly, "Cal? It's Sara."

He was silent for so long that she thought he had hung up. Finally he said, "Sara...how are your feet?"

"Sore. I won't be able to wear shoes for a week."

"No hikes around the lake."

No, but I could swim with you, Cal, she thought. *Or sit on your back porch and drink tea.* She gathered all her courage and said, "I wondered if some weekend we could go to a movie or go to the beach together?"

The silence this time had an intensity that frightened her. "I don't think that would be a very good idea."

"Or if you'd rather you could come here for supper one evening with the whole family." *Say yes,* she prayed inwardly. *Please say yes.*

"No, Sara. I don't think so."

She swallowed the last of her pride. "After the way you kissed me last night I figured we at least deserved one normal date. Instead of all these chance meetings."

"It's nice of you to think that. But I really can't."

She took heart that he seemed to be finding the conversation as difficult as she. "I don't usually ask men for dates."

"I'm sure you don't have to."

He added nothing more. Knowing she could not bear another of those long, charged silences, she said, "Well, I'd better go, then. I—I just wish I understood, that's all."

"I'm sorry," Cal said heavily.

"Goodbye then, Cal," she managed to say through the tightness in her throat. "Take care of yourself."

"Goodbye, Sara."

She had never heard two more final words. Tears were crowding her eyes as she put down the phone and went to stand by the window, so that all the bright colors in Cornelia's flower garden ran together like blobs of paint in a watercolor wash.

Laird was wrong. She was wrong. Cal wanted nothing from her.

SUMMER PASSED; it was brief, as Nova Scotian summers are, yet for Sara as slow moving as the pair of red-flanked oxen Mr. Murtridge owned. The last few days of July dragged past. She looked after the children for a week in August so that Laird and Cornelia could go away together. She tended the garden, read her books, swam and bicycled and jogged. She assiduously avoided going into town at times when she thought she might meet Cal, and she often took the roundabout route to the lake so she would not have to drive past the gray saltbox house.

Her tactics worked. She did not see him. She could only hope that eventually he would disappear from her thoughts.

But then September arrived, and with it Sara's move to the cottage next door to Cal's. She chided herself bitterly for having signed her name to the lease, a binding legal contract, and although she went through the motions of cleaning and of arranging her books and pictures to best advantage, the final effect was not one of home but of yet another temporary dwelling in a lifetime that had seen too many of them. She was tired of cleaning other people's windows and getting used to the quirks of other people's stoves. She was tired of hearing the unfamiliar noises of unfamiliar houses in the night. And while the cottage was well designed and in good condition, it did not have pine floors hollowed from generations of wear or the deep, slow ticking of a grandfather clock punctuating the September hours.

School started, with its attendant first-day nervousness and the effort to learn the array of new names and disparate personalities that would face her for the rest of the year. Sara genuinely loved teaching, and after two years' experience she was not afraid to take a few risks and use unorthodox methods to challenge her students. She could also be firm when the occasion demanded, and during the first week established that she, rather than the duo of gangly, leather-jacketed boys in the back row, was in control of the class.

Merrill Webster oversaw one of her classes and pronounced himself pleased, and Sara in her heart of hearts was glad to be busy after the lingering disappointments of the summer.

Once a week she was on duty in the school yard at lunch hour, because most of the students were bussed in from outlying areas and consequently ate in the cafeteria next door to the gym. The school comprised grades seven to twelve, so that there was everything from skinny twelve-year-olds playing rowdy games of basketball to supercilious final-year students wreathed in cigarette smoke. On Sara's first day of duty the sun was shining. She wandered around the school yard with her hands in her pockets, enjoying the fresh air after the combination of floor wax and chalk dust that seemed to permeate her classroom, wondering absently why adolescents seemed to find communication at normal voice levels so impossible. Because they had been permanently deafened by rock music? Because their hormones were in an uproar? She turned the corner of the building, into the cover of its sharp-edged shadow, and saw a circle of teenagers jostling each other in the corner. There was a black-haired girl in their midst.

As Sara stood still, her senses alert, the jeers and taunts that drifted across the Tarmac made her flinch. Crudity she could excuse, obscenity she had grown used to even if she did not condone it, but cruelty she could not abide. She walked closer. A denim-clad boy pushed the girl. Sara could not hear what he said, but the other boys laughed and the girls tittered, one of them blowing smoke into the black-haired girl's eyes, another making a very graphic gesture that caused more laughter. Feeling her temper rise, Sara called clearly, "Is anything wrong?"

Heads swung toward her, a circle of pale, blank faces. Without a word being spoken, a drifting away began, a moving from the center; Sara was reminded of a flock of birds that consists of individuals but moves as one. The black-haired girl was left isolated in the shadow of the building.

Sara came closer. She was not an attractive girl. Her clothes were ill-fitting on her dumpy figure and her hair needed washing. It framed a face mute with resentment.

Sara smiled and said conversationally, "I'm Miss Deane, the new teacher of 9B. They were giving you a hard time, weren't they?"

The girl scuffed at the Tarmac and said nothing.

"People in a group will say and do things that individually they would not...you might keep that in mind. What's your name?"

"Bonnie Dawson."

"Hello, Bonnie. What grade are you in?"

The girl's sneaker kicked viciously at the asphalt. "7C."

Sara hid her surprise, for Bonnie looked far too old to be in grade seven. "Do you come on the bus?"

"Yeah." Bonnie did not volunteer where she lived.

Above their heads the bell fixed to the brick wall pealed its shrill summons. While rationally Sara saw the necessity for bells, she hated them. Prisons had bells to regulate the day. As did factories. Schools should be different. She said, "I guess that means both of us have to get back to work," and gave Bonnie her best smile. "Goodbye, Bonnie, I expect we'll see each other again."

Bonnie grunted a reply and hurried off ahead of Sara. Sara watched her ruefully. She knew it did a student no good in the eyes of his or her peers to be seen talking to a teacher in the school yard, but had Bonnie needed to escape quite so eagerly?

For some reason the girl's sullen, inexpressive face stayed in Sara's mind. She caught a glimpse of Bonnie in the corridors after school, and in the staff room next morning at recess said casually to the room at large, "Does anyone know a student called Bonnie Dawson?"

"One of the Dogpatch Dawsons?" queried Mike Landry, the grade-eight social studies teacher.

Sara had heard the term Dogpatch before and knew it referred to the sprawl of shacks on the east side of the river in Haliburton, but it was not a term she cared for. "She could be."

"Of course she is," Jean MacPherson said waspishly. "You only have to look at her."

Courtney Burns, who taught grade-twelve economics and political science, said, "She's in your grade, isn't she, Jean?"

"More's the pity."

Mike grinned. "That bad, eh? Basic lack of soap and water?"

Courtney said in his deep, slow voice, "You can't blame the child for that. Look at the environment she comes from."

"Cleanliness is not difficult to achieve, Courtney," Jean retorted. "Even in these days of inflation you can buy three bars of soap for a dollar. They just don't care, that's all."

Courtney, unruffled, said, "A lot of them don't have running water, and they certainly don't have electric hot water tanks and built-in showers."

Sara stirred her coffee and kept quiet. Her more-or-less innocent question had opened the proverbial can of worms. She liked Courtney. In his early fifties now, he was a native of Haliburton who had taught in Ontario and British Columbia and then returned home when his youngest child had started university. She sensed in him a more balanced point of view than in someone like Jean, who had never lived anywhere but Coates Mill.

"It wouldn't matter if they had Jacuzzis," Jean snapped. "They don't care, Courtney. You know that as well as I do. Not that you have much to do with them, hardly any of them get as far as grade twelve."

"Understandably so."

"Because they're born stupid! You know what they're like, they breed like rabbits," Jean added triumphantly. "If they didn't like the way they lived, they wouldn't keep on having children, would they?"

"Birth control pills cost money."

Jean looked affronted by Courtney's bluntness. "Every one of them is on welfare; they've got money. Our money."

His movements very deliberate—he reminded Sara of Cal in some ways—Courtney took out a cigarette and lit it, then blew a cloud of blue smoke toward the ceiling. "You're oversimplifying the problem, Jean. Yes, some of the children in Dogpatch are born stupid, as you put it. There's been inbreeding and poverty for generations in some of those little hamlets. But all those kids are defeated before they start. The parents are seasonal farm laborers. They might make enough in the summer to go on unemployment but if not, they're on welfare. They don't understand basic nutrition or health care, they have too many children, and sooner or later the children become seasonal farm workers to put some money in the pot." In spite of himself, Courtney's voice was growing impassioned. "They can't get ahead, they're damn lucky if they can break even. If the kids don't have toilets or running water in the house, they sure don't have books."

Jean put her coffee mug down on the table with an angry crack. "They've always lived like that. If they didn't like it, they'd do something about it."

Courtney ran his fingers through his graying hair. "Jean, Jean, you haven't heard a word I've said. Take Bonnie Dawson, for instance. I don't know her mother, but years ago I taught her father, Everett. He dropped out of school in grade eight. He's functionally illiterate. He can't read the want ads or fill in the unemployment forms, so he ends up picking tobacco and working in the orchards. He's got no use for school. As for Bonnie, she's not very clean, not very pretty, she wears secondhand clothes donated by the church, which means she's never trendy or in style. What hope has she got of fitting in and of being even minimally happy in school? She's just filling in time until she's sixteen and she can legally quit."

"She'll get pregnant first," Jean said shrewishly. "All those girls do."

Courtney tapped his cigarette on the ashtray and ignored Jean's last comment. "She hasn't got a hope, poor kid." He gave Sara a twisted grin. "Does that answer your question?"

Sara understandably looked dazed. "I met her in the yard yesterday. Some other kids were being mean to her."

"The group always exiles the ones who don't fit in. The runts of the litter."

Even though Jean's tightly pursed mouth and Mike's nonchalant whistling were giving Sara the message to drop the subject of Bonnie Dawson, she persisted. "Are you saying her parents could be illiterate?"

"Oh, yes. Most of the inhabitants of Dogpatch are."

"But that's disgraceful!"

Courtney smiled at her flushed, indignant face. "That's life, Sara. It's a long way from middle class suburbia. That's where you taught last, isn't it?"

"Rockwood, in Halifax."

He stated the obvious. "Rockwood is not Dogpatch...ah, there's the bell. Back to the grind." Courtney stubbed out his cigarette, then said as he said most days, "Filthy habit, I must quit," and ambled out of the room, a stoop-shouldered man at home in his own skin. Jean left right behind him, her heels tapping irritably on the tiled floor. Under her brown sweater her shoulder blades protruded sharply, like rocks from thin soil.

Sara rinsed out her mug, wiped it with paper towel and replaced it in the cupboard. Her simple question, far from banishing Bonnie from her mind, had only implanted her all the more deeply.

SARA'S NEXT DAY for noon-hour duty was also sunny and exceptionally warm for mid-September. In the staff room she gave Jean MacPherson a perfunctory smile, grabbed her bag of sandwiches and decided to eat outdoors. She wanted to mull over a project for her creative writing class, and she also wanted to enjoy the sun. As autumn took hold, she always felt warm days were numbered and duly to be cherished.

Most of the students were in the cafeteria, no doubt eating French fries and drinking Coke. Sara bit into her sandwich and wandered toward the boundary of the yard, marked by a row of gnarled maple trees, their trunks bearing the initials of lovers past and present. Cal came to mind, as he still did too frequently for her liking. His initials, she thought grandiloquently, were carved on her heart, yet had not their relationship been as transitory as many of the romances confronting her now?

Something moved between two of the trees. "Oh hello, Bonnie," Sara said, recognizing the girl. "How are you?"

Bonnie came a little closer. Her hair was bundled into a rubber band and her sweatshirt was torn. Her eyes were small and dark and set too closely together; they fastened themselves on Sara's sandwich. "Fine," she said.

She did not look fine. An inarticulate, all-pervasive unhappiness hovered over her, a shadow among all the other shadows, yet one the sun could not disperse. Sara said gently, "You don't like school, do you?"

"Nope." The dark, secretive eyes followed the progress of Sara's sandwich to her mouth, then looked away.

"You don't eat with the other kids?"

Bonnie shook her head. Sara reached into the pocket of her linen jacket and took out a shiny red apple. "Would you like to have this?"

Her hunch had been right. Bonnie seized the apple and took a huge bite out of it, her face as near to animation as Sara had seen it. She neglected to say thank-you.

Thoughtfully, Sara looked down at the sandwiches in her hand. She had two left. She said casually, "Why don't we walk along the fence? It's nice in the sun, isn't it?"

The apple had disappeared by the time they reached the corner of the school yard. Just as casually Sara held out the sandwiches in their waxed paper. "Have one," she offered, "I'm not very hungry."

Many years ago Sara's father had looked after a husky dog for a neighbor; the husky had gulped its food in much the same way Bonnie did now. Sara proffered the second sandwich, waited until Bonnie had finished it and said with a careful lack of emphasis, "You wouldn't have had any lunch if I hadn't come along."

"I forgot it," Bonnie said defiantly. "Left it home."

Knowing the girl was lying, Sara added, "A meal card for the cafeteria is pretty expensive."

Bonnie eyed her warily and did not answer. They turned back and walked toward the maples again. Because the other students were starting to trickle out into the yard, Sara knew she had to cut their meeting short. She said, "I don't think you forgot your lunch today, Bonnie, I don't think there was any lunch for you to bring. Please don't think I'm prying or trying to interfere; that's not my intention. But right after school I'll go to the office and buy a meal card for you, and I'll give it to you tomorrow morning as soon as your bus gets in. That way you can go to the cafeteria when you want to.''

Bonnie stared at her suspiciously. ''Dad's pickin' apples. But he don't get paid till next week.''

It was the girl's longest speech so far. ''You don't have to pay me for the ticket, Bonnie,'' Sara said patiently. ''It'll be a secret between you and me, just so you don't have to worry about lunch anymore.'' She smiled into the girl's blank face. ''Get some salads and fruit to go with the chips and pop, though, okay?''

''Dad says when you pick apples, you don't wanna eat 'em.''

Delighted that she had evoked two whole sentences, Sara said, ''I've got to go. It's my day to keep an eye on the school yard. I'll see you tomorrow morning, Bonnie.''

Sara bought the meal ticket after her last class and, when she got home, told the whole story to Cornelia. ''She ate those sandwiches as if she was half starved. If I hadn't come along she wouldn't have had a bite to eat all day—and then people like Jean MacPherson wonder why Bonnie doesn't do well in school.''

''Jean MacPherson is a narrow-minded, life-hating bitch!''

''Really, Lia!''

''Well, she is. She'll never move from here and she's got years to go before she retires, which means both Caitlin and Malcolm will have her as a teacher. She doesn't even like children.''

Sara was always intrigued when her introverted sister spoke her mind. ''She certainly doesn't like Bonnie Dawson.''

''She likes her summers off and her paychecks.''

"All the teachers can't be like Courtney Burns."

Cornelia visibly relaxed. "Isn't he a sweetheart? If he and I weren't happily married to other people, I could go for him in a big way."

Sara laughed. "That sounds like a fairly safe approach to adultery."

"I'm not the adulterous type." Cornelia glanced out of the window. "Oh good, here's Laird."

Laird took off his work boots at the back door and looked from one sister to the other. "What are you two up to?"

Cornelia said primly, "I've just been confessing my unrequited love for Courtney Burns."

"Courtney Burns is not, I trust, inviting you for a wild weekend in New Glasgow?"

"Nobody is."

"I am."

Cornelia gave him the smile she reserved for him alone. "When?"

"Not this weekend but next. I've got a short business meeting Friday evening and one on Saturday morning, but the rest of the time would be free."

Sara said promptly, "I'll look after the children."

"And I could switch my Saturday-night shift with Marilyn. She owes me one." Cornelia clasped her hands with childlike pleasure. "I'd love to go, Laird. Courtney is forgotten."

"I should hope so. Turn your back, Sara." And Laird put his arms around his wife and proceeded to kiss her very thoroughly.

Sara did not immediately turn her back. Laird and Cornelia were not a demonstrative couple, and while she would have staked her life on the durability of their marriage, she was not used to seeing physical manifestations of it. There was familiarity in their embrace, the confidence of a love both bound and liberated by marriage. Disturbingly, there was also an intimation of acts committed in private in the big bedroom at the head of the stairs. Sara found herself thinking of Cal and of the long winter ahead. She wanted Cal to hold her the way Laird was holding Cornelia, wanted it just as much now as she had a month ago, and to tell herself she must forget Cal seemed useless, irrelevant and infinitely discouraging.

But if Sara could not forget Cal, neither did she forget Bonnie. The next morning she stationed herself by the back door of the school, where the big yellow buses disgorged their noisy cargoes, and waited for Bonnie. Bonnie was one of the last students to get off the bus. She slouched over to Sara, plainly ill at ease that a teacher should be waiting for her. Sara passed her a small white envelope. "The ticket's inside," she said.

Bonnie shoved the envelope in the pocket of her jeans; she had circles under her eyes. "I gotta go," she said.

Sara watched her push open the school's orange door and disappear from sight. A good thing she had not done her good deed expecting to be thanked, Sara thought, slowly following Bonnie through the door and letting the school envelop her in its seethe of young people and its constant stirring of dead air. Maybe Bonnie had never learned to say thank-you because nothing had ever been done for her. Maybe she preferred to hang around in the school yard and go hungry rather than face the crowded cafeteria where students mingled in groups that would never include her. Maybe she'd sell the ticket and buy cigarettes. Or drugs.

Thoroughly depressed, Sara went to the staff room to hang up her jacket.

CHAPTER SEVEN

CORNELIA AND LAIRD left for New Glasgow right after school on Friday afternoon, Laird unaccustomedly smart in a three-piece suit, Cornelia as pink-cheeked as a bride. Sara and the children waved goodbye from the window, then Sara said briskly, "I got paid today, so why don't we go to the bank in Coates Mill and then have supper there?"

"In a restaurant?" Caitlin asked.

"Can I have anything I want?" Malcolm added.

Malcolm's order included French fries, hot chili, a banana split and a raspberry soda, none of which seemed to adversely affect his digestive system. They went shopping after supper, Malcolm buying a plastic boat for the bathtub and Caitlin a book about elves in the forest; she had read three-quarters of it by the time Sara insisted on turning off the bedroom light. Sara went to bed soon afterward herself. Although she would not have acknowledged it to anyone else, she had hoped she might see Cal in town that night.

The following afternoon Caitlin went to play with her friend Jessie, taking the new book with her. "Jessie believes in fairies and gnomes and elves," she confided to Sara on her way out of the door, her face very serious. "Not many kids do. All they want to do is watch TV. TV's okay, I guess, but I like books better."

Caitlin will be beautiful when she's older, Sara thought with sudden prescience, but she won't find life smooth because she'll always be going against the tide. She said easily, "Then I'm glad you have Jessie for a friend. Be home by five, won't you? Roast chicken for dinner."

Sara liked having the house to herself. She played recordings of the Quebec composer André Gagnon all afternoon, enjoying the fluency of his piano playing and the vibrant rhythms of his backup band. She baked and iced a chocolate cake, prepared dinner, read from Ruth Rendell's latest thriller and kept an eye on Malcolm and Tony, who were engaged in complicated feats of engineering in the sand pit in the backyard. A considerable amount of sand had to be removed from Malcolm's person before she would allow him in the back door; once his hands were washed she cut him a small slice of cake.

"Where's Caitlin?" he asked, licking icing from his fingers.

Sara glanced at the clock. "She was over at Jessie's but she'll be home any minute. No more cake until after supper."

At twenty past five Caitlin still had not arrived home. Sara rinsed her hands—she had been carving the chicken, a job she detested—and rang Jessie's number. Jessie answered.

"Would you tell Caitlin to come home, please, Jessie?" Sara asked. "Supper's ready."

"She left a long time ago."

Sara frowned. "What do you mean?"

"She went home a long time ago," Jessie repeated, as if Sara was being rather slow witted.

"She couldn't have—she's not here," Sara said sharply.

"Well, she did."

Sara took hold of herself, for Jessie could be led but not pushed. "Is your mother there, please?"

Mrs. Duncan came on the line. "Is there a problem, Sara? Caitlin left for home at least an hour ago."

Sara was clasping the receiver so tightly that the skin was stretched tight over her knuckles. "She's not here yet. I told her to be home by five."

"Oh, dear. Could she have gone to the store, d'you think? You know what she's like, she'd get looking at the magazines and forget the time."

"She doesn't have any money," Sara said. "She spent it all in Coates Mill last night."

"Hold on a minute, I'll ask Jessie if she has any idea where she could be."

Sara listened to the murmur of voices in the background, trying her best to ignore the cold knot of fear in the pit of her stomach. Caitlin, dreamy Caitlin, had wandered off somewhere and would turn up any minute, full of apologies. She was only half an hour late. There was nothing to worry about.

"Jessie doesn't seem to know where she'd be," Mary Duncan said, her voice echoing Sara's inner and unspoken anxiety. "Why don't I send Kevin over to stay with Malcolm so that you can look around a bit? You might want to check out the store, for instance." Kevin was Jessie's fourteen-year-old brother.

"I'd really appreciate that, Mary. If she gets home in the meantime, I'll call."

As Sara put down the phone, Malcolm grabbed her leg. "Where's Caitlin?"

"She's late, Malcolm. She's probably sitting under a tree somewhere between here and Jessie's, daydreaming." She added grimly, "But she won't do it again, I'll tell you that."

She turned the oven off, lowered the heat under the vegetables and cut Malcolm another slice of cake. "Kevin's coming over for a few minutes so I can go and look for Caitlin. Offer him a piece of cake, won't you?" Then she ran upstairs to check Caitlin's room, half expecting to see the child curled up on her bed with her nose buried in a book. No Caitlin. At the back door she yelled her niece's name with all the force of her lungs. Still no Caitlin.

Kevin arrived a couple of minutes later, puffing because he had jogged the three-quarters of a mile between the two houses. His hair was almost as vibrant a red as Sara's, which had always predisposed her in his favor, while his plain face was redeemed by extraordinarily beautiful green eyes. He grinned at her. "I heard you from way down the road yelling Caitlin's name. I'll check out the garden and keep on calling her. Malcolm can yell, too. When she gets home, I'll call Mum."

His use of the word "when" rather than "if" was immensely comforting; sensitive Kevin, Sara decided, would make someone a fine husband someday. "Thanks, Kevin. If I'm more than fifteen minutes, help yourselves to supper."

Sara left the house and walked slowly down the drive, then onto the shoulder of the highway, stopping every few yards to peer into the undergrowth and call her niece's name. She checked the gas station and the little general store, but no one had seen Caitlin. Finally she arrived at Jessie's neat white bungalow with its rose garden that Mr. Duncan tended with fanatical zeal in between his sales trips. Mary was in the kitchen. "No sign of her here," she said. "And I just talked to Kevin and she's not there, either."

Sara sat down heavily in the nearest chair. "What will I do, Mary? Should I call the police?"

Jessie's eyes grew wider and she huddled a little closer to her mother's apron; she was not normally a clinging child. With a sudden inspiration Sara knelt so that her eyes were level with Jessie's and said, "Jessie, Caitlin started for home through the woods, didn't she?"

In a loud voice Jessie said, "She's not allowed to do that."

"I know she's not. And if she had, you wouldn't want to say so, because that would be telling tales, wouldn't it? But, Jessie, we're all very worried. Caitlin's over an hour late now and it'll be getting dark soon, so if you know something you must tell us."

Jessie cowered against her mother. "She's not allowed to go through the woods," she repeated stubbornly.

Sara held tightly to her temper, her impulse to shake the truth from the child, and heard Mary say very calmly, "Jessie, your father and I have always brought you up to speak the truth, even if it means admitting to something you've done wrong. If Caitlin did go home by the woods, then she probably threatened you not to tell. But you must tell, because Caitlin might be lost in the woods and we have to go out looking for her before it gets dark. Do you understand?"

Jessie gave a loud sob, burrowed her face in her mother's lap and wailed, "She told me the wicked witch would get me if I told!"

Mary put her arms around her daughter's heaving shoulders. "The wicked witch won't get you while I'm here. So did Caitlin go home by the woods?"

"Yes, s-she did," Jessie sobbed. "We read this new book she had, and she wanted to find the tree spirits, they live in little hollows under the roots and they only come out at d-dusk because sunlight makes them disappear."

"All right, Jessie," Mary said briskly. "It would have been better if you'd told me this half an hour ago, but I'm glad you've told me now. And I'll have a word with Caitlin about this wicked-witch stuff. Now, Sara, I'd suggest you go home through the woods, you know the path, don't you? If you don't find Caitlin, then I think you should call the police as soon as you get home."

Sara stood up. She must have looked as frightened as she felt, because Mary added comfortingly, "I wouldn't be the least bit surprised if you find her sitting under a tree just up the hill waiting for those darned spirits to appear—you know Caitlin!"

Sara managed a smile. "You'll be the first person to be told if I do."

In the Duncans' back garden a white picket fence held the wilderness at bay; Mr. Duncan did not care for unruliness. Sara closed the gate behind her and walked up the slope. Moss cushioned her feet. The trees enveloped her in shade and whispering boughs, so that when she called Caitlin's name her voice sounded faint, muffled by the layered leaves and the still, dark trunks.

She picked her way along the path, which wound between gaunt gray rocks and contorted roots. Her throat was soon sore from shouting, her heart racing and her palms damp. For Mary Duncan was wrong.

Caitlin was not sitting under any of the trees, her back to the trunk, her voice crooning to the innumerable creatures of her imagination. Caitlin was nowhere to be seen.

Sara walked faster, her eyes darting this way and that, her hoarse voice calling Caitlin's name over and over again. She tripped over a root, bruising her hand against a rock. A broken branch that was as sharp-pointed as a knife caught at her arm and left a thin trail of blood. She scarcely noticed. Her whole body seemed to have become an unvoiced prayer that she would find Caitlin. Nothing else mattered.

Ten minutes later she emerged from shade to sun in the clearing behind Laird and Cornelia's house. "Caitlin!" she called, her voice cracking with desperation. "Caitlin, where are you?" Then, her feet sliding on the path, she ran for the house. Caitlin might have come home while she was in the woods.

When Kevin met her at the door, one look at his face told Sara that her niece had not returned. She said with false calm, for Malcolm, big-eyed, was perched on a stool at the counter, "I'll telephone your mother, Kevin, to make sure Caitlin's not there. Then I think we'd better call the police." On her way to the phone she ruffled Malcolm's hair. "Did Kevin get your supper?"

"I wasn't hungry," Malcolm said, his lower lip stuck out.

She took a moment to give him an extravagant hug. "Malcolm, it will be all right. We'll find her," she said, but could not have told whom she was trying to convince, him or herself.

Caitlin was not at Mary's. Furthermore, the two teenage boys who lived next door had gone in the direction of Coates Mill on their bicycles and not seen her. "Call the police, Sara," Mary said. "We've done all we can. They'll send out a search party."

So Sara called the police. The constable she spoke to was very polite, took down some details and said the officer on patrol should be at her house in fifteen minutes. Exactly twelve minutes later a big blue-and-white car pulled up the driveway. Malcolm cheered up. There was a real patrol car in his backyard, a real policeman with a gun at his hip in the kitchen.

Swiftly Sara went through her story, describing all they had done. "I'm afraid she's wandered off into the woods," she finished, and with an immense effort managed to keep her voice from trembling.

The officer, who had curly brown hair in a military cut, said, "We'll organize a search party with the volunteer fire department. A tracking dog should be here in half an hour. I'll get you to give me some of her clothing, and we'll start the dog from the other house. Now, what was she wearing?"

"Denim shorts and a green shirt. Brown leather sandals."

"Okay. Show me something she's worn recently, then I'll head over to the fire hall."

The fire hall had a high-pitched siren that echoed in the hills around the village. Sara heard it as she sat with Malcolm in her lap and knew the majority of the able-bodied men of the community would be jumping into their cars and trucks to drive to the hall. It was nearly seven o'clock. She had decided that if Caitlin had not been found by ten she would phone Laird and Cornelia, a prospect that tied her stomach in knots but which had to be faced.

She cleaned up the kitchen, putting on a big pot of coffee in case any of the volunteers ended up at Laird and Cornelia's. She read to Malcolm without attempting to put him to bed. She answered half a dozen telephone calls from curious neighbors, each of which set her heart pounding. She waited. The hardest part was the waiting. She would have preferred to be a member of the search party tramping through the woods, but knew she owed it to Malcolm to stay home.

The minutes crept by. Seven-thirty. Eight. Eight-thirty. Darkness fell, the velvety darkness of September that yet carried a slight chill in the air, the first hint of the long months of winter that lay ahead. Stars punctuated the black tent of the sky. Nine o'clock. Nine-fifteen. Nine-thirty.

Malcolm had fallen asleep on the kitchen couch, his thumb in his mouth, his teddy bear hugged to his chest. Sara sat by the window, the phone number of the motel where Laird and Cornelia were staying running through her mind over and over again, an ominous litany that brought her no comfort.

At nine-thirty-six a car came up the driveway. A police car. Caitlin's dead, she thought, and for the first time in her life was afraid she was going to faint.

The back door opened. Frozen to the chair, Sara heard deep male voices, one of them hauntingly familiar. Then the door to the kitchen was pushed open.

The brown-haired policeman was carrying Caitlin in his arms. Her face was tear streaked and very dirty, and her arms and legs were blotched with fly bites. But she was alive. Quite definitely alive.

The kitchen windows soared toward the ceiling and the floor rushed up to meet Sara. Dimly she felt someone grab her shoulders and shove her head between her knees. Blood rushed to her brain. The floor resumed its usual relationship to her feet, and the horrible sick swoop of her stomach settled into normalcy. She pushed against the hands still holding her shoulders and croaked, "Caitlin?"

The policeman put the child in her lap. Sara buried her face in Caitlin's hair, wrapped her arms around her and said, "Caitlin, I love you. Don't you ever get lost again." Caitlin, predictably, began to cry.

Eventually Sara looked up. The policeman was revealing his youth by looking embarrassed; the man who had pushed her head to her knees was Cal. She stared at him as if she had never seen him before and said, "Did you find her?"

He shook his head. "No, the police dog found her. But I was searching nearby and I figured maybe you could do with a bit of company, so I came along."

He looked very large and solid, like someone she could lean on. "I'm glad you did," she said, and meant every word.

The sound of voices woke Malcolm up. He sat bolt upright on the couch, rubbing at his eyes and, when he saw his sister, ran across the room and scrambled up into Sara's lap, as well. Sara put her arms around both of them and fought back a deluge of tears. She said with creditable clarity, "I think we should all have some chocolate cake and coffee."

Cal grinned. "Great idea," he said, and began opening cupboards and taking out plates and forks as if he had always lived in the house. Sara directed the constable to the mugs and cream and sugar for the coffee, and in no time they were seated around the kitchen table talking and laughing, the unbearable emotion of a few moments ago dissipated by chocolate cake.

The constable ate two large pieces, drained his mug of coffee and said, "Got to get back on the road, ma'am. Thanks a lot."

Sara transferred Caitlin from her lap to Cal's, stood up and shook the policeman's hand. She said fervently, "Thank you. I'll write a letter to the detachment and to the fire department, but you're the one who headed up the search." She could feel the tears crowding the back of her eyes again. "I hope you'll get promoted."

"Not likely—not for this. Goodbye, Caitlin, glad we found you." He put his hat back on, made a feint at Malcolm, gave Cal a quick salute of his hand and left via the back door. On his way down the driveway he flashed the red and blue lights on the top of his car and sounded the siren, which made Sara jump but delighted Malcolm.

She wiped the cake crumbs from Caitlin's mouth. "Bedtime for you, young lady. And for you, Malcolm. Do you realize it's past ten-thirty?"

"Want a hand?" Cal offered.

It seemed the most natural thing in the world to say, "You carry Caitlin and I'll carry Malcolm."

They trudged upstairs. Sara turned on the bath water, sent Malcolm for his pyjamas and had him in and out of the tub in record time. She passed him over to Cal. "Can you read him a story while I'm bathing Caitlin?"

Cal picked the little boy up. His back to Sara, he said, "I'll tell him one of Dougal's bear stories. Get a couple of shots of whiskey into Dougal, and he'd go through all his bear stories regular as clockwork."

Sara put baking soda into the water to soothe Caitlin's fly bites. Because she felt the evening's events had to be discussed in some way, she asked, "Did you find the tree spirits?"

"No. I never did."

Sara wiped the dirt from her niece's face. "Maybe they don't appear to little girls who threaten their friends and disobey their parents' rules."

"I didn't mean to be so long. But it started getting dark and everything looked the same, and I couldn't find my way back to the path." Caitlin's lips quivered. "I was scared."

A child with Caitlin's vivid imagination must have been terrified in the black-shadowed, never-silent woods. But for the moment Sara withheld her sympathy. "That's why your parents have rules, to save you from being scared like that," she said. "And you frightened me, as well. I was very worried about you."

Caitlin hung her head. "I'm sorry."

"I'm sure you are," Sara said matter-of-factly. "And I'm sure you won't do it again."

"Never!" Caitlin exclaimed so vehemently that Sara had to laugh. Caitlin peeped at her through long, wet lashes. "Will you tell Mum and Dad?"

"I'll have to. If I don't, one of the neighbors will."

"Like old Mrs. Murtridge," Caitlin said vindictively.

"Or any one of the volunteer firemen."

"Oh." Caitlin's eyes widened. "I'm sort of famous, aren't I?"

"Fame is fleeting," Sara said dryly. "Hop out, and I'll put some lotion on your fly bites."

Caitlin looked down at her red-spotted arms. "Why do you s'pose God invented mosquitoes?"

"To keep us humble," Sara replied promptly. "Pass me the powder."

Caitlin's lids were drooping by the time she was dressed in her frilly white nightgown with her hair falling sleekly over its collar, and Sara knew there was no need for a bedtime story. She tucked her niece in, kissed her good-night and, as Caitlin's eyes closed, breathed a heartfelt prayer of thanks that the child was safely in her bed.

Cal was still in Malcolm's room, sitting quietly by the bed, for Malcolm, too, was asleep. Despite the little boy's presence Cal looked very much alone, and somehow aware of that aloneness. Cal should have his own son, Sara thought fiercely, a wife and children to bring the old saltbox house to life again.

He must have sensed her presence in the doorway. He looked up, then crossed the room toward her and took her by the elbow. "I should think you need a good strong drink," he said.

There was a small triangular tear in his shirt. Sara thought foolishly, he should have the kind of wife who'd mend his shirts. *I never would. I hate mending.*

The emotion that she had held back all evening was filling her throat. She swallowed hard and said, "You should get married, Cal... your shirt needs mending."

He ushered her out of Malcolm's room into the bright light of the hall. "Doesn't seem like much of a motive for marriage," he replied. "Sara, it's okay to cry."

She pulled away and headed for the stairs. "There's no reason to cry now. She's safe," Sara muttered, and nearly tripped on the last three stairs because her vision was so blurred by tears.

Cal pulled her into his arms just as the first tear-drop plopped from her lashes to her cheek. She sagged against his chest and wept for all the fears of the past few hours, for her terrified conviction that Caitlin was dead, for the dread sense of her own responsibility.

Sara was never one to do things by half measures. Her storm of weeping was violent if short-lived and left her floating on a vast, calm sea of exhaustion. She said, "I've got to sit down."

She collapsed on the chesterfield in the living room. Cal disappeared, returning in a few minutes with two glasses of amber liquid. Sara took a big mouthful and nearly choked. "That's pure rum!"

"It'll be good for you . . . are you feeling better?"

She gazed at him in the semidarkness, at the clean, strong line of his jaw and the intent gray eyes. "It makes you wonder why anyone has children—you're suddenly so terrifyingly vulnerable. Caitlin isn't my child—she's only my niece—but if something had happened to her tonight, I'm not sure I could have borne it. Let alone thinking how Cornelia and Laird would have felt." She took another swallow of the rum, grateful for its slow burn down her throat. "I felt responsible, as though it was all my fault. And yet rationally I know it wasn't."

Cal looked away, his big hands curled tightly around his glass. "Guilt's a terrible emotion," he said somberly. "You shouldn't feel guilty, Sara, you have no reason to."

There was a note in his voice that should not have been there. She rested a hand on his shoulder, where the muscles were tightly bunched. "I said something to upset you, didn't I?"

He hunched his shoulders as if her touch was repugnant to him. "For eleven years I've felt guilty for something I did," he said in such a low voice she had difficulty hearing him. "I wouldn't want you to do that to yourself."

She made a rapid calculation. "But you were only fourteen!"

"Old enough to know better."

"What happened, Cal? Was it the car accident you told me about?"

"No. No, not that." He put the glass down on the coffee table and rubbed at his forehead with the heels of his hands. "It doesn't matter what I did. I just don't want you to feel responsible for something you couldn't have helped."

She felt a flow of energy from a source deep within her, which, had she been wiser, she might have called love. "Cal, do you mean to tell me that for eleven years you've been carrying a burden of guilt around with you? Did Dougal know?"

"I never told him. Dougal wasn't much for talking about emotional stuff."

"Your parents . . . did they know?"

"They're part of the cause."

"You've never told anyone, have you?" she said gently. "You mentioned once that your parents were dead . . . is it something to do with them?"

His face still hidden in his hands, he nodded. Then he raised his head. His hands were not quite steady and his voice almost inaudible. "I had a sister, too."

Frightened that the slightest move on her part would scare him into silence, Sara waited, her hand feather-light on his shoulder. He flexed and unflexed his fingers, his vision lost in the past. "I was wild as a kid," he said. "When I was thirteen, fourteen, I was big for my age and hanging around with guys who were sixteen and seventeen. Three or four of them had motorbikes or souped-up old cars. We drank too much, tried drugs, hung around with a bunch of girls who were tougher than we were. I was young enough to think I was pretty smart. Cool. With it. And of course I was big enough that no one dared to argue with me." He came to a sudden stop.

"Where did you live?"

"On the South mountain, about thirty miles from here. We were poor, you see, dirt poor, so we lived in a little wooden shack back in the woods at the top of the mountain. Out of sight of all the prosperous folk." There was another painful pause. "Four of us. My parents, myself and my sister. She was younger than me. Her name was Annalise, my mum had heard that name on the radio and thought it was pretty...and Annalise was pretty. She had blond hair and blue eyes, and she was sort of fragile looking." He gave a mirthless smile. "Not a bit like me. I loved her more than anyone else in the world."

Sara had noticed his use of the past tense. So Annalise was dead; and Cal in some way felt responsible.

"Mitch came to pick me up on a Friday night in February. Mum didn't want me to go because she knew we were on the lookout for trouble. Annalise didn't want me to go, either. But I wouldn't listen to anyone in those days, not even her, so off I went with Mitch. We started off at the tavern and ended up at an all-night party. It was five in the morning when he took me back up the mountain." Cal's voice was toneless, as if he was reading a series of meaningless words on a page. "I knew there was something wrong as we turned the last corner. There were cars parked along the side of the road, and the fire trucks were just leaving. But the police were still there, and the ambulance...the shack had burned to the ground. Nothing left but the old brick chimney and the metal frame of my parents' bed, all bent out of shape by the heat.''

"Cal..." Sara took his hands in hers, although she was not sure he even noticed the contact; he was lost in the past, his eyes reseeing the unimaginable.

"The fire chief figured out the oil stove had exploded—they found bits of it scattered all around. They'd have died instantly, he said...I hope to God he was right." He looked over at Sara. "So they were all dead. My dad, my mum and Annalise. If I'd stayed home that night, if I hadn't gone out drinking with Mitch and the boys, maybe I'd have been able to get them out in time. Even if it'd just been one of them. Or at least I'd have died with them, where I belonged. But I was downtown drinking myself silly on draft beer and cheap wine, and by the time I got home it was too late."

Abruptly he picked up his glass and drained half of it. "I don't know what the hell I told you all that for," he said roughly. "It was a long time ago and best forgotten."

"But you haven't forgotten," Sara said. "And you haven't forgiven yourself."

"How can I? They're dead, Sara. Dead. And I wasn't there."

"If you had been there, you'd have died, too," she protested. "Why would you have been able to get them out when they weren't able to get themselves out? Do you think your mother would have wanted you to die along with the rest of them? Of course not. She'd have wanted you alive. She'd have been proud of you now, of what you've made of yourself. And so would Annalise."

"Dougal made me what I am."

"Sure, Dougal helped," Sara said vehemently. "But Dougal couldn't have taught you about woodworking if you hadn't wanted to learn. Give yourself some credit, Cal."

His hand wrapped itself around her wrist like a steel manacle. "I should have been home, Sara."

"But you weren't! It was a terrible tragedy, Cal. Terrible. But instead of blaming yourself, maybe you should blame a society that allows people to live in wooden shacks with old oil stoves that can explode in the middle of the night."

"That's the fashion today—shift the blame from yourself to society, or from yourself to the government."

"I'm sure your parents didn't want to be poor."

He let out his breath in a long sigh. "They were farm laborers. My dad drank more than was good for him, and my mum had no education."

"You can't blame yourself for that," Sara said tartly.

"No, I guess I can't."

"Darn right you can't." She added apologetically, "You're hurting my wrist."

He loosened his hold, massaging her flesh, and produced the semblance of a smile. "I can feel your pulse . . . do you know what the worst thing is, Sara? Sometimes I can't remember what they looked like. My dad and mum, even Annalise."

"You wouldn't have had any photographs?"

He gave a short laugh. "What would we have been doing with photographs? It's terrible not to remember what your sister looked like."

She frowned. "There would have been school photographs, wouldn't there?"

"We could never afford to buy them."

"But they should still have copies at the school."

"Would they? I never thought of that. Sara, would you go with me some day to find out?"

"Of course."

"I'd love to have a photograph of her." He was still rubbing Sara's wrist. "You realize you've done it again."

"Done what, Cal?"

"Got me talking about things I decided years ago were better not talked about. I've never told a living soul what I've just told you."

She gave him a slow smile. "Why do you suppose I do that?" she asked innocently.

"Because you're a witch." He leaned over and kissed her, a kiss as light as the fall of a butterfly on the petals of a flower.

"I'm not sure I'm complimented!" she replied, a little breathlessly, and related to him Caitlin's threats concerning the wicked witch.

"Oh, you're not wicked." He traced the curve of her cheek with his lips. "Sexy, but nice."

"Cal," she gasped, "if you keep that up, you can forget the niceness."

He took her by the shoulders, the laughter leaving his face. He said huskily, "Kiss me, Sara," and bent his head again.

He had never kissed her with such naked longing before; it was as if the unlocking of memory had freed him from other restraints. She fell back on the cushions, felt his weight press her into their softness and parted her lips to the slide of his tongue. He shifted his weight, his mouth more urgent, more demanding, his knees separating her thighs under her cotton skirt. Her fingers explored the silky thickness of his hair, digging into his scalp, holding him to his kiss. A kiss she wanted to last forever. A kiss she wanted to move inexorably toward a more complete possession.

As though he had read her mind, his hand moved to the fullness of her breast. The shock of his touch, delicious, infinitely pleasurable, raced through her body. She held him close, nibbling at his lips with tiny murmurs of delight; it seemed very natural that she should undo the cord at the neck of her blouse and guide his hand beneath the thin cotton and the lace of her bra to lie on her warm, supple flesh. He was impatient. She heard the fabric tear and would have had him rip it from her body, for the brush of his fingers on her nipple was agonizingly sweet and she knew he must not stop there. Frantic with haste, she reached for the buttons on his shirt.

He leaned on one elbow, helping her, struggling out of his shirt and letting it fall to the carpet, then unlacing the ties on her blouse and unsnapping the clasp on her bra. Almost reverently he pulled the clothing away from her body, baring her breasts to his gaze. "You're so beautiful," he whispered. "How will I ever forget you, Sara?"

His choice of words was strange to her; she did not want him to forget her. She wanted him to make love to her, to acknowledge the kinship between them that had struck her from the beginning. "You don't have to," she said, and unconsciously her eyes pleaded with him to talk not of forgetfulness but of love.

He raised himself on his other elbow so that his body hovered a foot above hers, cutting off the soft fall of light from the hall, casting her in shadow. She shivered. She did not want to inhabit the world of half shadows that was Cal's domain; she wanted the light of noonday and the full warmth of the sun.

He said harshly, "You're cold."

"Then warm me," she said, and because the flush on her cheekbones was invisible, she might have seemed shameless.

"You make everything sound so simple."

Although she was almost certain she had lost him once again, she looped her arms around his neck. "Life's only as complicated as we make it."

"Then it's complicated." His smile took any sting from his words. "Let go, Sara. This is the last thing we should be doing, anyway, with the children upstairs."

He was right, of course, which did not improve her mood. She unlinked her fingers, grabbed the two edges of her bra, and yanked them together, and as the hall light fell across her face, her pink cheeks were all too visible. But Cal was putting on his shirt. He turned away to tuck it in his waistband. Sara drew the soft pleats of her blouse across her body and wondered how she could have plummeted from desire to despair so quickly. She was a fool. She'd encouraged him and then was devastated when he rejected her.

When he turned back he must have seen the forlorn droop of her head. "I'm sorry, Sara," he said with genuine compunction. "It's happened again, hasn't it? There's something about you.... I don't know what it is, but you can cut through my defences as if they were made of paper.''

"But why do you need defences?''

"I don't want closeness. I decided that long ago.''

"Because your sister died?''

"For all kinds of reasons. Annalise is one of them, I suppose.'' He raked his fingers through his hair. "It's best we stay away from each other, you and I. Otherwise I end up hurting you, and I hate doing that. I hate staying away from you, too—but it seems the only way.''

"You act like a monk who's taken a vow of chastity!''

"Oh, I'm no monk,'' he said bitterly. "You've taught me that. Sara, I'm truly sorry. But it is really better if we don't see each other anymore.''

"You're in and out of my life just as my father was,'' she said with cruel insight. "He could never be depended upon for anything—just when you wanted him he wasn't there. I don't want a man like that. I want someone who's not afraid to commit himself, who's willing to be open and vulnerable and to share himself with me. A man like Laird. That's what I want.''

"Then it would be even more wrong of me to keep on seeing you,'' Cal said flatly. "I'll let myself out . . . and thank you for listening about my sister.''

He strode across the room. She heard the click of the back door, and not until then did it occur to her that he would have to walk home. There was nothing she could do about it; she could not leave the children. She went to stand by the window that overlooked the road and watched the ghostly gleam of his shirt move swiftly out of sight.

CHAPTER EIGHT

CORNELIA AND LAIRD came home on Sunday, Caitlin's escapade was duly dealt with and Sara returned to her cottage on the lake road. The cottage seemed so empty and Cal so disturbingly close that she was glad to go back to school on Monday morning. She kept an eye out for Bonnie all week but did not see her, not even in the cafeteria at noon. On Thursday in the staff room she very casually asked Jean MacPherson, "Is Bonnie Dawson sick? I haven't seen her for several days."

"You won't see her for a month or so. She's picking apples."

"During the day? But she should be in school."

"Those people don't worry about school, Sara. It's not one of their priorities." Jean daintily dropped her tea bag into the wastebasket.

"But that's truancy," Sara protested.

"Call it survival," Courtney said, raising one eyebrow.

Sara turned to him. "Just to pick a few apples? How will she ever hope to graduate to the next grade if she misses a month of school right at the beginning of the year?"

He sat back in his chair, crossed his legs and lit a cigarette. "Bonnie's a husky girl, she can certainly pick as many apples a day as her mother can. So she can

probably add twenty dollars a day to the family income. Multiply that by five days a week if the weather
holds, and you've got a hundred dollars. Not to be
sneezed at. A lot of the farmers' kids take time off
during planting and harvesting, and the school offi-
cials turn a blind eye. It's the way things are done
around here."

"A hundred dollars a week isn't very much," Sara
said argumentatively. "That's below the minimum
wage."

"They get paid by the amount they pick. Used to be
nine dollars a bin, although it might be more now. A
man can probably pick four or five bins a day if he
works really hard. That's around minimum wage."

Sara sighed. "It still doesn't seem right to me,
Courtney. I'm only a beginning teacher, but I can already earn in a week five times what Bonnie can earn,
and if she keeps on missing school she'll never be able
to better herself."

"She's lazy," Jean interjected. "She never answers
questions or takes part in discussions, and her home-
work is always in a disgraceful state. I've tried sending
notes home to her parents, but it doesn't do a speck of
good."

"Her parents can't read the notes, Jean," Courtney
said mildly.

"They could take them to a neighbor." Jean began
scouring her mug at the sink.

Courtney winked at Sara, took a letter out of his
pocket and began to read it. Sara finished her coffee
and went back to her classroom. After work she drove
to the orchard on the outskirts of Haliburton.

Slatted wooden boxes were piled untidily beside a
small bulldozer equipped with a forklift. Tire tracks

indented the grass between the rows of trees, the nearest of which had been picked clean. Sara could hear the sound of voices over the hill and began walking in that direction, picking her way between the trees, the tall grass swishing against her legs. The sun was shining and the air smelled clean and fresh; there could be worse jobs, Sara thought, and tramped down the slope.

Bonnie was halfway up a wooden ladder in one of the outermost trees, her body twisted at an awkward angle as she reached for the round red apples and deposited them carefully in a canvas bag slung around her neck. A radio was blaring from the ground a couple of trees away; the girl looked more contented—or, rather, less discontented—than Sara had ever seen her. Sara walked closer. "Hello, Bonnie," she said.

Bonnie looked down. When she saw Sara she dropped the apple from her hand and said a very crude word.

"I didn't mean to startle you," Sara said apologetically, picking up the apple and proffering it to her.

"That one's no good. It's bruised. Get too many bruised ones in your bin and the boss'll reject the whole lot. Only good for juicers."

"Oh. You mean you don't get paid as much for them?"

"Chances are you won't get paid nuthin'."

Feeling humbly that she had a great deal to learn and that she would never again view fruit pickers through the colored lenses of romance, Sara heard Bonnie say from her perch in the tree, "I'm not goin' back to school till pickin's done with."

"I didn't come here to get you to go back."

"Why'd you come, then?" Bonnie clambered up one more rung and reached for the topmost apples.

"Just to see what you were doing," Sara said lamely. "What kind of apples are they?"

"Cortlands. Good pickin', 'cause they're big. Takes twice as long to fill a bin with McIntoshes."

The bins she was referring to were obviously the slatted wooden boxes, of which Sara could see several filled to the brim. "How many bins can you pick a day?"

"Two. Two and a half." Bonnie climbed down the ladder, emptied the bag into the bin nearest the tree, shifted the ladder and climbed back up again. To Sara's eyes the contents of the bag did not appear to change the level in the bin at all. She wondered how many bags made a bin. "Are your parents working here, as well?"

"Yeah. Mum don't get good trees, 'cause the boss don't like her." Bonnie added cynically, "You gotta be nice to the boss to get good trees."

Did niceness involve sexual favors? Sara was very much afraid it might. Discouraged, she decided to eat the fallen apple, and rubbed it on her skirt. A yellowish film transferred itself from the apple to the skirt. "What's on the apples?" she asked, puzzled.

"Spray," Bonnie said laconically. "They spray the trees ten or eleven times the course of a summer. A couple of the pickers wear masks. I don't. They cost money."

Sara dropped the apple, which disappeared among the long blades of grass. "You like it better here than in school, don't you, Bonnie?"

Bonnie grunted as she stretched for an apple at the very end of a limb. "Yeah. I like the people here better than the kids in school."

Somehow it did not seem the time or the place for a sermon on self-advancement. Sara said, "Well, I'd better be going. I'll see you when you get back to school, Bonnie."

"I guess so," Bonnie replied, without much enthusiasm.

As Sara walked to the road across the grass, a burly red-faced man in a greasy cap emerged from between two trees and stationed himself in her path. "You looking for someone?"

She disliked him on sight. "No," she said shortly.

"This is private property, you're trespassing."

"Oh. Do you own it?"

His eyes narrowed. "No. But I'm the foreman."

If this was the boss then she, Sara, would never get the good trees, because she could not have stood to have those beefy hands anywhere near her. "I see. I'm from the city," she said, more or less truthfully, "and I was curious to see how apples get picked."

"You a reporter?"

"No, I'm not." She gave him a perfunctory smile and walked around him.

He said with what could only be described as a leer, "You want a job, you come and see me."

Hell would freeze over first, thought Sara. "Thank you," she said politely, and kept on walking. She could feel his eyes on her back and was glad her outfit was businesslike rather than seductive. It seemed to take a long time to reach her car, and when she looked back he was still watching her.

Sara drove home in a thoughtful mood. The visit to the orchard had given her a better understanding of Bonnie. Bonnie felt more at home among the other apple pickers than she did at school. Bonnie had talked more in five minutes in the orchard than she probably would have all day at school. So did one abandon the

Bonnies of the world, Sara wondered, on the premise
that they were happier where they were? Or did one
challenge them, push them, urge them to do better, so
that they could rise above the deficiencies of Dogpatch and seasonal farm labor? After all, what lay
ahead for Bonnie if she quit school? Poverty. Preg-
nancy. A shack in a rural slum. Or maybe, even worse,
the fate that had overtaken pretty, blond-haired Annalise.

ON SUNDAY AFTERNOON, Bonnie still very much on her
mind, Sara put on her oldest pair of jeans and a plain
blue shirt and drove across the river to the cluster of
trailers and houses where Bonnie lived. She asked
directions of a couple of boys playing ground hockey
and was sent to the farthest building, set near the river
bank among roof-high alders. She had never liked alders very much; they were the starlings of shrubbery.
She turned off the ignition and got out of the car.

Even the soft light of late September did little for the
houses of Dogpatch. Defeat hung in the air like river
mist. Rusted cars, chained dogs, ragged children, junk
scattered over the ground without reason or design:
Sara saw them all. A tattered white cloth fluttering in
the bushes was like a flag of surrender.

She crossed the road and walked along the planks
lying over the trampled brown mud that led to the door
of Bonnie's home. The walls were plywood painted a
once-jocular shade of blue; the roof was flat, pierced
by a metal chimney. Taking a deep breath, she raised
her hand to knock on the door and knew that she was
afraid.

What was she doing here, involving herself in lives
she knew virtually nothing about? She had never gone

hungry a day in her life. She knew nothing of the constraints of poverty, even though at this moment she was surrounded by them. But they were external to her, not bitten into her soul.

Come on, Sara, she chided herself. *You can't stand here forever, in a dither about knocking on the door. After all, what will the neighbors think?*

She rapped on the wood panels with her fist. The door was opened so suddenly that she knew the man had been waiting on the other side of it. She said her words in a rush, before she could lose courage, "My name is Sara Deane. I'm a teacher at Bonnie's school. I wondered if I could talk to you and your wife for a minute?"

The man looked at her unwinkingly. His hair was as black as the plumage of a crow, and the stubble of beard on his chin was the same dead shade. Although he was not quite as tall as Sara, he was in no sense overpowered by her; he was a force to be reckoned with, a concrete wall around which she had to insinuate herself.

He said, "You the truancy officer?"

"No! I'm just an ordinary teacher. I wanted to see if there was anything I could do to help Bonnie with her schoolwork."

"Everett, who is it?" A woman had ranged herself at the man's side, creating a double barrier.

Bonnie was her father's child, not her mother's. Mrs. Dawson was a bony woman, pared to the essentials, her eyes a clear, depthless turquoise that gave nothing away. She was not very clean, her jeans making Sara's look the height of respectability.

Gamely Sara began again. "My name is Sara Deane, Mrs. Dawson, and I teach at Bonnie's school. I was wondering if I could give Bonnie a little extra tutoring while she's working in the orchard, so she won't get too far behind in her schoolwork.''

"The name's Marlene," the woman said, her voice as sharp as broken glass. "What d'you want to go doin' that for?''

"I . . . I'm sorry?''

"What's in it for you?''

Sara met the turquoise eyes squarely. "There's nothing in it for me. I understand why Bonnie has to pick apples, but I don't want her to fail her grades as a result. That's all.''

"You better come in.''

With the feeling she had just made it past the first hurdle, Sara walked into the house, trying not to stare. The room was neither particularly dirty nor particularly clean. But the furnishings were so sparse, so bare of even the smallest unnecessary touch of beauty, that she felt she had passed from freedom into a prison cell. There was an old claw-footed wood stove in one corner; she thought of Annalise and shivered.

Everett hooked a wooden chair with his boot and sat down. Marlene pulled out a chair for Sara and sat down herself, her tanned ringless fingers clasped on top of the board table, exposing joints swollen with arthritis. "Why d'you care what happens to Bonnie?''

"She done somethin' wrong?'' Everett chimed in.

"No, she hasn't done anything wrong." Sara ran her finger along a gouge in the tabletop. "I don't know why I care about Bonnie," she said truthfully. "The other kids were picking on her one day in the yard, and I've talked to her a couple of times since then. I went to see her in the orchard on Thursday. I'm afraid that she might fail her Christmas exams if she doesn't get some extra help, and I'd be willing to give her that help."

Everett scraped back his chair and put a couple of logs in the stove, rattling the cast-iron lid. The crackle and snap of the flames should have been cheerful and was not. "She'll get by," he said. "I got no use for book learnin'." Marlene said nothing.

Realizing Bonnie could not have told her parents about the meal ticket, Sara labored on. "Bonnie has to stay in school two more years. Surely it would be better for her to succeed in those two years rather than fail?"

"She hates school," Marlene said.

Sara's natural reaction, thinking of Jean McPherson, was one of complete empathy. "School doesn't have to be hateful, or a place of failure," she said. "I love teaching. I know I'm new at the job and I have a lot to learn, but perhaps I can show Bonnie that schoolwork doesn't have to be dull or frustrating, that it can be fun. Learning can be the most exciting thing in the world." She stopped, afraid that she had spoken too emphatically, even though she believed every word she had said.

"Bonnie's in the orchard all day, and she's tired at night. We all are," Marlene replied in the same flat voice.

Sara looked from one to the other. She would have appreciated even the smallest sign of friendliness, but in Everett's dark-browed stare and Marlene's unflinching gaze her own eyes met only distrust and a deep, protective reserve. They were ranged against her, united against a common threat. Their attitude spoke volumes to her. Schools and bureaucracies and institutions could not have dealt kindly with them over the years, nor could she hope to erase that distrust in one short visit, no matter how sincere her offer to help.

She said calmly, refusing to look away, "I'm free on Sundays."

"What if she don't want to?" Marlene said.

"Then I guess we can forget it." Not until she had spoken did Sara realize how disappointed she would be. if Bonnie were to turn down her proposal.

Everett said truculently, "If we tell her she's gonna have lessons, then she'll have 'em."

You can lead a horse to water but you can't make it drink. The power of clichés, thought Sara wryly, lay in the truths they represented. "It would be much better if she wanted them," she said peaceably. "Better for both of us."

"Where is she?" Everett demanded.

"Lookin' after Nellie's kids. She should be back soon."

Sara said quickly, "But first of all, are you agreeable? She and I could get together once a week during the time she's working at the orchard. If everything went well, the lessons could continue through the winter."

"We can't pay you," Marlene said.

"If I can help Bonnie be a little happier in school, that will be payment enough."

"Charity don't sit good with me," Marlene snapped.

"But I'm not doing this for you. I'm doing it for Bonnie."

They all heard footsteps tramping up the front path. *Enter Bonnie,* thought Sara, *right on cue*. The door creaked open.

Bonnie saw Sara immediately. Her heavy features, normally so inexpressive, registered surprise, guilt and repudiation in quick succession. Before she could speak, Sara said pleasantly, "Hello, Bonnie. I came here to suggest to your parents that I give you a little extra tutoring on Sundays while you're working in the orchard, so you won't get too far behind in your schoolwork."

"I don't want no tutorin'."

Marlene said, "Your dad and me both think you should."

Sara kept a straight face and avoided looking at Everett. "Bonnie, I know Sunday is your day off. It's my day off, too, and if the lessons are a drag for you, they'll be a drag for me, as well. I don't want that any more than you do. I think we could have fun together."

"I'm gonna quit school soon as I'm sixteen."

"That's two years away. Have you made up your mind to be miserable for two years, or are you willing to try and get some fun out of them?" Sara gave her a winning smile, hoping against hope that Bonnie would agree to the proposal.

But then Marlene said, "You're goin', Bonnie. It won't hurt, and it might do some good."

Sara's heart sank. A Bonnie who had been ordered to learn was a much tougher proposition than a Bonnie who had volunteered. She said tranquilly, "Why don't you come outside with me for a minute, Bonnie, and we'll discuss what I had in mind?" Standing up, she added, "Thank you, Mr. and Mrs. Dawson. I'm glad to have met you."

Everett grunted. Marlene gave her an inscrutable look. Sara ushered Bonnie out of the door and down the plank walk. Then she turned to face the girl. "Bonnie, I know you're not very keen on these lessons and that you dislike school. But maybe between the two of us we can change that just a little bit—don't you think it's worth a try? We haven't got much to lose and a lot to gain.''

"Do we have to do it at the school?"

"Goodness, no. At my house. I'm renting a cottage on the lake road. If we started in the morning we could break for lunch, and then I'll bring you back sometime in the afternoon.''

The smallest gleam of interest brightened Bonnie's eye. "How would I get there?''

Sara looked around. There was no vehicle other than her own parked near the Dawson home. "I could come and get you and bring you home. Your dad doesn't have a car, does he?''

"He can't drive." For once Bonnie's close-set eyes met Sara's directly, malice in their depths. "He can't read or write. So he never got his license."

Sara stared at Bonnie, dumbfounded. The scene was forever etched in her brain as if a camera had recorded it on film: the girl's dark eyes, the plank walk and the blue plywood walls, the greedy alders with their toothed leaves. "What did you say?''

With rather overdone patience Bonnie repeated, "Dad never got his license because he couldn't read all the stuff you gotta know to pass your test."

One by one the thoughts clicked through Sara's brain. Everett Dawson couldn't drive because he had no license. He had no license because he couldn't read or write. Cal did not drive. Cal had thrown her book at the wall. Cal hired Peg to do all his bills and letters. Cal said he never read novels.

The conclusion was inescapable. Cal was illiterate. Cal Mathieson could not read or write.

Bonnie said suspiciously, "You okay, Miss Deane?"

The girl's dark eyes and the blue-painted walls were just as they had been, even though Sara felt as if the whole world had shifted under her feet. "Yes, I'm fine," she stammered. "What you said made me understand something that's been bothering me for weeks. Don't ask me to explain, because I can't." Her smile was brilliant. "Bonnie, I'll pick you up at ten-thirty on Sunday morning, okay? Now I've got to run. I've got another visit to make. Bye."

She reversed the car and drove carefully along the rutted road, leaving behind her the unkempt clutter of Haliburton's ghetto. She did not allow herself to think of her discovery. Intuitively she knew her conclusion had to be correct. It explained so much. It explained everything.

A few minutes later she turned into Cal's driveway and turned off the ignition. The square-paned windows of the saltbox house were reflecting the gold of the sun, blinding her to the interior. From the barn drifted the sound of a radio. Cal must be working. That made sense; he would not be spending Sunday afternoon reading the newspaper or the book she had given him, not if she was right. And she knew she was.

She walked through Peg's office and into the shadowed, wood-scented barn. The radio was louder, playing a tango, sensual and disturbing music that made Sara remember how Cal had made love to her in the living room at Cornelia's, and afterward had talked of defenses and of his aversion to intimacy.

He was standing by the bench holding a chisel. He had turned at the sound of her steps. "Sara," he said, and her name fell like a sigh from his lips.

"Hello, Cal." She walked closer. He was carving a design of leaves and grapes on the curved back of a chair. "That's very beautiful," she said.

He put down the chisel and said with a crooked smile that did not quite reach his eyes, "I can't concentrate with you here, and I don't want to make any mistakes at this stage. Did you come to pick up Cornelia's footstool?"

"No. I didn't even know she had one here." Cal was taking off his leather apron, his movements slow and deliberate, as if he wished to very carefully control everything he did. Her convictions wavered. He looked so solid, so capable. Was she not being immensely egotistical to assume he had been avoiding her because he was illiterate and feared discovery? Maybe it was much simpler than that. Perhaps he didn't like her. Or he was afraid to love anyone since the death of his family.

Sara cleared her throat. "I came to talk to you. To ask you something."

He was neatly replacing each tool in its canvas slot. "Go ahead."

Her heart was pounding as hard as if she had run from Bonnie's house to here. She thought of Bonnie, fought back panic and said as calmly as she could, "I made arrangements this afternoon to tutor a girl in grade six who lives across the river in that little group of houses by the bridge. She's missing school because she's picking apples. When she told me her father doesn't have a driver's license because he can't read or write, I couldn't help making the connection with you, Cal. You don't drive the truck. Is it because you can't read?"

He picked up a tool with a viciously sharp point and poked it in the case. "I told you why I don't drive. I was once responsible for an accident."

She walked round the end of the bench to face him. "But there's more to it than that. I was so hurt that you'd damage the book I gave you. I couldn't understand why you would do such a thing. But if you can't read, then your action makes sense. And of course you'd be short with me the day Joel and I were reading out of that book, and of course you'd be reluctant to go into a restaurant with me, because restaurants have menus, don't they, and menus have to be read. Don't you see, Cal, it all makes sense!"

He said evenly, "I think you should be writing novels, not reading them—you certainly have the imagination."

She flushed. "There's no shame in being illiterate, Cal. Your parents were poor. They wouldn't have been able to afford books. Books are luxuries, aren't they? I always used to take them for granted, but I never will again." Her voice was persuasive. "It so happened I was born the child of an officer in the armed forces while you were the child of seasonal farm workers. I can't take any credit for that, I was just lucky. We're not born equal, that's one of the myths of our society. It's blatantly obvious that you didn't have anything like the opportunities I had. From the little you've told me about your upbringing it's a wonder you've ended up doing as well as you have."

"You should go into politics," Cal said unpleasantly. "You can talk a lot and say absolutely nothing."

Sara gripped the edge of the bench and said hotly, "When you talk like that, I feel like bashing you over the head with a piece of two-by-four."

"I wouldn't advise you to try."

"Cal, please don't shut me out!"

"Listen, Sara, you march in here and accuse me of being illiterate and expect me to applaud? For God's sake!" He rolled up the canvas bag of tools and tied a very tight knot around them.

Rather the tools than my throat, she thought. "You as much as said you were wild in school, and after your family died in the fire, I'm quite sure English and history and mathematics wouldn't have been high on your list. That's why you're so grateful to Dougal, because he rescued you from your parents' fate, he gave you work that you love and a home and a way of earning your living and holding your head high. Of course you'd be grateful!"

Cal leaned forward. She had never seen such naked fury in a man's face before; it took all her willpower not to retreat. "Go home, Sara," he snarled. "And take your cute little theories and your patronizing attitudes with you. I don't need them. I don't need you. Get out!"

Cornelia and her mother had always bemoaned Sara's lack of good sense. She stood her ground. "Then explain to me, Cal Mathieson, why you've kissed me as if I was the only woman in the world and then pushed me away as if you couldn't stand the sight of me."

"You're not a bad-looking woman," he drawled. "And you made it fairly obvious you were available. I'd have been a fool not to kiss you."

"Now who's being patronizing!" she said, gritting her teeth. "So why didn't you take me to bed, Cal? Don't tell me you're impotent as well as illiterate!"

Across the width of the bench he grabbed her arm and shook it. "I'm neither one!"

"I'm not interested in proving your sexual prowess," she said wildly—and inaccurately. "But your literacy I am." She scrabbled in her purse and pulled out the first thing that came to hand, a pamphlet on new books for teenagers that she had picked up at the library in Coates Mill. She folded it open to a paragraph that described recent trends in literature for young adults and held it out to Cal. "Read this to me," she said.

He made no attempt to take the pamphlet. "There's no reason why I should have to play your little game."

"There's every reason, Cal. I really like you. I have from the first night we met, when you rescued me from the dog. I'm going to sound very conceited and say that I think you like me. I know you do. You showed me the flowers in the meadow . . . and I don't think you're the kind of man who would kiss a woman if he didn't care for her in some way. But then each time you get close to me, you retreat. Run. Hide. And I've never understood why." She managed a weak smile. "I'm assuming you don't have a wife and ten children hidden in the attic."

His mouth was a thin line. "No wife. No children."

"But if you are illiterate, you'd probably be embarrassed to admit it to me. Particularly as I'm someone who teaches, of all things, English. It's taken for granted, isn't it, that everyone in our society can read and write. Until I came here and talked to some of the teachers in the staff room, I took it for granted. How humiliating to be unable to order the special in the restaurant because you can't read the menu! Or to be unable to decipher shipping labels on your orders from Ontario. Oh Cal, don't you see, I understand how you feel."

"This is a ridiculous conversation," he said in a clipped voice. "Do you do this often, Sara—make huge assumptions about people and then go on the attack? If you do, then it's a wonder you have any friends left."

Her stomach was churning, and the pamphlet was shaking like a leaf in the wind. "Then explain to me why each time you and I get close to each other, you push me away."

"My mum and dad used to fight a lot. So a long time ago I figured I'd never let anyone that close to me. Dougal never married, and he was okay."

"Dougal treated you like a son because he never had one of his own."

Cal's breath hissed between his teeth. "You have an answer for everything, don't you?"

"So your rejection of me is because of your family, not because you can't read?"

"That's right."

She held out the pamphlet. "Then read me that paragraph!"

Although the radio was playing an old Sinatra song, the silence between Cal and Sara could have been cut with a knife. Very slowly he took the paper from her and looked down at it, and the paper shook in his hand just as it had in hers. A light sweat broke out on his forehead.

"I can't," he said.

She had won. But the victory was like ashes on her tongue, for a bitter shame was etched in Cal's face, and an anger deeper than words. Because she could not bear to see his hands trembling like an old man's, she took the pamphlet from him and put it in her purse, and wondered if he would ever forgive her for what she had just done.

He rubbed his palms down the side of his trousers and said in an almost conversational tone of voice, "Get out of here Sara. And don't come back."

"Cal, I can help—"

"I don't want to see you again."

"But now we know what the problem is, we—"

"Get out, Sara."

He was rocking back and forth on the balls of his feet like a boxer about to strike, and the force of his will hit her like a blow. She could have stood and argued. But she knew it was useless. She had won, and she had lost. She turned away and walked out of the barn.

The wind had sprung up, driving gray-edged clouds to shroud the blue of the sky. Sara got in her car, drove to the cottage, went inside and locked the door behind her. Then she sat at the kitchen table, resting her chin on her hands, and stared out at the trees. In the swamp the maples were turning color, a gallant, flamboyant death. She remembered the look on Cal's face as he had held the pamphlet and winced. Death can come in many forms.

If only he had been able to admit to her voluntarily that he could not read, how much easier it would have been. But his defenses and his shame went too deep for that. So she had yelled at him and insulted him and badgered him until he had told the truth, and her reward was to be banished. She scarcely blamed him. She had exposed to the light of day something he had kept hidden for years; naturally he would project on her all his anger for his own failure. His pride must be in shreds—and whom could he blame but her?

She should have come home after the revelation at Bonnie's, and considered a plan of action. But, oh no, she had barged into Cal's workshop and announced her great discovery without a moment's thought, and then had been disconcerted when he had reacted with fury rather than gratitude. *You're a naive fool, Sara. Cornelia's told you more than once to think before you act. When are you ever going to learn?*

As the wind moaned in the chimney and the sky darkened, her thoughts carried her inexorably forward. Her depression had deeper causes than her sense of having failed Cal, for more than she had failed him. His parents had. His school most certainly had. An education was considered the right of every child born in the land, yet Cal had emerged from the system at sixteen unable to read. While some of the fault must lie with him, not all of it could. Was the system set up for the average child, the son or daughter of a Rockwood family with an adequate income, a two-car garage and a recreation room scattered with books and magazines that were read as a matter of course? Did the system ignore families like Bonnie's, fathers like Everett who had no use for book learning, mothers like Marlene who had to pick apples to put food on the table, children like Bonnie who were happier in the orchard than at a desk in school? Put Bonnie beside the daughter of the local doctor, and what did you have? A most unequal competition, and one with no handicaps. Bonnie would be the loser every time.

Although Sara had learned a lot in her two years in Rockwood, she had never been confronted by the bleak realities of a dwelling like Bonnie's; her naïveté and idealism had escaped largely intact. She had known in theory that poverty existed in Canada, but her mind had conveniently relegated this poverty to city slums, or Indian reserves, or Inuit communities in the far north. She had not thought to find illiteracy in a pretty little hamlet thirty miles from the university where she had obtained her education degree. That was too close to home. That could never happen.

Sara sat for a long time, until the red leaves on the maples blended into the shadows and the sky turned black. Her thoughts had gone full circle, because they ended up where they had begun, with Cal. His property and her rented one were only separated by a band of trees, so that she could have walked to his house in five minutes. But far more than trees lay between them: bitter words and an even more bitter discovery. She would never again sit in the lamplit kitchen or smooth the grain in a pale pine board in the barn. *We strive for intimacy,* she thought painfully, *but we are infinitely separated one from the other. Love can bridge the gap, certainly. But love has to be shared.*

These were not uplifting thoughts. Sara heated some leftover lasagna and went to bed early, listening to the wind whisper around the house, the same wind that would be prying at Cal's windows and speaking to him of the loneliness of the human soul.

CAL WAS NOT IN BED. After Sara had left he had gone for a swim in the lake, thrashing around in the wind-ruffled water and diving beneath its surface to a realm where he had always felt protected from the everyday world to which he did not belong. But in the barn Sara had ripped from him all protection, so that his soul was now as naked as his body.

He jogged back to the house, his wet hair flopping on his forehead. He prepared a meal and ate it, and afterward could not have said what he had eaten. He cleaned out the wood stove and carried in kindling and freshly split logs. And it was still only eight o'clock. Too early to sleep. Too late to go for another swim.

He stood at the window, unmindful of the swaying branches of the apple trees. She had held out a pamphlet to him, a sheet of paper covered with words, row upon row of meaningless symbols that had blurred in front of his eyes. It was the actual recurrence of a nightmare he had had since he was seven years old. In the dream a deep male voice, firm and authoritative, would speak from above him, and a disembodied hand, covered with black, springing hair, would hold out a book, open to two pages of printing. No pictures or photographs, no clue as to the meaning. "Read to the class, Calvin," the voice intoned. Cal would grasp the book with fingers that shook and feel sweat dampen his skin as he stumbled through the first few lines. Some words he missed altogether, others he mispronounced. A girl giggled first, then a couple of boys guffawed, then the whole classroom broke into gales of laughter. The voice could have quelled the noise, for it had the authority. But it never did. It allowed the laughter to engulf Cal in shame and a helpless, consuming rage, and he would waken to the echo of that laughter in his ears, to find the sheets tangled about his body and his heart racing.

Sara now knew of that shame. A young woman with hair like flame and eyes the color of lake water, a woman of quick temper and ready laughter whose body he craved and whose spirit could match his own; it was she who had breached his defenses. No one else had done so, not even Dougal, with whom he had lived for six years. It had taken Sara a scant three months. He wondered what she would do with her new knowledge. Tell Cornelia and Laird? Tell Peg, which meant the whole community would find out? Or would she keep it to herself, a secret shared between them and never to be spoken of again?

He did not want to go to bed, for tonight of all nights he feared the dream. He cleaned out the back porch, a job long overdue, then pulled on a flannel shirt, switched on the barn lights and went outside to split wood. The swish and bite of the ax and the thunk of falling wood soothed him. He chopped until his shoulders began to ache, and then he stacked the logs in a neat crisscross pattern beside the barn. When he went back in the house, it was after midnight, and he thought he could sleep.

He slept. He did not dream. But he was wide awake at five o'clock, and as so often had happened through the summer, he woke to an image of Sara. What would it be like to find her bright tousled curls on the pillow beside him, her warm, responsive body curved to his side? He could only imagine it, and imagination brought no surcease to the unruly demands of his body.

He got out of bed, dressed and went outside to replenish the bird feeders that were strung on ropes between the trees. He fed the birds summer and winter, probably learning more about their behavior by observing them than he could have by reading books. This morning the chickadees were calling in the apple trees. When he made a low, whistling sound with his lips, holding his arm out from his body, a tiny black-headed bird landed on his finger, picked up a seed in its sharp little beak and flew back to the nearest tree, where it began banging the seed against the trunk to dislodge the casing. Two other chickadees followed suit before a loud screeching announced the arrival of the blue jays. Cal told them, rudely, where they could go. They paid no attention to him, instead scattering seed profligately from the tray of the feeder. He had long ago decided that blue jays were the most ill-mannered of birds, no matter how elegant their plumage; they reminded him of certain of his customers, who took for granted that he would be delighted when they telephoned at eight o'clock on a Sunday morning to discuss antique chairs. The cowbirds, who sneaked their eggs into other birds' nests, must be related to Percy Gillis; the redpolls, he thought ruefully, were like Sara. Sara, who now knew he could not read.

After he had gone back in the house, he took the bird book that a grateful customer had given him some months ago from the shelf in the living room and leafed through its pages. He recognized many of the sketches, and from the maps could discern the distribution patterns of the birds. But he could not read the written description; he did not know what the book said about the chickadee.

After replacing it on the shelf, he took down the book about furniture that had been Sara's present to him, which, because the binding was split, always opened to the same page, a complicated set of instructions for the case of a grandfather clock. The grandfather clock that ticked away in the corner had been made by Dougal's father, but Dougal had never deemed Cal skillful enough to pass on the directions for its production. The book could tell him how; but he could not read the book.

His knuckles tightened on the binding. He could fling the book at the wall again. He could rip it into shreds. He could burn it in the wood stove. But he could not destroy every book in the world, and even if he could he would still be left with the knowledge of his own failure, a knowledge that was seared into the very fiber of his being.

He shoved the book on the shelf and went out to split more wood. Next time he heard a woman scream for help, he thought venomously, he would ignore her, no matter if she was being attacked by a dozen dogs.

CHAPTER NINE

ON MONDAY AFTERNOON after school Sara went straight to Jean MacPherson's classroom, for she had decided if she was to tutor Bonnie she would do it openly. With some trepidation she told Jean her plan.

Her trepidation was justified. Jean wrinkled her nose as if a particularly bad smell had assaulted her nostrils and said, "Tutor her? Whatever for?"

Sara had already given her reasons. She repeated them patiently. "I'd hate her to fail the next set of exams."

"Of course she'll fail them. She's a hopeless case, that child, not a spark of initiative or drive."

Sara mentally counted to ten and with great geniality said, "I don't like to think that any child in this school is a hopeless case, Jean. Can you let me have her texts and scribblers until she comes back? Obviously I'll ensure that they don't get lost."

"When you see the state of her scribblers you'll understand what I mean," Jean said nastily. "I'm telling you, Sara, you're wasting your time."

She opened a cupboard near the blackboard and brought back half a dozen scribblers, which she put down on the desk in front of Sara. Quickly Sara glanced through the top two; Bonnie's work would have discredited a grade-two student. With a sinking heart she asked, "Does she do well in any subject?"

Rather than looking guilt-stricken that a pupil in her class should do so poorly, Jean looked triumphant at having proved her point. "She shows no interest in anything other than boys, which is exactly what you'd expect."

Sara knew she would say something exceedingly crude if she did not leave immediately. "I've got my work cut out for me, haven't I?" she said instead, gathering up the pile of textbooks and dog-eared scribblers. "Thanks, Jean. See you tomorrow."

She spent the rest of the week familiarizing herself with the grade-six texts and with the astonishing deficiencies in Bonnie's knowledge. On Sunday morning when she ushered the girl into the cottage, she was still not sure where she was going to begin.

The living room of the cottage was typical of a thousand such cottages found on the shores of Nova Scotian lakes, for it was complete with mail-order furniture, braided rugs and polyester easy-care drapes in autumnal colors. The only difference was that the picture windows, in Sara's case, overlooked trees rather than the next door neighbor's cottage. Sara had strived to give the room a touch of individuality with plants, posters and books, but had not wholly succeeded, for department store middle-of-the-line merchandise could subdue personalities stronger than hers.

But to Bonnie the room was obviously a palace. As she stood, a graceless lump of a girl with greasy hair, and looked around her openmouthed, Sara saw the room with fresh eyes as a repository of color, cleanliness and plenty, of objects that Bonnie would see as useless luxuries. The warm flesh tones of Sara's Renoir reproductions, the clutter of brightly jacketed books, the tropical lushness of the schefflera plant she had kept with her, not without difficulty, for the past four years, would all be outside Bonnie's limited experience, as exotic to her as the furnishings of Windsor Castle had been to Sara on her trip to Britain the summer before last. Feeling curiously humbled, Sara said, "Do you like the room? I'm only renting the cottage for the winter, because after next spring I may be out of a job again."

"Yeah, it's nice," Bonnie said, and looked over at Sara with the air of one who expects to be told what to do next.

"I made chocolate chip cookies this morning. Would you like some with a glass of milk? I thought we'd work at the table by the window. Maybe you could tell me where you'd like to start, Bonnie. Do you have a favorite subject?"

"I hate school," Bonnie said categorically.

"Do you hate any of it less than the rest?"

Bonnie pursed her lips in unaccustomed thought. "Nope."

Sara had not expected the sessions to be easy. "English is pretty basic," she said cheerfully. "Maybe we should start there." So she began with a short story that Jean's class had covered last week, and within five minutes realized that Bonnie's scribblers had not lied. The girl could read no better than she could write, and any spark of meaning in the first paragraph of the story was extinguished in Bonnie's attempts to pronounce the words.

"Do you read aloud in school very often?" Sara asked.

"Miss MacPherson don't usually ask me."

Sara could see why, for the whole class would be held up while Bonnie staggered through the maze of letters on the page. "I think we'll change tactics. Why don't you write the letters of the alphabet on this piece of paper while I hunt up some magazines. We'll start a scrapbook."

To Sara's relief Bonnie eventually produced a legible array of letters representing objects from ambulances and apples to ants. Bonnie had cut out the pictures and pasted them in the book while Sara had sounded out the letters, then printed questions beneath them for Bonnie to answer verbally and in writing. After the exercise they both relaxed a little, and by the time they broke for lunch the first three letters of the alphabet had been thoroughly dealt with. They did some simple mathematics after lunch, Sara taking change from her purse and setting up imaginary situations in a store, and then they went outside, where a science lesson was incorporated into their ramble through the woods. Back in the house, the letter *d* was added to the scrapbook. Then Sara gave Bonnie a brief tour of the dictionary and explained the best way it could be put to use.

Bonnie was starting to look tired. Sara closed the dictionary and said briskly, "Would you like to borrow two or three of the magazines until next week, Bonnie?"

Bonnie picked up the latest issue of *Seventeen*. The girl on the cover, pearly-toothed, glossy with cleanliness, laughed up at her. "I'll never look like that," said Bonnie.

"We all have to make do with what we've got," Sara replied gently. "The thing is, to make the most of it."

"I'm ugly. The kids at school say so." Sullen-browed, Bonnie dropped the magazine on the table.

"If you see yourself as ugly and act as if you are, then probably you will be."

Bonnie gave her a blank stare. "I gotta go now."

Condemning the sunny-faced girl on the magazine to perdition, Sara said calmly, "Okay. I'll get my keys."

She was shrugging into her sweater when a knock came at the door. Bonnie, without asking permission, opened it. The man on the step was Cal. Sara stared at him as if she were seeing a ghost.

"May I come in?"

She grabbed him by the arm, which was quite definitely made of flesh and blood, and pulled him into the room, saying breathlessly, "I'm so glad to see you! I was afraid we'd never see each other again."

"You have company."

"Oh." She dropped Cal's sleeve and hastily introduced Bonnie and Cal. "Bonnie and I have been doing some extra schoolwork. I was about to drive her home. I'll only be gone ten minutes. Why don't you wait here until I get back?" Her smile was ingenuous. "You won't disappear, will you?"

"I'll wait for you."

He would, she knew. "All right, I'll see you in a little while."

She and Bonnie went down the steps and got into the car. As they drove away Bonnie said with the first curiosity she had shown about Sara, "Is he your boyfriend?"

"I don't think so."

Bonnie heaved a sigh. "I wish I had a boyfriend."

"You're young yet," Sara said, and could have bitten her tongue, for it was the sort of reply her mother would have made when she herself was fourteen, and fourteen does not want such replies.

"Laura Schneider's got a boyfriend and she's younger than me."

"I'm considerably older than you, and I don't have one."

"The kids at school say Mr. Pinkerton's got a crush on you."

Mr. Pinkerton taught geography, had rampaging acne and was absurdly shy. "Well, he's not my boyfriend," Sara said firmly. "Bonnie, I enjoyed our session today. I hope you did, too."

Bonnie was not skilled in diplomacy. "It wasn't as bad as I thought it'd be," she said, and with that Sara had to be content. When she dropped Bonnie off in front of the blue house, the girl bolted up the plank walk without a backward look. Wondering if she were crazy to be attempting to improve Bonnie's dyspeptic view of herself and the world, Sara turned the car around and headed home.

She had forced herself not to think about Cal's unexpected arrival while Bonnie was in the car with her, but now her imagination went wild. He had come to apologize for sending her away. He had come to berate her for her interference. He wanted her to move fifty miles away. He wanted her to move in with him. He loved her. He hated her. Or, worse, he was indifferent to her.

But here Sara's imagination ran up against a strong streak of realism. However Cal regarded her, it was not with indifference.

She parked the car by the cottage and ran up the stairs, frightened despite his promise that Cal might have vanished as mysteriously as he had appeared. But he was standing by the living room window, where the books and papers were still spread on the table. He said without preamble, "Bonnie's from east of the river, isn't she?" Sara nodded. "Why are you helping her?"

Sara explained about the apple picking. "She's nowhere near the grade six level, I don't see how she can possibly pass her Christmas exams. But at least we'll give it a try."

He said soberly, "That's good of you, Sara."

"Oh, I don't know. I guess I feel sorry for her because she's such a misfit, although I'd never tell her that." Her smile was wry. "I wish she wanted to learn to read as badly as she wants a boyfriend."

"You'll be good for her."

"I'll try. If she'll let me." Sara had been tidying the papers as she talked. She knew Cal had not come here to discuss Bonnie. "Can I get you a cup of tea or some homemade lemonade?"

"No. I came to talk to you, Sara."

She bit her lip and asked in a small voice, "Are we still friends?"

"I'd like to think we are."

"Then do me a favor," she said in a rush. "Come over here and give me a hug. You seem so far away, and not quite real and—"

The rest of what she had to say was muffled in his shirtfront. His hug was bone-crackingly sincere. Sara hugged him back and wailed, "I'm so sorry for the way I yelled at you last week, Cal! I didn't mean to lose my temper. I meant to be cool and calm and rational, but I said such dreadful things to you. Cornelia always says I talk before I think . . . ouch!"

He had squeezed her ribs tightly enough to silence her. "I'm the one who came to apologize," he said.

She raised her head. "Is that why you're here? I thought you might have decided to wring my neck."

The beginnings of a smile softened his face. "If I ever decide to wring your neck, I won't wait a week. No, I came to say I'm sorry for the way I spoke to you. And I'm so damned stiff-necked it took me a week to get up my nerve. You were only trying to help, I see that now, and I said some unforgivable things to you."

"Then if we're both sorry, I think we should kiss and make up," she said recklessly.

He kissed her with a hesitancy that was very touching. Stroking her cheek, he said, "You're the only person in the world who knows the truth about me, Sara."

She sensed an implicit question in his words. "I'd never tell anyone, you know that. But Peg's never guessed?"

"God, no! If she had, everyone in Haliburton would know."

"Will you tell me how it happened, Cal?"

As he sat down on the tweed-covered chesterfield, his arm draped along its back. Sara sat beside him, very conscious of that arm, conscious, too, of a deep contentment that he had come to see her. He said softly, "It's a story much like Bonnie's, I imagine, except that I had the added disadvantage of being twice the size of everyone else in the classroom. My parents were illiterate. Mum used to get her neighbor to fill out the welfare forms. Dad could sign his name on the unemployment cheques and then as often as not head for the bootlegger's with the money. He certainly never headed for the bookstore. They didn't really care if I went to school or not. School was an alien world to them, a place that sent home notes they couldn't read, that told them to phone for appointments when they didn't have a telephone. They didn't have the right clothes for parent-teacher interviews, they couldn't even read the names of the teachers on the classroom doors. How could they have found the courage to expose themselves to almost certain humiliation? So they never went near the school. And if I played hooky on the first sunny days in spring, they didn't care. Of course, once I got big enough to work I'd be picking whatever crop was ready. School couldn't compete with money in your pocket. I failed a couple of the early grades, I grew like a bad weed, and by the time I was in grade five I was taller than the teacher." He gave a faint grin. "I used to sit in the very back row and make paper airplanes and spitballs and see how many of the other kids I could get into trouble."

Sara pulled a face. "Every teacher's nightmare."

"I never looked at it from the teacher's point of view...well, I told you how I got in with a gang of much older boys and graduated from spitballs to sniffing glue. I was a smart aleck kid who thought he knew it all—school couldn't teach me anything I didn't already know. And then there was the fire..." Cal picked at a flaw in the knee of his jeans. "I went crazy for a while after that. Drank myself silly, stayed out night after night, drove Lonnie's motorbike as if the devil himself was behind me. Maybe he was. When I look back, I reckon I was trying to put an end to myself without ever using the word suicide. No foster home would keep me more than a month or two, and I can't say I blame them...in my black leather jacket on a borrowed motorbike, I was headed straight for reform school. Or hell, depending on your point of view. But in the fall I got into industrial arts and discovered the fit of a hammer in my hand, the smoothness of a planed piece of pine and the smell of shavings. It was the first time in my life anything made sense. And then Dougal came to the school. The industrial arts teacher had known Dougal for years and used to invite him to the school each January to show the class some of the techniques of cabinetmaking. I doubt if Dougal in his whole life ever told anyone he loved them, but he sure loved wood and the things he could make out of it. Right away I knew what I was going to do when I was sixteen, so I sobered up and stopped trying to kill myself on the highway, started keeping to myself a lot. Lonnie soon gave up on me, and the rest of the gang followed suit. In a few short weeks I went from a hell-raiser to a loner, and I reckon the whole community breathed a sigh of relief. I got all the odd jobs I could and bought my own set of tools, and the day I turned sixteen I got on the bus, came to Haliburton and asked Dougal to take me on. I've never been back there. Since the night of the fire I've never gone up the mountain to see where we used to live...."

His voice had died away. Sara said softly, "When you came here no one knew you were illiterate, and you've kept it a secret ever since."

"Yeah. Dougal was never one for books, everything he knew was in his head and his hands. And after he died, I hired Peg to do the bookkeeping and to drive the truck for pickups and deliveries."

"Everyone else you kept at arm's length."

He shrugged. "I'm a loner, Sara, I always have been. Annalise was the only person I could ever talk to."

"But you get lonely sometimes."

He looked full at her. "Don't we all?"

She thought of some of the long evenings since school had begun when she had been tempted to call Joel because she was lonely. To her credit she had not done so, but she had been tempted. Wanting a change of subject, she said, "So there never was a car accident. You don't drive because you don't have your license."

"That's right. Couldn't face the test, all the forms you'd have to fill out. I've known how to drive for years—anyone who hung out with Mitch and Lonnie knew how to drive... I'm sorry I lied to you, Sara."

"That's okay." She took the plunge. "Cal, I could give you some lessons, the same as Bonnie. I could tutor you in reading and writing."

He shook his head. "There's no need. I manage fine as I am."

"If it would bother you to take lessons for nothing, I'd charge you." She grinned impishly. "Charge you plenty. I'll need a new car next year."

His face gave nothing away. "Why should I bother, Sara? I've got my business and my house. I'm happy as I am."

She narrowed her eyes. "So if you're happy as you are, why did you throw the book at the wall?"

"I've always had a bad temper," Cal said shortly. "That's another reason I keep to myself. Once when I was in grade seven I beat a kid up so badly he ended up in hospital."

Sara kept her expression studiously blank. "Why did you lose your temper?"

"Oh, he was mistreating a kitten. I can't stand that kind of thing."

"It sounds like a fairly normal reaction to me." Methodically she moved in for the attack. "So why did a book about furniture make you lose your temper?"

"You missed your vocation. You should have been a lawyer."

"Pretend you're under oath and answer the question."

"Okay," he said irritably. "I didn't like the fact that you'd give me a present that wasn't the slightest bit of good to me."

"You could look at the pictures and the plans."

"But I couldn't read the instructions!"

"So you do care."

"I'd like to know how to make the grandfather clock," he admitted grudgingly. "Five pages of written instructions."

"I'll read them for you."

"As if I was blind, or an idiot."

"You're neither of those things, Cal. You're an intelligent man who's had a raw deal. Now it's up to you whether or not you remain hampered by that for the rest of your life."

"I can't take lessons from you, Sara. I just can't."

His refusal hurt. She said in a low voice, "You kept avoiding me because you were afraid I'd find out you were illiterate . . . am I right?"

He nodded. "You're not exactly stupid, you know. And in the end you found out, anyway."

"So now there's surely no reason why we can't have normal dates, like any other couple."

"Listen, Sara, while you were driving Bonnie home, I took a good long look at this room. The furniture isn't up to much—"

"The furniture's not mine," she retorted, stung. "Mine's in storage in Halifax."

"But the books are yours, and the magazines. You've got two university degrees and you're a full-fledged teacher. I'm a carpenter who bluffed his way through grade eight. Functionally illiterate is the term they use for people like me. So don't talk about normal dates."

Her color was rising. "Are you calling me an intellectual snob?"

"I'm trying to be realistic."

"We have a great deal in common."

"Come off it," he said rudely.

She ticked off her fingers. "We both love Haliburton. We love the outdoors. We share an eye for beauty. We're both perfectionists—I care about the quality of my teaching just as much as you care about the finish on a mahogany table. We can't stand people who mistreat animals, we're orphans, and if you have a temper, so have I."

He was not amused. "My skill is all in my hands. Yours is in your head. Forget it, Sara."

"Cal, you're a very intelligent man who was totally frustrated by the school system. Don't give me the Simple Carpenter routine."

He got up and strode across the room, leaning his back on the beachstone fireplace. "How do you think I feel when I look at all your books, shelf after shelf of the damn things? I feel like a goddamned ignoramus."

"Don't be silly! Remember the day in the restaurant when we talked about the lumber industry in British Columbia? You were far better informed than I."

"I listen to the radio a lot while I'm working," he said impatiently.

"You're not just listening, you're learning. You've got a darn good vocabulary and you know how to use it."

"But I can't read!"

"Then do something about it!" She tried to soften her tone. "I'll help you to the best of my ability."

"No!"

Sara had had a long day, for her attempts to spark interest and initiative in Bonnie had been tiring, as well as largely unsuccessful, and she was not in the mood for more rejection. "Fine," she snapped. "Then we're wasting each other's time, aren't we? We have nothing in common, we can't have a normal date and you're determined to wallow in the martyrdom of illiteracy. So why don't you get the hell out of here and don't come back!"

She stomped over to the window, staring at the trees as if she had never seen a tree in her life before, her fists clenched at her sides. She expected to hear the thud of Cal's work boots across the floor and the slam of the door. Instead there was silence.

Sara had never been very good at handling suspense, and her curiosity had often led her into trouble. She turned around. Cal was still standing by the fireplace, a most peculiar look on his face, compounded of chagrin, dismay and surprise. She said crossly, "Didn't you hear me? Go away, Cal."

"I don't want to." His voice held the same surprise as his features.

"That's not what you said the last time we were together."

"No, it's not, is it?"

"I do wish you'd make up your mind."

"I have. When you told me to get out, I knew I didn't want to. Just like that. So I guess I'll have to learn to read."

She tried to harden her heart. "I thought women were the ones who were supposed to be illogical. Seriously, Cal, there's no point in you staying if you're going to have a huge inferiority complex the whole time you're around me."

As he crossed the room and clasped her by the shoulders all the mixed emotions in his face had coalesced into an intense seriousness. "I was wrong. I do want to learn to read. Will you teach me, Sara?"

"Oh, yes," she said, her head whirling. "Yes. I'll do my best."

"And I'll do my best to learn." Solemnly he held out his hand, and just as solemnly she shook it.

He dropped her hand rather abruptly, clearing his throat. "When shall we start?"

"Not tonight!" she replied so feelingly he had to laugh. "How about one evening this week? Tuesday?"

"Peg and I do deliveries on Wednesday, so Tuesday would be fine." He shifted his shoulders restlessly. "Sara, you look tired. Why don't you come to my place for supper? We can eat yesterday's stew."

She too felt a need for action after a decision that was, she knew, momentous. "Sounds wonderful."

"Come on, then."

They walked to the saltbox house side by side but carefully not touching, and throughout the meal the unease between them persisted. They covered it with small talk, laughing and joking a great deal, Sara hiding a hollow ache of disappointment under a somewhat overdone vivacity. She had felt closer to Cal when they were yelling at each other in her living room than she did now. She helped him wash the dishes, trying to ignore the overtones of domesticity in that most ordinary of tasks and, when they had finished, said with a brightness that she hoped did not ring as false in his ears as it did in her own, "Well, I'd better be going, workday tomorrow. Thanks for the meal, Cal, I'd recommend your stew to anyone."

"I'll walk you home."

She could not bear to hear herself artlessly chatter on for another five minutes. "No need. This is Haliburton, not Halifax."

"Haliburton has its fair share of roughnecks. I'll walk you home, Sara." As she glared at him rebelliously, debating whether or not to argue, Cal added, "Don't scowl. I can always throw you over my shoulder."

As Sara was five-foot-ten and weighed 130 pounds, the number of men who could throw her over their shoulders was limited. "Caveman stuff," she said with a gleam in her eye.

"You unquestionably bring out the primitive in me."

"I'd never have known it, judging by the past couple of hours," she responded provocatively.

He thrust his hands in his pockets and did not smile. "I don't know if I've ever felt as strange—and as strained—with anyone as I have with you right here in this kitchen this evening. Don't you see, Sara? You know the truth about me, you know me as I really am. No masks, no inventions or social lies. You know the real Cal, the school dropout, the wild kid with the uncontrollable temper who grew into the man who can't read." He looked at her somberly across the width of the table. "I wonder if you have any idea what it's like to be illiterate in a society that revolves around the written word. It's a sense of isolation so deep you can't imagine bridging it. A conviction of your own abnormality—you're the outcast, the one who doesn't fit. And along with that goes the secrecy and the lying, the endless, complicated deceits because you can't bear the thought of being found out. People will laugh at you. You'll be humiliated, or pitied, or scorned. So you're always afraid. Such simple little things can happen. A customer holds out a bill she can't understand. The dentist shows you your chart. The stationmaster wants you to read the invoice. And you break out into a sweat, and your heart begins to race, and you want to run as far and as fast as you can, because you're afraid... I have nightmares of being found out, Sara, and when I wake up I can still see the fingers pointing at me and the circle of faces jeering at me with all the cruelty of those who belong toward those who don't."

Sara stood very still on the other side of the table. She belonged, she thought humbly. She always had. Because of an accident of birth she was one of the lucky ones. But Cal had not been so lucky; he had been born into poverty in a shack on a mountain. She said shakily, "How you must have hated me when I stuck that paper under your nose and told you to read it."

"I did, yes. But now I feel as though I'm standing in front of you naked, Sara. As naked as the day I was born, and just as vulnerable."

Impulsively she walked around the table. Looking up at him and making no attempt to hide the tears in her eyes, she said, "I understand, Cal. Because of your vulnerability, I have a tremendous amount of power, don't I? I swear I'll never abuse that power, and, just to keep the record straight, I neither pity nor scorn you. It takes courage to speak to another human being the way you just did—I'm complimented that you chose me."

Very deliberately he lowered his head and kissed her, a long, slow kiss that somehow conveyed both his vulnerability and his trust. He said soberly, "I sometimes wonder if we haven't chosen each other."

She knew exactly what he meant, and in her innermost heart could only agree with him. She found herself wishing she could stay with him all night and hold him close and keep at bay the nightmares. Swiftly she lowered her eyes so that he could not read her thoughts.

She must have succeeded. He said with an attempt to restore normality, "I was going to walk you home, wasn't I?" As she nodded, he crooked an eyebrow. "What, no arguments?"

"Nary an argument."

"How dull of you."

"I wouldn't want you to get a hernia carrying me over your shoulder."

He swelled out his chest and flexed his arms. "You insult me."

His T-shirt was short sleeved and tight fitting; Sara controlled various wanton impulses and said primly, "Walk me home, Cal Mathieson."

He kept an arm around her as they tramped along the side of the road; she decided she fit very nicely into the curve of his shoulder and was sorry when they reached her front door. He said in a businesslike voice, "What time on Tuesday?"

"Seven?"

"I'll come over here, shall I?" He kissed her on the cheek, a kiss she could not call anything other than restrained, and said awkwardly, "Sara, thank you."

To mask the feelings his closeness aroused, she answered flippantly, "You're the one who provided dinner."

"Thank you for listening, that's what I meant. It's almost as though I've found Annalise again."

I am certainly not your sister, Sara thought, and clamped her mouth shut so she would not say the words out loud. When the danger was over she said temperately, "Sharing a problem is often the first step to solving it. I'll see you Tuesday, Cal."

He made no attempt to kiss her again, and by the time she had unlocked her front door, he was halfway down the driveway. She closed the door and leaned against its varnished wood, wishing he had indeed swept her into his arms, wondering why, if she aroused the primitive in him, he was walking back to his house, leaving her alone in hers. They should be in bed together. That's exactly where they should be. She heaved a monumental sigh and went to clean her teeth.

CHAPTER TEN

THE FIRST LESSON with Cal was an unmitigated disaster from beginning to end. When he arrived, Cal looked steeled for the worst, like a man with six cavities entering the dentist's office. He did not seem to know what to do with his hands. Sara, who had thought of nothing else but this lesson for two days, was trying much too hard to be at ease; her nonchalance was assumed but her nervousness was not.

She knew her first task was to assess the extent of Cal's knowledge. In Bonnie's case she had had scribblers and textbooks as starting points, in Cal's case, nothing. So she had borrowed books of different reading levels from the school library. Picking out an intermediate one, she asked Cal if he could read it.

He opened the book. It had line drawings of children in a playground. The print was large and the sentences short. Something tightened in his face. He stumbled through three or four pages, his voice a monotone, missing words Sara would have thought were obvious, ignoring the punctuation as if it were not there. Sara was quite sure that whatever meaning existed in the pages passed him by completely. She tried a simpler book, wincing as he struggled with the infantile activities of Johnny, Mary and their little dog, Patches.

When he finally put the book down, his cheeks were flushed with embarrassment. Sara said apologetically, "These books were all I could find in the school library, Cal. I realize they're for children. But I needed to get some idea of what you could and couldn't read."

"Now you know. I can't even read a book intended for a seven-year-old."

"That's all right," she said strongly. "If you could read, we wouldn't be here, would we? Let's just try one more, and then we'll do some writing."

With fierce determination, his big hands clutching the book as if it were a recalcitrant slab of mahogany, he desecrated the syntax of a chapter about the St. Lawrence Seaway. Sara was appalled, although she was trying very hard to keep her face expressionless. On a lined piece of paper she printed some questions about what he had just read, then passed him the paper and a pencil.

A chisel or a hammer fit Cal's hand, became an extension of it, but a pencil looked awkward between his fingers, and he pressed so hard on the paper that the lead point snapped. He could have split a dozen logs with less effort than it took him to write one-line answers to her questions. The letters strayed across the page like deformed children.

The contrast between her own neat printing and his ramshackle efforts was painful. Reluctantly Sara decided she would have to adopt the same methods with him as she had with Bonnie, and set him to work printing the letters of the alphabet while she collected a pile of magazines, the scissors and the glue. But whereas Bonnie had enjoyed looking through the magazines, her eyes lighting covetously on clothes and bronzed young men alike, Cal simply did as he was told, finding photographs of Arabs, artists and abbeys, cutting them out, pasting them beside the letter *a*. He inscribed laborious sentences beneath them; he read the sentences to Sara; they used the dictionary to check meanings, phonetic values and spellings; and through it all Sara had no sense of connections being made, of the vibrant excitement that true learning could kindle. Cal was trying very hard—she could not fault him for that—as was she. Were they trying too hard? Or was her methodology wrong? What had worked for Bonnie would not necessarily work for an adult. Scrapbooks of the alphabet seemed incongruous in Cal's callused hands, while to hear a man six-foot-four sounding out the letters in a word had all the elements of black comedy. At the end of two hours Sara had a headache and Cal looked exhausted. She said, fighting to keep discouragement out of her voice, "I think that's enough for one night, don't you?"

He put the dictionary down with the alacrity of a little boy on the last day of school and kneaded his forehead with his fingertips. "Yeah. Give me a cord of wood to split any day of the week."

"The first few lessons are bound to be the hardest," Sara responded, as much to convince herself as him.

"I guess you're right." He got up and stretched, rolling his head to ease the tension in his shoulders. "When's the next one?"

"We could get together on Thursday. Friday's a fairly easy day for me at school."

His agreement was polite rather than enthusiastic. "Why don't you come to my place for a change?"

Maybe he would feel more at ease in his own kitchen; certainly she was willing to try that. "Okay. Same time?"

He nodded. Not quite meeting her eyes, he said, "Thanks, Sara. You put a lot of effort into the last couple of hours. You must be tired. I'll see you Thursday." He pulled on his jacket and went out of the door without a backward look.

Her shoulders sagged. She had never felt so inadequate in her life as she had this evening. Goodwill and the desire to help were not enough: somehow she had to reach the real Cal. But she had no idea how.

THE EVENINGS WERE COOLER NOW, so a fire was chattering in the wood stove in Cal's kitchen, and the curtains were drawn against a fine, misty rain that gathered like tears on the windowpane. Sara hung her rain jacket by the back door and pulled off her boots. The kitchen welcomed her like an old friend, and she knew with a lift of optimism that the evening would go well. "Hi, Cal!" she said. "Don't you love the smell of the woods in a night like this? Fallen leaves and damp earth . . . heavenly!"

"Not to mention rotting ferns, deer droppings and earwigs," he said gravely.

"Earwigs don't smell."

"They live in places that smell."

"I have a feeling this conversation isn't going anywhere."

He kissed her rain-damp cheek. "How are you, Sara? You look wonderful."

She knew her eyes were shining and her cheeks glowing because she was happy to be with him. "Thank you," she said pertly. "You don't look so bad yourself." *That's the understatement of the year, Sara. Admit that you'd like to tear the clothes off him.* She said briskly, "We start with the letter *c* this evening, don't we? I found some back issues of *National Geographic* at Cornelia's, so I brought them long. I didn't tell her why, of course," she added hastily.

They sat down at the kitchen table and began to work. Although the magazines provided cheetahs, coral, catacombs and crows, Sara knew within ten minutes that she and Cal were on the wrong track. He did exactly as she asked. But his heart was not in the exercise, and a half an hour later when they tried reading another of the books she had borrowed from the school library, she was somehow not surprised that he should break off in the middle of Johnny and Mary's tobogganing expedition and slam the book on the table. "I can't read this stuff!" he said violently.

She was sure Cal would have used a much stronger word than stuff had she not been present. She could not really blame him, for Johnny and Mary were children of saccharine virtue, their conversation such as she had never heard between normal boys and girls. Nor has she missed the danger signals in Cal: the tightness of his jaw, his restless movements in the chair, his ferocious grip on the yellow pencil.

He scraped back his chair. "Look, Sara, why don't we admit that we're wasting each other's time? I'm truly grateful to you for trying, but I can't hack this any longer. I feel exactly as if I'm back in grade school, all this c is for cat and Johnny-and-Mary nonsense. I just can't handle it, I'm sorry." As abruptly as he had stood up, he sat down again, burying his head in his hands. She could hear the harsh rhythm of his breathing.

"We can't give up!" she said.

"Why can't we? If I'm no better off after these two lessons, I'm no worse off. Let sleeping dogs lie." His mouth twisted in a mirthless smile. "And don't tell me *d* is for dog."

"But, Cal, you have to know the letters and the way they sound. They're as important for language as the musical notes are for a composer."

He banged his fist on the table. "I don't give a damn! Neither you or anyone else is going to make me feel like an eight-year-old again. I hated school. I failed in school." Contemptuously he flicked the primer with his nail. "All this does is remind me of that failure."

"So you're going to quit."

His mouth thinned. "Yes, I'm going to quit."

"Again."

"Shut up, Sara."

"No, I won't! You can't quit, not when we've scarcely started."

"If we keep on as we are, I'll start to hate you. Just like I hated my teachers in school."

He was indeed looking at her with something like hatred in his eyes. Making a sudden, last-ditch decision, Sara seized him by the wrist. "You come with me."

"What the hell are you—"

"Come on." She tugged at him with all her strength; somewhat to her surprise, he followed her. She led him out the back door and across the driveway to the barn. "Unlock the door," she ordered. "And hurry up, I'm getting wet."

He fished in his pocket for the keys and snapped, "There's a word called please."

"Spelled p-l-e-a-s-e," she retorted, the effect rather spoiled when a drop from the roof splashed on her nose. She dared him to laugh, her eyes blazing.

He did not laugh, which was probably wise of him. After unlocking the door, he flipped on the light switch. Sara herded him through Peg's tidy office to the workshop. Only then did she drop his arm. "Now," she said militantly, "we'll change roles. You're the teacher and I'm the student. Teach me to saw a plank into pieces and nail them together."

He frowned. "I don't know what you're getting at."

"You will."

He was looking at her as if she had gone crazy, but at least the baffled humiliation that Johnny and Mary had evoked had disappeared from his eyes. He pulled out a short pine board from a heap of scrap wood in the corner and laid it along a sawhorse. Then he selected a saw from the array of tools on the wall.

Sara had had time to collect herself. "Why that particular saw?" she asked amiably.

He looked surprised at the question. "We're cutting across the grain, so we use a crosscut handsaw. If you cut along the grain, you use a ripsaw. The difference is in the teeth." Putting his knee on the board, he made a mark on it with a pencil, then drew the saw toward him, using his thumb as a guide.

"But you're cutting backward."

"This is what you call the kerf, this groove in the wood. The first one's always started with a backstroke, and you make it on the waste side of the line. If the piece you want is a little bit too long, you can always shorten it. But if it's too short, you're in trouble."

"It's a lot more complicated than I thought," Sara remarked with a certain disingenuousness.

"Most things are." He straightened and gave her a smile of singular sweetness. "I begin to see where we're headed."

"Cut the piece of wood, Cal."

"Okay. Always keep the saw at a forty-five-degree angle for crosscutting, and when you've nearly finished the cut, support the end piece, or you'll get splintering." With smooth easy strokes he cut through the board. Then he marked another notch and said, "Your turn."

Sara had watched carefully, and the operation had not looked particularly difficult. She braced her knee, made the first cut and began to saw up and down. But the cutting line did not stay straight, as it had with Cal, and partway through the board the saw buckled. He showed her how to correct her errors, and she tried again. But she forgot to support the end piece, so that it snapped off, leaving jagged splinters. She set her jaw. "Let me try again."

Her second cut was minimally less crooked than the first. "Now I want to nail the pieces together," she announced, her hands on her hips.

Cal took a hammer from the rack and showed her how to grasp it near the end. "A good hammer balances well. Most of mine are probably too heavy for you. We'll use common nails, because we're not worrying about appearance. Steady the nail in your left hand and tap it lightly to start it, then strike it hard to drive it into the grain. If you don't hit it squarely you can damage the head, or drive the nail in crookedly."

Again he made the process look both natural and easy. With beginner's luck Sara drove her first nail into the plank with three clean blows. But the second one bent, the third took eleven strokes and on her fourth attempt she hit her thumb a resounding blow.

She clutched it, grimacing. "I did not do that on purpose."

Although Cal was concerned, she could also see he was trying to hide a smile. "I think you'd better stick to teaching."

"I've always been clumsy with my hands...I swear there's a connection missing between my hand and my brain." She gave him a rueful smile. "Do you get the message, Cal? The path of learning rarely runs smooth. You can use a hammer and saw without thought, but I can't even cut a straight line, let alone drive in a nail. And it's difficult for you to explain to someone else how to do something that you do automatically. I can read without even thinking about the process involved—and I'm finding it impossible to figure out how best to teach you."

"Halfway through the first cut I got the message. But what are we going to do about it, Sara?"

She pursed her lips. "I'm not sure," she said honestly. "My friend Ally in Halifax is a reading specialist. I could visit her on the weekend and see if she could help out...I've always taught junior high, you see, so I've never been involved with the actual teaching of reading." Absently she rolled a couple of nails between her thumb and finger. "Cal, what would you most like to be able to do that you can't because you can't read?"

"Drive the truck," he replied promptly.

"Well, maybe that's where we should start. I could get the driver's manual and the forms from the Registry of Motor Vehicles, and we could try reading them."

She had his full attention. "I always feel like a fool having Peg drive me around. It'd be wonderful to be able to get my license."

"Why don't we try that, then? It would beat Johnny and Mary."

"And dear little Patches chasing that damned toboggan." Cal ran his fingers through his hair, his eyes bright. "Would you be willing to try, Sara? Get the book and go over it with me? I know the mechanics of driving, that's no problem. It's the rules of the road that would be the hang up."

"Of course I will."

He looked as excited as a small boy. "I'd feel like a normal person if I could drive my own truck, make all my own deliveries. It would be a huge step forward."

Sara made a silent vow that even if the driver's manual presented ten times the problems of Johnny and Mary, she would see that Cal got his license. His use of the word *outcast* a couple of days ago had struck her deeply, and she would give anything to see him take his rightful place in the world.

ON FRIDAY SARA got all the materials from the Registry of Motor Vehicles and discovered that Cal could take an oral exam rather than a written one. On Saturday she went to Halifax, where she bought a flame-colored shirtdress that would cheer up herself and her class in the dark days of January. Then she had dinner with Pete and Ally.

The Nasebys lived in the north end of the city and had been married just over a year. Pete was a radio announcer whose mellifluous voice on the air gave the impression of a broad-shouldered gentleman in tweeds holding back a brace of large, hairy dogs. Pete, however, was exactly two inches taller than his wife, which made him five-foot-six, and he disliked dogs. But he was entirely comfortable with his lack of height, becoming neither excessively aggressive nor overly virile in the presence of women like Sara, who towered over him. She liked Pete very much; he anchored Ally's changes of mood, so that the febrile gaiety of Ally's college years had softened to a serenity that was very appealing.

After fettuccine Alfredo, an exotic fruit salad and impassioned discussions of everything from media responsibility in cases of terrorism to the best recipe for pasta, they took their coffee into the living room. The furniture was a whimsical blend of Ally's preference for American colonial and Pete's minimalist tastes; black leather nudged antique pine. Sara and Ally settled in Windsor chairs while Pete stretched out on the black leather, putting his coffee on an angular chrome table. "So how's your love life in Haliburton?" he said lazily to Sara.

She had intended to introduce the subject of Cal with great discretion. "I'm in love," she blurted. "He's illiterate. That's why I came to see you."

Pete gave the deep laugh that had endeared him to many a housewife. "So you want my advice about love and Ally's about illiteracy."

However, Ally looked aghast. "*Illiterate?* Really, Sara, it's time you moved back to Halifax, all those orchards and cows are getting to you."

"No, they're not," Sara protested. "I love it there. Cal had a dreadful childhood, which meant he never got beyond grade eight, but he's a very accomplished and totally self-supporting cabinetmaker."

Pete's eyes followed the swaying movements of a steel mobile over his head. "So when's the wedding?"

Sara sighed. "He doesn't know there's going to be one yet."

"What does he look like?"

"Six-foot-four and rugged," she said dreamily. "Blond hair, gray eyes, altogether gorgeous. Pete, you can be an usher."

"I'd need stilts."

"He's the first man I've ever met that I can wear high heels with and still look up," Sara said with a fine disregard for the niceties of grammar.

"There's more to marriage then being able to look up," Ally demured. "And any psychologist worth his salt would warn you about marrying a man with a dreadful childhood. But if Pete's going to be an usher, you must have me as a bridesmaid. We could stand on boxes. Like Prince Charles."

"Of course you'd be a bridesmaid. You and Cornelia. And Caitlin, too, I suppose."

Pete said dryly, "Considering Cal has not yet proposed, I feel this wedding is getting a little out of hand. How long have you known him, Sara?"

"I'd met him before I had lunch with Ally in July. But the start of the relationship wasn't really what you'd call smooth. In fact, at that point I didn't even think we had a relationship—which is why I didn't tell you about him, Ally. He was afraid I'd find out he was illiterate, you see."

"There's more to him than the fact that he's illiterate and six-foot-four," Pete persisted. "Come on, Sara, tell us about him."

Sara did her best; and the gentle curve of her lips and the sparkle in her eye told the rest. Unseen by her, Pete winked at Ally, who winked back. Then Ally said, "So what's to be done about the illiteracy, Sara? Because it would be nice if he could sign the marriage license."

Briefly Sara described the two abortive lessons and her commitment to help Cal get his license. "I don't know if I've done the right thing," she confessed. "But I didn't know what else to do. I'm teaching a fourteen-year-old, as well." And she told them about Bonnie.

"So do you want my advice?" Ally asked.

"Yes, I do. That's why I came to see you."

"Okay. Here goes." Almost visibly, Ally slipped into a professional role. "Several years ago, say up to 1960, word recognition was the established method for teaching reading. But when Cal was in school reading would have been taught by phonics—the decoding of print to sound. Unfortunately, with both methods large numbers of children failed to learn to read, so that as many as thirty per cent needed remedial assistance. So if you're using essentially the same method with Cal now—scrapbooks, reading from school primers—you could be reminding him very strongly of a previous failure. If it didn't take the first time, why should it the second? Bonnie might feel more comfortable with that method, more secure ... but not Cal."

"He more or less told me that himself," Sara admitted. "And we both felt pretty stupid reading grade-two books."

"Of course you would. But the driver's manual is an excellent idea. You see, it's Cal's choice. Cal is an adult. He should surely be encouraged to make his own decisions about what he wants to read, and having made the decision himself, he'll be strongly moti-vated. If he wants to drive his truck, if that's what will give him a sense of belonging in society, then he'll do his utmost to read the manual.''

"That makes a lot of sense."

"It goes along with what we call the Whole Language, or psycholinguistic approach, which is essentially the way reading and writing will be taught in the schools in Nova Scotia from now on. Rather than reading for sounds and specific words, where accuracy is stressed, students will be taught to read for meaning, to understand the context of what they're reading. As you near the end of reading a particular sentence, the number of words that will make sense is strongly reduced; and similarly reading a paragraph, the final sentences will become more and more predictable. The emphasis is on understanding rather than accuracy. In writing, as well, there's not as much slavish attention on correct spelling, grammar and punctuation. Rather the ability of the student to organize ideas and to communicate concepts is important."

Sara said slowly, "So a fair bit of guesswork is involved."

"That's right. Risk taking. That's why the Whole Language approach is admirably suited for adults, because it encourages them to take risks and to make their own decisions. You're not forcing grade-school stuff on them. The school primers purposely use a limited vocabulary and very short sentences that are often quite disconnected . . . it's much more difficult to read for meaning in a series of short sentences than in longer ones. Instead, our method allows the adult to choose his or her own areas of interest whether they be the driver's manual, how to carry out simple banking, how to write a résumé, how to read the job ads or whatever. It's all tied in with a concept called empowerment, Sara. What you're doing is giving the student more power to direct his or her own life. To be able to handle his own particular set of problems whatever they may be." Ally ended off her speech with a self-conscious laugh. "You shouldn't get me started! I'm a strong advocate of this method, so I tend to go off the deep end."

"It all seems very logical. But does it work in practice?"

"It's based on studies of how children learn to read—cognitive psychology and linguistics—and yes, I think it will work. A lot will depend on the teachers, because more initiative will be demanded of them and less dependence on the highly structured reading programs that the publishers put out. The teacher is addressing the needs and interests of the student—which means he or she has to know what those interests are. Basically, the teachers will have to be more flexible, more willing to go out on a limb and take a few risks themselves."

Sara crinkled her brow. "In view of all this, I wonder what I should do about Bonnie?"

"If a more traditional method is working with her, go for it. Or combine the two. Use whatever works. You see, the predominant method for literacy volunteers in Nova Scotia is the Laubach method, which is based on phonics and word recognition. The volunteers are given detailed manuals of instruction and tests for evaluation. But I'm sure a lot of Laubach tutors don't follow the workbooks word for word, because as they get to know their students they adapt to the student's needs. And these volunteers do a tremendous amount of good. They, like you, are willing to dedicate some of their free time to teaching adults to read, teaching them to function more effectively in today's society. I know I've come on strong about the Whole Language approach, but we certainly can't afford to get into a war over methodology. There are too many people needing help—eleven thousand in Halifax County alone—and far too few volunteers." Ally paused for breath. "Gracious me. I really climbed on the soapbox, didn't I?"

"You're opening my eyes."

"I can lend you some materials to get started. I have a couple of manuals for the Whole Language approach, and I can give you some background reading. I'll lend you Jonathan's Kozol's latest book, too. Are you familiar with it? It's called *Illiterate America*. If it doesn't shock you, it should."

Said Sara feelingly, "Pour me another coffee, Pete, I can see I'm going to be up half the night reading."

She left Pete and Ally's an hour later with an armload of books and did indeed read well into the night. Some of the statistics in Kozol's book shocked her as much as Ally had intended that they should, while the manuals filled her with enthusiasm. When she finally went to sleep she had a new sense of direction for her lessons with Cal. No longer was Cal going to be one of the millions of North Americans whom Kozol called "the prisoners of silence." Cal was going to learn to read.

CHAPTER ELEVEN

SARA SLEPT LATE the next morning and had to rush to pick Bonnie up on time. She had given Bonnie's situation considerable thought over the week. She did not have to be a psychologist to realize that Bonnie held herself in low esteem. A poor self-image was the term mental health professionals used. But what to do about it?

Bonnie, Sara had decided, was in the age group where appearance was all-important. At fourteen one has to belong, and one's clothing must allow one to blend into the protective coloration of the group, for a longing for individuality comes later. Bonnie did not belong. Bonnie might never belong. But Bonnie could look better than she did, and while Sara was not a slave to outward appearances she did believe that the way one looked said something about the way one felt about oneself. Would improving Bonnie's appearance be the first step toward improving her self-esteem? If even a modicum of pride and self-confidence could be cultivated in the girl, would she not take a greater interest in academic achievements?

Sara was not sure. But she felt the new approach was worth a try, and furthermore it could be combined with reading and writing in a way Ally would have approved.

Bonnie slouched up Sara's steps; her hair was as greasy as it had been last week. Sara sent up a silent prayer for tact and followed her into the house. She produced cookies and fruit juice, and for an hour they worked together on the scrapbook. Then Sara said, "Bonnie, I'd like to try something a little different this morning. I picked up some pamphlets from the home economics department about hair and skin care, and I thought we might read them together. Let's start with the one about hair. I'll read it first and you follow along. Then we'll try reading it together, and then you can read it by yourself."

The pamphlet had attractive colored pictures, and in relatively simple language it described cuts, permanent waves, shampoos and conditioners. Bonnie listened in a glum silence. Her only comment when Sara had finished was, "I got oily hair."

"You can get special shampoos for oily hair, Bonnie—in fact, I have some. After lunch, if you like, I could wash your hair for you."

Bonnie gave her the look of deep suspicion she seemed to reserve for all new ideas. "Yeah?"

"Maybe I could even get my sister to come over and trim the ends for you. I'd offer to do it myself but I'd end up scalping you. I'm a menace with a pair of scissors."

"I got no money," Bonnie said cautiously.

"Cornelia would do it for nothing, she likes cutting hair...do you remember what the article said about split ends, Bonnie? See this?" She held up the lank ends of Bonnie's hair. "Your hair would look neater if those were cut off."

Bonnie's heavy features were leavened with something that could have been excitement. "Okay," she said.

"Great! When we break for lunch, I'll give my sister a call. In the meantime let's read this together."

Bonnie followed along in a dull monotone, tripping over any words with more than three syllables, but on the third and fourth repetitions she read more confidently, and eventually she got through the entire pamphlet on her own.

Sara said warmly, "You did it all yourself—I didn't help you at all."

"Yeah, I did, didn't I?" Bonnie replied with what could almost be called a smile. "When are you goin' to call your sister?"

Corneila was perfectly agreeable to acting as a hairdresser. After the phone call Bonnie and Sara ate lunch, then did some mathematics, reading this time from a pamphlet on money management. Bonnie revealed she was allowed to keep five dollars of her weekly wages at the orchard for herself. "There's a sweater I want in the dress shop at Coates Mill. But it's thirty dollars."

"I've got a better idea," said Sara, who had hoped this conversation would arise. "Why don't we go to Mel's?"

"Mel's? They got junk."

Sara's smile was a model of innocence. "Do you like my blouse?"

It was turquoise cotton, stylishly wide-shouldered. Bonnie obviously suspected a trap, but said grudgingly, "Yeah, I like it."

"Seventy-five cents at Mel's. Don't get me wrong, Bonnie, you wouldn't want to buy everything there.

But if you take your time and poke around you can find some amazing bargains. If it's all right with your mother, I could pick you up from the orchard one afternoon this week and take you there. It would be fun."

"You mean I could find stuff to wear for school?"

"I'm sure you could."

Bonnie frowned. "You're a different kinda teacher than I ever had."

Although Bonnie may not have intended the words to be a compliment, Sara took them as such. "Thanks," she said lightly. "Learning doesn't have to be a drag, Bonnie. It can be fun, too." She rummaged among the papers on the table. "Somewhere here there's another of these pamphlets—here it is. Tells you how to pick the right styles for your build, why don't we read it while we're waiting for Cornelia?"

Bonnie tackled the pamphlet with more interest than Sara would have believed possible a week ago, and inwardly she blessed Ally for her advice. However, when Cornelia arrived all Bonnie's self-consciousness returned, so that she reverted to the sullen, monosyllabic child of the school yard.

Cornelia, nurse and mother, was not one whit put out. In no time Bonnie's hair had been shampooed at the sink, and she was sitting in front of Sara's mirror in the bedroom, a plastic cape around her shoulders. Thoughtfully, Cornelia tried various arrangements of the long black hair around Bonnie's face, all the while talking to Bonnie adult to adult, asking her opinion, questioning her about her various pursuits and finally saying, "I think we should take two or three inches off at the back and sides, that will still give you the length for a ponytail when you're in the orchard. But I'd like

to try a bang at the front, it would soften your forehead. What do you think?''

Sara doubted if Bonnie had ever had as much attention in her life. When the girl said solemnly, ''Go
ahead,'' Sara turned away, for her throat was tight. She
banged around in the kitchen making tea and raisin
toast, which she produced when the hair drier was
turned off.

Bonnie came back into the living room, holding her
head at an unnatural angle; her hair fell, sleek and
shining, to her shoulders, with dark wisps across her
forehead. Sara said sincerely, ''It looks lovely, Bonnie.''

Bonnie sat down very carefully in the chair by the
window, obviously not wanting to disarrange Cornelia's handiwork. In her smile was an element Sara had
never seen before: pride, as fragile as the buds of
spring, yet as full of promise. ''It looks okay,'' she
said.

Cornelia left after one cup of tea. As her car drove
away, Bonnie said with uncharacteristic loquacious-
ness, ''Your sister's neat. She said she'd cut my hair
again in a month or so, but that I gotta keep it clean.
I'll buy that kind of shampoo that you got outa my five
bucks. When'll we be goin' to Mel's?''

''How about Wednesday?''

''Okay. I get through 'round five.''

''I'll pick you up.'' Bonnie nodded. Sara said mildly,
''It's considered polite to say thank-you.''

''Oh. Thanks.'' Bonnie screwed up her face in con-
centrated thought. ''I oughta have about twelve
bucks.''

They did an hour of science, Bonnie twiddling a lock
of hair the whole time, then Sara took her home. As

Bonnie got out of the car she said to Sara, "See you Wednesday. If it's pourin' rain, I'll be home." As a definite afterthought she added, "Thanks," and traversed the planks with all the dignity of her new hairdo.

Full of self-congratulation, Sara went to Cornelia and Laird's for dinner. She helped put the children to bed, although she insisted that Laird read Malcolm's bedtime story. Then she went home, read the driver's manual, an uninspiring piece of literature, and was in bed herself by ten o'clock.

ON MONDAY EVERYTHING that could go wrong did. A girl in Sara's 9B class had a torrential nosebleed in the middle of *Who Has Seen the Wind*, and the girl seated next to her fainted at the sight of so much blood; the 9D class did so miserably on a short quiz Sara had sprung on them that she wondered if she had been talking to thin air for the past week; in the staff room at lunchtime Jean MacPherson went on a tirade against a student who just happened to live east of the river, a tirade that Sara cut short with a pithy retort that was neither tactful nor wise, no matter how satisfying; and when three-thirty finally came and she went out to her car in the teacher's parking lot, a practical joker had let the air out of her tires. Probably one of the 9D class, Sara thought sourly. Or else Jean MacPherson.

She got home at quarter after four tired and grumpy, her mood not improved when she discovered an ink stain on her new blue blouse, a garment that had not come from Mel's. A hot bath seemed the only suitable course of action.

She filled the tub with steaming water and bubbles and sank into it, deliberately turning off her brain. Half an hour later she washed herself with her most expensive soap, the excess water gurgling down the pipe as she sang old Beatles songs at the top of her lungs. When she climbed out on the mat, her flesh was bright pink and fingertips wrinkled. She felt much better. After using lavish amounts of powder, she pulled on her old green housecoat, the one she had had all through university, and wandered into the living room in her bare feet.

Cal was standing inside the door.

She suppressed a shriek of alarm, remembered how she had warbled away about Eleanor Rigby and Michelle, and said testily, "You're supposed to knock."

"I did. You didn't hear me, you were singing too loud." He then added with a perfectly straight face, "You should keep the door locked, Sara, you never know who could walk in."

"I see what you mean."

He smiled. "You look like an overdone lobster."

Belatedly Sara became aware that under the old green housecoat she was naked; her cheeks grew pinker. Trying to keep the conversation on mundane matters, she said, "I had an awful day at school—a hot bath is excellent therapy for a teacher with frazzled nerves. I first learned that when I was practice teaching."

"I wonder if it works for carpenters. I spilled some paint remover on a maple coffee table, so I'll have to refinish the whole thing."

"Happy Monday," Sara commiserated.

"I came to ask you to go for a walk. There's talk of a moose being sighted on the far side of the lake."

It was not quite what one would call a normal date, but it was close. "I'll go and put my jeans on."

He said quietly, "Come here first."

Sara scarcely hesitated at all. She crossed the carpet to stand in front of him, her face still flushed, her eyes very serious. He took her in his arms and kissed her.

It was a long and thorough kiss, and she loved every minute of it. His skin smelled of after-shave, his body fitted the length of hers as if they had been made for each other. She slid her arms around his neck and, for the second time that afternoon, turned off her brain for the joy of sheer sensation. But she knew when his hands left her waist to roam her body and knew that he must be aware of her nakedness. When his palms cupped her breasts she shivered with delight, and when he drew open the neckline of her housecoat, his urgency aroused her as much as the sureness of his long fingers on her skin.

The housecoat, which was not meant for such rough treatment, gaped open to the waist. Cal's lips drifted down her throat, discovered the smooth hollow of her collarbone, then sought the fullness of her breast. She threw back her head and whimpered with pleasure, fondling the hard bone behind his ears and the thickness of his hair.

He looked up, seeing her dazzled face and drowned eyes. "Sara," he said huskily, "beautiful Sara...what am I to do with you?"

With her fingertip she traced the line of his mouth. "What would you like to do with me?"

His gray eyes were very direct. "Take you to bed."

"Would that be so very wrong, Cal?"

He captured her hand in his, rubbing it against his cheek. "Yes. Right now it would."

She trusted him enough to match his directness. "Why?"

"I've said this before, and you accused me of being an intellectual snob. I don't mean to sound like a snob, Sara. But there is a huge gap between you and me, you can't deny that. Unless I can break out of this—this prison I'm in, I can't get involved with you. It would be wrong for both of us. I'd always feel inferior and you'd come to hate my limitations, I know you would." Unconsciously his hand had tightened around hers. "I've got to learn to read...but I'm afraid. Afraid of failing. I don't know if I can describe how rotten I felt last week during those two lessons."

"Try."

He took a deep breath. "I felt like a kid again, pushed to the back row, scared to death of being laughed at and called stupid. Clumsy, bigger than everyone else, wanting to belong but always feeling an outsider, the kid from up the mountain...I never want to feel like that again, Sara, and if learning to read means I've got to feel that way, I don't think I can stand it. I won't last. I'll never learn."

She tugged at her hand. "You're hurting me."

"God, I'm sorry!" He dropped it as if her flesh were scalding him.

She pulled the edges of her housecoat together, belting it more tightly about her waist. "Cal," she said quietly, "I know you can learn to read. We just have to find the right method, that's all—because I'm as new at this as you are. But we will find a way. I know we will."

He said, trying to joke, "I've noticed something about you . . . your eyes turn green whenever you feel very strongly about anything."

"Then they can hardly ever be gray when I'm around you," she said wryly.

He digested this in silence for a moment. "You feel sorry for me."

"Don't insult me, Cal."

Another long silence. "You'd go to bed with me, wouldn't you?"

"Yes."

"Why, Sara?"

She sensed he was searching for answers that went beyond words, and that she was venturing into territory for which she had no maps. Instinctively she chose the truth. "The first time I met you I had the strangest sensation, as if you were right for me, the other half of me, the one who would make me whole. I can't explain why, Cal. I can only tell you how I felt. Your house felt like home. You felt like home... as if after years of wandering I had found the person to whom I belonged, the place where I was rooted—"

She broke off abruptly, terrified. She had done it again. Spoken without thought, bared her soul when a lighthearted answer about lust would have sufficed. She took a couple of backward steps, muttering, "I'll go and get changed. Or it'll be too dark to go for a walk."

Said Cal, unmoving, "I felt it, too, Sara."

She was unwilling to trust the evidence of her own ears. "Felt what?"

"There you were, red haired, green eyed, fierce as a lion when the dog was trying to kill the deer, gentle as the light of dawn when your sister arrived. You think I was indifferent? You think I didn't notice you?"

Remembering the long empty summer days, Sara said, "You gave a good approximation of a man who was indifferent!"

"The only way I could handle my feelings was by staying away from you."

"At which you did a marvelous job."

He hesitated. "Are you willing to keep on with the lessons? A couple of times a week?"

She nodded, trying to sound practical. "I got some new materials over the weekend, and I think we'll do a lot better."

"Until I get the feeling that I'm progressing I'll probably still stay away from you. I have to. You can call it cowardice or self-protection, I don't really care. But I can't get involved with you the way things are now."

He sounded very vehement. To convince himself? With a glimmer of humor Sara said, "You're certainly giving me an incentive to teach you to read."

His smile, as always, touched her to the heart. "I like you, Sara."

She was content with that, for liking, she had always felt, was equally as important as loving. She and Cal went for a very energetic walk along the lakeshore, during which the moose did not appear, and Cal went straight home afterward.

He arrived sharp at seven on Tuesday evening for their third lesson. Sara had decided to start with the section of the driver's handbook that dealt with highway signs, because there were a lot of pictures and much of the text was self-explanatory. She followed the same technique she had used with Bonnie, reading passages aloud herself, having Cal read along with her, then having him read the passage alone. At the end of each page she wrote out some questions for him to answer in writing. Apart from the basic method, however, there was not much resemblance to the sessions with Bonnie.

Johnny, Mary and the little dog Patches were creatures of the past: Cal was desperate to learn. His memory was phenomenal. He soaked up the information on the page as moss soaks up rain water, and by nine o'clock knew every one of the highway signs and could give her at least the gist of the text. Although when answering her written questions his spelling was atrocious and his grammar haphazard, he could reproduce neatly and without error the printing on each sign.

Finally Sara sat back in her chair, looking dazed. "Time to quit," she said. "Cal, you've done wonders."

He gave an incredulous laugh. "It's useful, that's why." He flicked the brightly colored diagrams. "I need this information to get my license. So I want to learn it as quickly as I can."

"On Thursday we'll go over the scoring form used by the examiner and then do the rules of the road."

"Sara, if I brought over a tape recorder, could you tape some of the chapters? That way I could practice them at home on weekends."

"That's a good idea. Of course I could."

"And maybe after one or two more lessons we could go to a store and buy a dictionary."

"I'll lend you one of mine in the meantime. Cal, are you still convinced you'll never learn to read?"

He grinned. "Not quite as convinced as I was last week."

"You have an amazing memory."

"They say blind people develop their hearing to compensate for the loss of sight. I've developed my memory to ward off embarrassing situations. To function as best I can in a world where all the signposts and the instructions are a meaningless jumble. Pure self-preservation.''

"Useful, nevertheless.'' She suddenly gave a huge yawn.

"I'd better go, you're tired. Sara, I feel so much better than I did when I arrived. Thanks.'' Cal's lips brushed her cheek and then he was gone. The room seemed larger without him, and very empty. He was right; she was tired. Feeling oddly depressed, Sara went to bed.

MEL'S WAS LOCATED in a brown-shingled shed on the outskirts of town and was not for the fainthearted; the clothes were squashed together on racks, tumbled into big bins and sprawled over wooden tables. There was a degree of organization. Women's sweaters were separated from men's trousers. But only a degree. One had to have a spirit of adventure and a great deal of time to shop at Mel's. Sara that Wednesday afternoon had both, and Bonnie under her tutelage soon acquired the spirit of adventure.

They rummaged through piles of jeans and canvas pants, and although some were out of date, others made Bonnie's eyes gleam with acquisitiveness. Sara restrained her from buying anything too tight fitting, and soon two pairs were selected with the requisite labels, buckles and colored stitching. In a round bin in the back corner Bonnie found a pink lamb's wool sweater for a dollar and a half and a man's blue shirt for fifty cents. Sara dug through a new bale to discover a bundle of neon-colored socks, while Bonnie picked out a very respectable pair of running shoes.

They repaired to a couple of rickety chairs by the dressing rooms, where Bonnie, noisily chewing on her pencil, added up the total. Eleven dollars. With an air of momentous decision she said, "I'm savin' up for a hair dryer. So I guess I won't buy nothin' else."

"Anything else," Sara corrected. "You've done really well, Bonnie." She had debated about buying Bonnie another shirt as a present, but had decided not to. It would be only too easy to slip into the role of Lady Bountiful with someone who owned as few of the world's goods as Bonnie, and that was not the role that Sara wanted in Bonnie's life.

"I'm not goin' to wear these to the orchard. I'll keep them for when I go back to school."

Bonnie had said "when," not "if"; and perhaps the combination of Sara's tutoring, a new hairdo and clothes that, chameleonlike, would allow Bonnie to blend in with the other girls would make the return to school a pleasure rather than an ordeal. So thought Sara optimistically. And so she hoped.

CHAPTER TWELVE

AUTUMN PASSED, October in a blaze of gold and red, November stripped to gray and dun. The birds had long ago flown south. The lake skimmed over with ice. The first snowfall blinded the eye with whiteness.

Sara was far too busy to mourn the loss of the color and fruitfulness of that briefest of Nova Scotian seasons, summer. She was doing a great deal of reading to keep ahead of her grade-nine English class; she had attended Laubach and Whole Language workshops in Halifax; she continued to tutor Bonnie on Sundays and Cal on Tuesdays and Thursdays. And as the weeks passed and the days grew shorter, she knew she was falling more and more deeply in love with Cal. She did not speak of this love, chiefly because he gave her no opportunity to do so. He was a man obsessed, but not by her. By the written word.

Cal was accustomed to spending a lot of time alone, and he now spent that time with his nose in a book, a pamphlet, a newspaper or a catalog. Sara taped and erased and retaped. She started him on books about carpentry. She had him read in the daily paper the news he had already heard on the radio. She went over shipping bills and order forms. And section by section they reviewed the driver's manual, until she felt she could recite the entire book with her eyes shut. There were evenings when Cal got frustrated, when the pen in his hand looked as out of place as the hammer had in Sara's, when the letters on the pages were as mystifying to him as a blueprint would have been to her. But there were also evenings of incredible achievement, when the written word blossomed into meaning. He understood. The little boy in the back row became a man.

Sara had never known anyone to focus so fanatically on learning. Yet although Cal was punctilious in expressing his gratitude for her help, she sometimes felt as if she had ceased to exist for him as a person. She was the voice coming out of the tape recorder, the pronouncer of words, the corrector of misspellings. She was the teacher. But she was no longer Sara, the woman.

Meanwhile, Bonnie had gone back to school in October. No miracles happened. The teenagers who had ignored her in September continued to ignore her. But Bonnie, so she reported to Sara, occasionally spoke up in class now and she ate in the cafeteria every day.

For a month or so after her first haircut Bonnie was cooperative with Sara in their Sunday sessions, although her grammar and her manners improved rather more than her knowledge of science and geography. But as the ragged red leaves fell from the maples, Bonnie grew dreamy. She wanted to read nothing but *Seventeen* magazines, mooning over the lipstick ads and the articles on dating. Her attention span shriveled as drastically as her motivation. Unfinished projects lay about her like the dead leaves on the ground, and she noticed them as little.

Sara, frustrated always, enraged occasionally, plodded on with grim determination. The fault must be hers, she reasoned, because she knew she'd had Bonnie's attention and then, somehow, had lost it.

Jean MacPherson corrected this assumption of guilt one afternoon in November.

Sara had gone to the staff room in a free period to read her class's offerings on the subject of *Romeo and Juliet*; Jean, coincidentally, had the same period free. Sara smiled at her politely, made a commonplace remark about the weather, which was November at its dreariest, and took out her papers and her red pen. Jean said with a twitch of her nose, "I assume you've given up tutoring the Dawson girl."

"No. We still meet every Sunday."

"You're wasting your time."

There had been several Sundays when Sara would have heartily agreed. She said lightly, "I keep hoping."

"She's boy crazy, of course—you know that."

"Show me the fourteen-year-old girl who isn't."

"She's got her eye on Danny Koneski. They're those immigrants who've settled by the mill." An immigrant was an undesirable to Jean, a foreigner who should have stayed where he belonged.

"I wish her luck. When I was fourteen I was madly in love with the colonel on the air base. At least she's being a little more realistic."

"So realistic that she'll end up pregnant."

Sara bit her lip and, metaphorically, her tongue. "I must get at these papers, Jean. Poor old Shakespeare would turn in his grave at some of my students' interpretations of his play."

"Bonnie Dawson will go the same way as her mother, you'll see. I remember Marlene; she quit school in grade seven because she had to get married to that no-good Everett Dawson.''

Romeo and Juliet were abandoned. Sara said tightly, ''Look, Jean, it's all very well for you and me to sit in judgment of Marlene, Everett and Bonnie. We've had a good education, we can earn a decent salary, we've got sick leave and pensions and a place in the community. There is no place for Marlene and Everett. They're condemned to live on the fringes of society, to scrape the bare soil for a living. And because they can't read or write at a level where they can function as capable, decision-making adults, they have no power. I want a different life for Bonnie! I want her to be well enough educated to have a few choices. She won't be assured of a permanent job if she can read, but she'll certainly never get one if she can't.''

''My, my,'' said Jean nastily, ''a proper little crusader.''

''We need a few crusaders,'' Sara replied hotly. ''Five million Canadians are functionally illiterate. Sixty million Americans...one-third of the population. Think of the waste, Jean! Think of the cost in welfare payments, lost earnings, prison upkeep—sixty percent of the men in federal prisons in the Atlantic provinces are functionally illiterate. Sixty percent! The whole democratic process is put in jeopardy because illiterate citizens rarely vote, and if they do, they can scarcely make informed decisions. Illiterates can't read menus, can't read the warning on a can of poison, can't read the notes we wonderful teachers send home to them about their children, can't handle a bank account, read a recipe, look up a telephone number...on and on it goes. And everything I've said applies to five million Canadians. Of which Marlene is one and Everett is one, and Bonnie could well become one . . . oh yes, we need crusaders."

Jean's nostrils were pinched with temper. "You're exaggerating!" she snapped. "Anyway, those people wouldn't be any happier if they could read and write."

Sara had heard that line before; she closed her eyes, letting out her breath in a long sigh. "That's comparable to rich people saying money doesn't make you happy," she said. "Look, Jean, I've got to start marking these essays. Excuse me, please."

She took out the first paper, although she was so worked up that the words made as little sense to her as they would have to Cal. Was she just a middle-class do-gooder activated by guilt? A crusader, as Jean had suggested? The Crusaders in their zeal for the Holy Land had done tremendous damage, and their motivation by religious principles did not excuse them in Sara's eyes. Was she harming Bonnie? Giving her, as Jean would put it, ideas above her station?

"Romeo and Juliet's parents didn't get along," she read. "There was a feud and lots of fighting in the streets, which was why they couldn't get married."

Cal would write a better sentence than that. She uncapped her red pen. She was right to help Bonnie. And right to help Cal. To hell with Jean MacPherson and her narrow little soul that could only see Bonnie as a representative of "those people" and not as a person in her own right. She wrote in the margin of the page in front of her, "Who couldn't get married?" and settled down to work.

ON THE LAST TUESDAY in November, when Sara was waiting for Cal to arrive for their regular lesson, she heard the sound of a car engine over the drumming of rain on the roof and old-fashioned fiddle music on her radio. When she opened the door Cal was standing there in his yellow rain slicker, his truck parked in the driveway.

"Hi, Cal, come in," she said. "I don't blame you for not walking, it's a lousy night, isn't it? Although it's the time of year when we should be grateful it's not snow, I suppose. Let me hang up your jacket."

He closed the door but made no move to take off his jacket. "I didn't bring the truck because it was raining," he said.

There was a peculiar note in his voice. She glanced at him curiously. His eyes were laughing at her and a smile was pulling at his lips. "Are you in a law-breaking mood?" she asked in a puzzled voice. "You really shouldn't drive without your license, even if it is only—" Her voice broke off. "Cal, you got your license!"

The smile became a wide grin. "I thought you'd never catch on."

She grabbed his sleeve. "You mean you did?"

He threw back his head and gave an exultant laugh. "Yep! This afternoon at four o'clock. Passed with flying colors. I am legally entitled to drive my truck anywhere in the country."

"Oh, Cal, I'm so glad!" Sara flung her arms around him and hugged him with all her strength.

He grabbed her around the waist and began to waltz her around the room to the tune of the fiddle music. He was still wearing his work boots and there was rather a lot of furniture. They were soon laughing breathlessly. "I've got to take my boots off," Cal puffed. "If I tramp on your toe you'll know it."

"This calls for a drink. I wish I had champagne! All I can offer you is a beer. But I have some ripe Brie and green grapes, I'll put those out, as well."

He had hauled off his boots and was hanging his jacket over the back of one of the chairs. "No caviar?" he asked in mock complaint.

"If I'd known, we'd have had a five-course dinner!"

"I wanted to surprise you."

She had not heard that note of excitement in his voice for a long time. "I'm so happy for you, Cal," she said softly.

"It's the first step forward."

"A huge step."

"I owe it all to you, Sara."

"No, you don't. I helped, yes, but you're the one who worked so hard."

"You're the one who badgered me into admitting the problem in the first place."

"That, certainly, is true."

"And you've done more than just help, Sara. You've cared. It's mattered to you that I learn to read. You've put a lot of time and energy into these sessions. Don't ever think I haven't realized that. I couldn't have got my license without your help." He ruffled her curls. "My red-haired, stubborn Sara."

His use of the personal pronoun warmed her heart, so that she was more than ready for him when he bent his head to kiss her, a kiss that started as simple gratitude but ended in something far more complex. Against her lips he muttered, "You've turned my life upside down. You've changed everything," and then he kissed her again with an almost desperate intensity, as if this was his one opportunity in life to kiss a woman and he must learn everything there was to learn.

When he touched her breasts, she shuddered with pleasure; when he said hoarsely, "Sara, I want to make love to you," the decision was already made. Briefly it crossed her mind that gratitude might not be the best basis for lovemaking, but she banished the thought as rapidly as it had arisen and her reply was full of a quiet confidence. "My bedroom's through there," she said.

He picked her up to carry her into the bedroom. Cal had carried her once before, the night her feet were blistered; but this time, because she knew where they were going and what they were going to do, the experience was very different. Her gaze was level with the corded muscles in his throat and the curl of his hair about his ears, while she was blazingly conscious of the hard strength of his arms against her back and under her knees. Briefly she closed her eyes, shy of showing him the happiness that she knew must be shining there.

He put her down by the bed and kissed her again. But there was a hesitancy in his touch that had not been there before and that she might almost have called fear. She discovered that she was nervous, as well. She had no idea how they were to make the immense transition from two fully clothed adults standing beside a bed to the intimacy of nakedness. The light seemed very bright, and Cal much bigger than usual, a man she scarcely knew, a stranger in her bedroom.

She could easily have made a false remark or a wrong move, giggling out of sheer nervousness, if Cal had not said, "Help me, Sara. Tell me what to do."

"You're as nervous as I am," she said with an air of discovery.

"You couldn't possibly be as scared as I am right now."

"Want to take a bet?" Sara smiled, feeling much better. "Why don't we just lie down on the bed and see what happens?"

He kicked the door so the room was shrouded in a welcome darkness, then stretched out on the bed. She lay down beside him, hoping the rattle of raindrops against the windowpane was drowning the thudding of her heart. He put his arms around her and drew her close, his hands rubbing her back as if she were a wild creature to be gentled. Then he began kissing her again, softly teasing her lips apart, his tongue dancing with hers.

They kissed for a long time, and even when Sara began unbuttoning his shirt there was no sense of haste. She rested her cheek against his chest, hearing the steady pound of his heart, discovering the warmth of his body and the roughness of hair. "You smell nice," she murmured, and felt laughter reverberate in his chest.

"So do you. I want to see your body again, Sara. I haven't forgotten how beautiful you looked that afternoon." He lifted himself on one elbow, shrugging out of his shirt, then helped her ease her sweater over her head and undo the clasp of her bra. "Lie down again," he said huskily. Gathering her into his arms, he held her close, breast to chest. "You're so unimaginably soft," he whispered. "Your skin is like the petals of a water lily... I'm scared I'll hurt you."

"You wouldn't hurt me, Cal."

"I want to see all of you. I've never seen you naked, Sara. Show me."

And because her body had the languor of milk-white petals in the sun, and because she wanted to please him, she drew her jeans down over her hips, tossed her panties to the floor and opened her thighs to him. With the first sign of impatience he had shown, he stripped off the rest of his clothes. Then he straddled her, tracing the outline of her body with his hands.

With infinite gentleness he entered her. Her body convulsed, seizing him, and fiercely he drove himself into her. But then he withdrew. At her tiny move of protest he said with an honesty that charmed her, "If I stay there, it'll all be over. Tell me what to do for you, what pleases you."

Drawing him down on top of her, she said gravely, "Everything you do pleases me."

"This?" He brushed her nipple with his finger as delicately as the spring breeze ruffles the marsh grass. "Or this?"

Her gasp of delight as his hand moved lower was all the answer he needed. Watching her face, he coaxed even wilder responses from her. He was a man of sensitivity who was not in a hurry. Sara had never known she could feel so wanton or plead so shamelessly for ever greater intimacies, or explore with such sweet joy another's body. She ached to be joined to the man who hovered over her, whose hands had brought her to a nakedness far more comprehensive than that of the flesh. In his workshop she had watched Cal seek out the grain in a piece of wood and bring its true beauty of design to the surface; now he was doing the same for her, exposing facets of herself she had not known existed, and delighting in his creation.

Between one moment and the next the tension became unbearable. Sara sobbed out Cal's name and took all the hardness that was his essence into her hands, guiding him to enter her, arching upward to envelop him, seeing an answering spasm in his face, a mingling of agony and dark, deep pleasure. Only then did she let go, her voice the broken cry of a falling bird. Swooping like a hawk to follow her, he met her in the place where sky and bird are one, the place of spiraling release, the small, still center that is timeless.

Very slowly Sara came back to herself, to the bed in the darkened room and the weight of Cal's body, still joined to hers, immeasurably dear to her. She kissed his shoulder, which was slick with sweat, and was suddenly shaken by the intensity of her love for him. She had thought she knew what it meant to make love to a man, but Cal had shown her differently. She murmured against his throat, "You took me to a place I have never been before."

He lifted himself on one elbow, his eyes scanning her face, and what he saw there must have satisfied him. "I've never been there, either."

"Then I'm glad we went together."

He eased his weight off her. "I must be heavy."

She did not want to be separated from him; and he had not spoken to her of love. Suddenly frightened, she burrowed into his chest, one arm across his ribs. "Don't go away."

"Nothing is farther from my mind." He gave a tiny laugh. "I don't think I could move, anyway."

Sara said intuitively, "It had been a long time for you, Cal."

"A long time." He nuzzled her hair. "Ten years."

He was not asking for pity; he was simply stating a fact. "But you were just a boy!"

"Fifteen. Old enough to know better."

"You'd better tell me about it."

"More true confessions?"

"What better time than this?"

"I'm not sure it's a story you'd want to hear, Sara."

"I want to know all of you, Cal." She craned her neck so she could meet his eyes. "Do you remember the night I walked to your place after Joel left me in the field, and I was embarrassed to show you my feet? You told me never to be embarrassed in front of you. That I didn't have to hide anything. Surely the same applies to you?"

"No masks. You want the real person."

She gave him a small smile. "I think it's called acceptance . . . what was her name, Cal?"

"Jen." Fractionally Cal withdrew from her, his eyes gazing over her head to the far wall. "She was nineteen when I first met her and I was fourteen. The autumn before the fire. She was Ray's girlfriend. Ray was the leader of our gang, and Jen was the type who'd always be the girlfriend of the leader."

"What did she look like?"

"I thought she was the most beautiful creature I'd ever seen."

Sara smothered a pang of what was undeniably jealousy. "I hope she didn't have red hair."

"Dyed blond. God knows what its natural color was. She wore a great deal of makeup, which I was young enough to see as a sign of sophistication, and skintight jeans that used to play havoc with my hormones. Blood-red fingernails that she filed into sharp points. Low-cut sweaters. Earrings dangling to her shoulders and a cigarette hanging from her mouth. I was infatuated. I was in love. But not so much in love that I told Annalise about her. Even though I was only fourteen I knew Jen was different from Annalise in a way that did not reflect to Jen's credit.''

"She sounds lethal."

"That's a good word. You see, at first I used to worship her from afar. She was Ray's girl, so she could never be mine. Or so I thought. But I gradually became aware that she had her eye on me. She'd sidle up to me when no one was looking and rub herself against me. She'd get me to light her cigarette and then blow the smoke in my face. Hollywood tricks. Or, worst of all, she'd lean so far forward to lace her boots that she'd just about fall out of her sweater...you can imagine what that did to me."

"I hate her already," Sara said unequivocally.

"Too bad I hadn't. I thought about her every minute of the day. I had lurid and quite unrepeatable dreams about her at night, and, of course, I had no one I could talk to about her. But then the fire happened, and for a while I forgot about her. She ceased to exist. I even bumped into her on the street one day and literally couldn't remember her name."

"She probably took that as a challenge."

"Maybe. In June Ray went to Montreal for a month and didn't take her with him. She was furious and out for revenge. So she invited me to the drive-in one night; she'd borrowed her brother's car. You can guess the rest. We made love in the back seat of the car."

"She seduced you!"

"I was willing to be seduced, Sara.'

Sara scowled. "Did you like it?"

"Sure I did. And she was clever enough to play me like a fish on a hook. She'd ignore me for a week, have a rip-roaring fight with me because I'd neglected her and then we'd make up."

"In bed," Sara said crossly.

He tweaked her nose. "I don't think we were ever in a bed together... whose would we use? I was in a foster home, and even Jen didn't have the nerve to take me to Ray's room. We made love in cars and fields, and on beaches. In an old deserted barn one day... but there were mice." His smile was malicious. "Jen wasn't scared of much, but she didn't like mice. And each time we made love—although I suppose there are cruder words for what we did—I grew more and more besotted with her. I had no basis for comparison other than X-rated movies, but when I look back I have the feeling she was pretty adept. And I was only fifteen."

"What happened when Ray came back?"

"For a while we carried on much as before, except that now it had an element of risk, the extra excitement of the forbidden—and the dangerous. Ray wasn't a man to fool around with; he knew more dirty tricks than the A-Team. I was a lot bigger than he was, but I was scared of him. I used to have fantasies about rescuing Jen from him, beating him to a pulp in a very public and spectacular fashion and then sashaying off into the sunset with Jen on my arm. Kid stuff, but real enough at the time."

"But instead he beat you up?" Sara hazarded a guess.

"No, it ended quite differently from my fantasies. Jen started ignoring me for real. No fights. No making up. Acting as if she'd never seen me before. At first I thought she was kidding or that she was being more cautious because of Ray, and I played along. I didn't want a confrontation with Ray any more than she did. But a week became two weeks and then a month, by which time I was slavering after her like a dog after a bone. I knew her habits, of course—I'd studied her minutely—so I suppose it wasn't surprising that I came across her as I did. She wasn't with Ray. She was with Dean, the newest member of the gang, who'd come back from Montreal with Ray because the cops were after him—not a very smart move on Ray's part, because Dean was the kind who'd want to be boss. Anyway what Dean and Jen were doing was bad enough. But what she was saying was worse.'' His eyes were like flint. "She was talking about me. Sneering. Telling him what a kid I was, that she'd only put up with me because I was the youngest she'd ever had. The general message, and I'll spare you Jen's exact words because she had a tongue on her worse than any hooker, was that I was no good in bed.''

Sara's arm tightened around him. A devastating message at any age, but to a fifteen-year-old boy it would have been the ultimate cruelty. There was a knot in her stomach, for she knew Cal's story had not yet ended. She whispered, "What did you do?''

"What do you think? I'd loved her as if she was an angel of virtue, and there she was in bed with another man and making fun of my sexual prowess. I burst in on them and went for her. I'd have killed her if I'd got hold of her. But Dean very neatly stuck out his foot and tripped me—at least I assume that's what he did— and when I went crashing to the floor, he clipped me with the side of his hand. I went out like a light. When I came to they were gone, and I was lying in a pool of blood with two broken ribs. Evidently Dean had gotten dressed and used his boots on me. Or maybe Jen had, I wouldn't put it past her.'' He cleared his throat, trying to sound more normal. "Shortly after that I met Dougal when he came to the school. Good timing.''

"Did you ever see Jen again?"

"No. I purposely avoided all of them." Abruptly he sat up, hunching himself over his knees. "I was scared of seeing Jen again. If Dean hadn't intervened I don't know what I'd have done to her, Sara."

Sara also sat up, rubbing one hand up and down the long curve of his spine, trying to ease the tension from his muscles. "She did a horribly cruel thing."

"She couldn't have known I was there."

"She could guess that sooner or later you'd find her."

"I suppose so. No excuse for me going at her the way I did."

Sara said with a careful lack of emphasis, "When our angels reveal themselves as devils, we're apt to react fairly strongly."

He raised his head, giving her a long, straight stare. "Ever since that night I've been scared to death of my own temper."

"You haven't made love to anyone since then." Her cheeks dimpled. "Except me, that is."

"No one."

"In Haliburton you didn't want anyone discovering you were illiterate…it's difficult to hide something like that when you become intimate on other levels."

"Oh, the illiteracy's part of it, no question of that," Cal said irritably. "But always I've had this underlying fear of what I might do to someone if I got in a rage. I'm a big man, Sara, and I'm strong. I could do a lot of damage. Remember the dog with the broken neck? And the book I smashed against the wall?"

"Cal, the dog was doing its best to rip my throat out. You threw it off me, and by chance it hit a rock and broke its neck. As for the book, it was just that...a book. Not a person. There's a difference, you know."

"But what if I got angry with you?"

"You were extremely angry with me in the workshop the day I'd discovered you were illiterate. You didn't throw me at the wall or hit me on the head with a hammer."

"You think I'm worrying over nothing?" There was a dangerous note in his voice; it was obvious that his fears were very real to him.

"That's not what I'm saying, no. But I think you've got to understand where that boy of fifteen was coming from, and forgive him. You were full of anger then, Cal. Anger at a school system that had stuck you in the back row. A terrible anger because of the deaths of your parents and Annalise...did you ever cry about that? Sit down and howl your eyes out?"

"Of course not," he said stiffly.

"Oh, of course not! Boy's don't cry, it's unmanly, a sign of weakness. So you had all that grief choking you and coming out as anger. And you were legitimately angry with Jen, who'd seduced you and deceived you and made fun of your sexuality. For God's sake, Cal, of course you went for her! You'd have been the angel if you hadn't."

"I never thought of it quite that way."

"You're too hard on yourself." She hesitated, clasping her hands together. "When my mother was so ill, and I was looking after her, there were a few times when I lost patience and said things to her that were thoughtless and unkind. Later, when she was dead, I felt so guilty. Why couldn't I have controlled myself, why hadn't I held my tongue? But at the time I was under a tremendous amount of stress because it's dreadful watching someone you love suffer, and if occasionally some of my pain escaped as anger, that's understandable. My mother understood, I'm sure... and forgave me, I'm sure of that, as well. But it's most difficult of all to forgive oneself.''

Cal put his arm around her bare shoulders. ''It's not easy for you to talk about her, is it?''

So he understood how raw she could still feel about her mother's illness and death. ''I hope I wasn't preaching,'' she said in a small voice.

''No. You've given me something to think about.''

Cal drew her down beside him and put his arms around her, and for a long while they held each other in a silence that was full of intimacy and a quiet happiness. Then he began kissing her again, teasing her about her red hair and tickling her ribs. Sara, being Sara, responded in kind. They made lively and unabashed love together, both of them much less shy than last time, much more ready to experiment. They laughed. They played. And as they did so Sara saw a new Cal emerge from behind the barriers he had constructed so many years before. He showed her tenderness, an awkward, diffident tenderness that disarmed her. He unleashed the sensuality she had suspected in him the day he had shown her the purple flowers in the marsh. He was so unrestrainedly generous that she had to coax him to make demands of his own and to seek pleasure for himself; she was delighted when, almost shyly, he did so. Knowing the story of Jen, she could understand his hesitancy. Jen had taught him the techniques of sex without any of its tenderness, its give-and-take, its sense of partnership.

Their lovemaking culminated in a tumultuous storm of emotion that took them both by surprise. They fell asleep soon afterward, arms wrapped around each other, and in the middle of the night made love again, dreamlike love, two people in a trance of sensuality. At 7:00 a.m. they woke to the loud peal of the alarm.

Sara rolled over and shut off the bell. Then she stretched, rubbed her eyes and moaned, "I could sleep all day."

Cal snuggled his face between her breasts. "If I were here, you wouldn't sleep all day."

His beard was rasping her skin, a by no means unpleasant sensation. She giggled, pushing his head away, and asked with mock innocence, "Oh? What else would we do?"

"I could teach you to play cribbage."

"I already know how. I'm a whiz at it," she added immodestly.

"We could have the reading lesson we didn't have last night."

Her lips curved in unconscious provocation. "We studied other things last night. Unrelated to reading and writing."

"So we did. Much more interesting things." He pulled a face. "And now we both have to go to work."

The prospect was not appealing. They kissed and cuddled for a while, until Sara caught sight of the clock. "I'll be late!" she cried, leaping out of bed and running for the shower. Fifty minutes later, respectably dressed and munching a piece of toast, she was driving to school.

She did not feel respectable. She felt as though everything she and Cal had done in the night was written on her face for the world to see. However, no one in the staff room paid her any more attention than usual. Jean MacPherson ignored her and her students were as self-absorbed as teenagers generally are. She got through the day and was in bed by nine o'clock that night. She slept for ten hours and woke thinking of Cal, remembering the warmth of his body against hers, the unexpected smoothness of his skin, the fierce, possessive passion in his eyes. When she had first met him she had intuitively recognized him as her complement, a recognition that had been borne out in their love-making, for with him, in this very bed, she had become part of a whole.

She rolled over, burying her face in the pillow, wishing he was beside her now, wishing he would phone and say good-morning and tell her he was as happy as she. But the spoken word did not always come easily to him; she knew that. And she would see him tonight, when he arrived for their regular Thursday session.

Her lips curving in an unconscious smile, Sara got out of bed and began to get ready for work. At quarter to seven that evening she was waiting for Cal in a state that her mother would have called a regular tizzy: cheeks flushed, heart racing, body unable to sit still.

CAL ARRIVED ON FOOT promptly at seven, his books tucked under the arm of his sheepskin jacket, his face red with cold. "Hello, Sara," he said. Then he put down the books and hung up his jacket, taking rather a long time to adjust the shoulders on the hanger.

She had expected him at the very least to throw his arms around her and kiss her, at the most, perhaps, to carry her off to bed; she would not have screamed for help. But as he turned to face her he kept a careful distance between them. "Feels like snow. I'm surprised we haven't had any yet."

"How are you, Cal?"

"Oh, fine. When we do have snow you'll have to park your car by the road. The driveway's much too long for you to shovel on your own."

She gave him a fulminating look. "I thought we had got past the point of talking about the weather."

"Yeah..." He bent and picked up the books, holding them against his chest as if for protection. "I should have remembered how direct you are." He took a deep breath. "Don't get me wrong, Sara, Tuesday night was marvelous. But it mustn't happen again."

Her jaw dropped. "Why not?"

He flinched from the stunned look on her face. "Sara, nothing's really changed. Sure, I can drive my truck now. But I'm still a carpenter with a grade-eight education and you're still a teacher with two degrees from university. We're not suited for each other."

She remembered Jen, sophisticated, amoral Jen, and paled. "I wasn't any good."

He took an involuntary step toward her. "Don't be silly, you were wonderful."

She could not doubt his sincerity. "Then what's wrong?"

"We should never have gone to bed together. I was excited about my license and grateful to you, but..."

He did not love her; that was what he was trying to say. An ice-cold hand clenched itself around Sara's heart. "Oh, I see," she said. "It was a one-night stand."

He took another step, near enough now that she could see a tiny cut on his chin where he had scraped himself with his razor. "It was nothing of the sort!"

"Then what was it, Cal?" she asked very quietly.

He put his free hand on her shoulder. "It was the most beautiful experience of my whole life," he said. "But it can't happen again. It wouldn't be right."

"It felt right to me."

He bit his lip. "I can't have a casual affair with you—take you to bed on Tuesday and Thursday nights just because we happen to be together. I can't do it, Sara. And we mustn't get any more deeply involved than we are now. It would be wrong for both of us. It would never work."

She had always sensed in Cal a stubbornness that matched the jut of his jawline and knew instinctively that it was useless to argue. "So are we going to sit down and read *Repairing Antique Furniture* as if nothing had happened?" she said with understandable bitterness.

"I'd suggest we do just that, yes."

She turned away and walked to the table by the window, where she straightened the pencils and aligned the pile of books. When he sat down across from her, her eyes, brilliant with unshed tears, defied him to offer her sympathy. He said formally, "I ran into quite a few problems on the first page, couldn't figure out what he was getting at. The list you made of all the carpentry tools was a real help."

For a moment Sara was not sure she was going to be able to respond. She wanted to stamp her feet and scream at him, throw *Repairing Antique Furniture* through the window and generally express her outrage that Cal should have made a decision on his own that so strongly affected them both. Because she loved him, her outrage was perfectly natural. It was only that cold inner conviction that he did not love her that kept her silent. Pride was very little comfort, but it was better than nothing.

"Perhaps," she said, after what seemed like a very long silence but was actually only a couple of seconds, "we should read the first page together."

She had to sit beside him in order to look at the same page as he. Cal still followed along the lines with his finger. She found herself staring at his hand, remembering how intimately it had touched her, and stumbled over the words on the page. But gradually, bolstered by pride and by an innate professionalism, she began to give her best to the task at hand, divorcing her emotions from the man she was teaching, doing all she could to help him find the meaning of the words on the page. When nine o'clock came she at least had the satisfaction of accomplishment. She said with a brief smile, her eyes not quite meeting his, "I'll tape chapter three tomorrow and drop the tape and the book in your mailbox. Then you can work on it over the weekend."

"You can come to the house, Sara. I still want to be your friend."

Her lashes flickered. "Friend can be a very cruel word," she said. "I'm not sure I can be friends with you the way we were. Tuesday night happened, Cal. We can't act as if it didn't."

"You think I'm finding this easy?" he retorted.

"You don't seem to be much bothered by it," she said in a voice that was not conciliatory. "I certainly don't think it was very fair of you to march in the house and announce a decision that affects both of us."

"What the devil was I supposed to do? Have a three-hour consultation with you?"

"Even three minutes would have been an improvement! You could spend all night in my bed, but you couldn't be bothered talking to me about it afterward? How do you think that makes me feel? It makes me feel cheap, that's how. Like I'm an easy lay."

"Don't, Sara."

"Can't take the truth, can you, Cal?" All the pain of rejection was in her voice. "Well, I've made a decision, too. I'll put the book and the tape in your mailbox, and I'll be here on Tuesdays and Thursdays from seven until nine. Other than that I don't want to see you."

She wanted him to argue but he did not. His eyes flat, like pieces of stone, he stood up, gathering up his books and papers. "I'll come over on Tuesday at seven."

"Good," she snapped untruthfully. She stayed by the table while he put his jacket on, her body braced against it because she was trembling, and she did not say good-night. The door closed behind him, and his footsteps clumped down the steps. She sat down again, rested her forehead on her hands and began to cry.

CHAPTER THIRTEEN

THE NEXT TWO WEEKS passed unbelievably slowly. The winter solstice was approaching, the shortest day of the year. The trees were stripped bare and the ground frozen hard. Christmas was also approaching, the time of jollity and peace. Sara felt neither jolly nor peaceful. She felt extremely unhappy.

She did not let Cal see how unhappy she was. In their lessons she was calm and businesslike, and because he was working very hard they achieved a great deal. But she never allowed the conversation to approach the personal, and she only saw him twice a week. Twice was more than enough. It was torture to be with him, sitting together at the table with the wood stove crackling cheerfully in the background, and feeling so distant from him. He was worse than a stranger. He was the man she loved—just how much she loved him she was painfully discovering—and he was equally the man who did not love her.

She lost weight. She was perpetually tired because she was not sleeping well. The bitterly cold December days seemed a personal insult, and Christmas an occasion to be dreaded.

Cornelia had invited her for dinner one Saturday night. When Sara arrived, Cornelia surveyed her from head to foot and said, "You look dreadful. What's wrong?"

Laird and the children had gone shopping in Halifax and were not home yet. Sara accepted a glass of wine and sat down by the counter. "I don't want to talk about it, Lia."

Cornelia topped up her own glass. "You're in love with Cal Mathieson, aren't you?"

By a miracle of self-control Sara managed not to drop her wineglass. "You're a psychic," she said. "Or else I'm totally transparent."

Cornelia patted her hand. "I could see it coming, love. He's a fine man, and I think you're very well suited."

"Tell him that."

"What's the problem?"

Sara took a very large gulp of wine. She had promised Cal not to discuss his illiteracy, and still did not feel she could break that promise. "Cal quit school when he was sixteen and apprenticed as a carpenter," she said with careful truth. "I have a Bachelor of Arts degree and a Bachelor of Education degree, and I'm a schoolteacher. He doesn't think the two mix."

"That's understandable . . . although he's a very intelligent man, and very intuitive, I would suspect. But, Sara, if you did marry him you'd have to live in Haliburton. I can't see Cal leaving here. Wouldn't you miss the city?"

"I love Haliburton, and it's near enough to Halifax to go in for movies and the theater."

"It would be lovely if you settled here."

"Well, I'm not going to. Cal's not in love with me."

Cornelia got up to check a couple of the saucepans on the stove. "He's not a man who'd show his feelings easily."

"He doesn't have any feelings to show."

"You sound very adamant. Have you discussed this between you?"

Sara gazed into the ruby heart of the wine. "We made love, Lia . . . once." Her voice raw with pain, she quoted Cal. "It was the most beautiful experience of my whole life. But since then he's decided we mustn't do it again. Because I'm a schoolteacher and he's a carpenter. So that's that." She refilled her glass. "Maybe I should get drunk."

"You'll hate yourself tomorrow."

"I was going to ask you if he could come here for Christmas. I bet he's never had a proper Christmas in his life . . . but I can't now."

Cornelia prodded the potatoes, her eyes calculating. "I'm sure he's not involved with anyone else."

So was Sara. Her own private concern, which she could not share with Cornelia, was that Cal would increasingly ease himself out of her life as he became more proficient at reading and writing. He would not need her help as he had over the autumn; he would be capable of working on his own. While her aim as a teacher should be to make herself redundant, she needed the twice-weekly sessions, painful though they were. If they were gone, she would not see Cal at all.

"I've scarcely started my Christmas shopping," she said dismally. "I haven't felt in the mood."

"Why don't you and I go one evening next week? Tuesday or Wednesday."

They agreed to go on Wednesday evening. The combination of the wine, the children's tremendous air of secrecy as they smuggled their parcels into the house a few minutes later and the cheerful confusion of a family dinner cheered Sara up, and she remained in a better frame of mind until she went to get Bonnie the next afternoon.

Usually Bonnie was waiting outside, perhaps, Sara reasoned, because she was ashamed of her home. Although Bonnie could not be said to approach her weekly tutoring sessions with joy, she was still more or less cooperative and by dint of Sara's perseverance the girl was improving some of her basic language and mathematical skills. For Sara it was always hard work. Bonnie did not have Cal's natural curiosity or burning urge to learn, and her attention could be distracted from the task at hand by almost anything. But faithfully, every Sunday, she was waiting for Sara in front of the dilapidated blue house.

Today she was not. Sara tapped the horn, not wanting to brave the cold wind. The front door opened, and Bonnie hurried over the frozen ground. Her hair still shone with cleanliness, and because she had lost a little weight during the autumn, her clothes were better fitting. To Sara's surprise she was not wearing a coat. She scrambled into the front seat of the car and said abruptly, "I'm not coming no more."

"Anymore," Sara said automatically. "What do you mean, Bonnie?"

"I don't want no more lessons."

Sara sat very still, for Bonnie's words were an unexpected blow. She quelled the dozen or so protests that came to mind, folded her hands in her lap and said calmly, "Why not?"

"I gotta boyfriend."

It was not the reply Sara had anticipated, although now that she looked at the girl she could see an air of ill-concealed triumph about her: Bonnie had achieved her heart's desire. "Oh? What's his name?"

"Danny Koneski."

So Jean MacPherson had been right. "Your very first boyfriend—you must be happy."

"Yeah. Ma likes him, too."

"I think that's wonderful, Bonnie. I'm happy for you. But just because you have a boyfriend you don't have to drop the lessons. All the more reason to continue them, I would have thought. What grade is Danny in?"

"Same grade as me."

Said Sara with low cunning, "You wouldn't want him to get ahead of you, would you?"

"Likely he won't graduate, either," Bonnie said complacently. "He don't . . . doesn't . . . speak English so good."

"Then the more you study, the more you can help him."

Bonnie stuck out her lower lip. "I gotta go to school five days a week already. The rest of the time I wanna have fun."

Sara knew she was fighting a losing battle. "I felt exactly the same way when I was your age," she remarked. "Why don't we renegotiate the time and the length of the lesson, Bonnie? We could meet one evening through the week, if you'd prefer, and perhaps just for a couple of hours. Let's try that for a week or two and then reassess the situation."

Bonnie looked as sulky as only Bonnie could. "I don't want no more lessons!" she exclaimed. "You been real good to me, my hair and takin' me to Mel's and all, but now that I got Danny I don't want no more of this book stuff."

It was a long speech for Bonnie, and unquestionably she meant every word of it. Sara was experienced enough to know that she could not teach where the mind was closed against her, for the relationship between teacher and student must flow both ways. She stared down at her hands in her lap and knew herself defeated. Her best efforts had not been enough. Bonnie did not want to learn.

Bonnie was not overly sensitive, but something in Sara's pose must have reached her. "I'm gonna quit school once I'm sixteen. I always told you that. So there's no use in you wastin' your time on me. I'm gonna get a job as soon as I can and get some money so as I can buy the stuff I want, what's school and book learnin' got to do with that?"

Everything in the world, thought Sara, and knew it was useless to say so. "Bonnie, promise me something," she said. "If you change your mind, will you let me know? Don't let pride stand in your way or a fear that I'll reject you. I'll always be glad to hear from you . . . and I do wish you well."

"Sure, I'd let you know," said Bonnie with the air of one who knows she will not change her mind. She did not have many of the social graces; not looking at Sara she said hurriedly, "I gotta go, Danny's comin' over. Thanks, Miss Deane. You been good to me."

She scrambled out of the car as gracelessly as she had scrambled in, and Sara's, "You're welcome," was lost in the slam of the door. Quickly Sara drove away, not wanting to meet Danny Koneski, the symbol of her defeat. For it was a defeat. She had tried her utmost to infect Bonnie with the adventure of learning and with the joy books could bring, and she had failed. Bonnie wanted money and a boyfriend, not books.

She parked the car on the outskirts of the village and walked across the fields to the river, the wind tugging at her hair and numbing her ears, the stubbled grass crunching underfoot. The tide was low, the riverbanks slick with red mud and littered with chunks of dirty ice. The drooping branches of the willows rattled in the wind like distant, sporadic gunfire. Her shoulders hunched and her hands thrust in her pockets, Sara walked along the river's edge. The crows scolding her from the treetops were the only other living creatures in sight.

Even though the rational side of her brain said otherwise, her emotions told her she had failed Bonnie. There must have been something more she could have done to have captured Bonnie's interest. The vital connection between teacher and student had not been made, and she could scarcely blame Bonnie for that. But Bonnie's defection was not the only problem. The lessons with Cal had become an ordeal she dreaded. With all her heart Sara wished she had never heard of illiteracy, let alone engaged herself in the struggle against it.

By the time she turned back to the car, she was chilled to the bone. Normally her sense of humor would have come to her rescue, or at least a sense of balance, and chided her for wallowing so flagrantly in self-recrimination, not to mention self-pity. But her sense of humor had ebbed like the tide, and self-pity suited the bleak, dun-colored landscape with its stripped trees and bleached grass. She trudged across the fields, drove home, and in an effort to dissipate her black mood, vacuumed the house from top to bottom.

SARA AND CORNELIA went Christmas shopping in Halifax Wednesday evening. The weather cooperated, giving them a clear, starlit sky and roads bare of snow.

The stores were loud with recorded carols and crowded with aggressive shoppers and overtired clerks, which presented something of a challenge to someone like Sara, who had not even begun to buy her gifts. She entered into the spirit of the evening, and by nine-thirty was loaded with parcels, long tubes of gift wrap sticking over her shoulder, Malcolm's shiny red fire truck digging into her hip. She and Cornelia battled their way to the car in the parking lot of the mall and then drove out of town, Sara describing what she had bought for the children and Laird, and dropping all kinds of misleading hints about Cornelia's present.

Turning onto the Bicentennial Highway, Cornelia said casually, "Did you get anything for Cal?"

The animation left Sara's face. "No."

"Not even a card? Or some little thing for a joke?"

"I didn't buy him anything, Lia!"

"But you're still in love with him?"

"Of course I am. I know my feelings for Joel changed, but Cal's different." Sara gave a mirthless laugh. "Or do people always say things like that?"

She was staring out of the window. Cornelia said carefully, "I hate to see you so unhappy."

Trying to make a joke of it, her sister responded, "I can stand anything but sympathy—so stop, or you'll have me bawling like a baby." Then, abruptly, she added in a voice filled with pain, "I don't know what to do, Lia. I just wish I could get on a plane headed for Australia. I hate living next door to him!"

"Isn't there anything I can do?"

"There's nothing anyone can do. That's part of the problem. I feel so powerless."

Cornelia was tapping her gloved fingers on the steering wheel, her face very thoughtful. "Well, to start with you can come and have dinner with us on Sunday. What are you doing Friday evening?''

''Marking exams,'' Sara said gloomily.

''At home?''

''Yes. Why?''

''Oh, no reason, really. I may come back into the city, to do some more shopping Friday evening.''

Sara made a valiant effort to sound more cheerful. ''No can do... my chequing account's at rock bottom after tonight!''

''It's fun though, isn't it? Remember the Christmas we spent at the chalet in the Laurentians?'' And Cornelia led the conversation away from Sara's plans for the weekend.

But on Friday morning Sara's phone rang before she left for school. ''Sara? It's Cornelia. How are you doing?''

''Oh, fine,'' Sara said without much conviction.

''You haven't fallen out of love?'' her sister asked lightly.

''No such luck.''

''Why don't you change your mind and come shopping with me this evening? It'd cheer you up.''

''I can't, Lia. I've got exams and book reports to mark by Monday, and I don't want to leave them all until Sunday. Besides, I really am broke.''

''I see. Well, maybe I'll drop in when I get home to show you what I bought.''

''I'll be here,'' Sara promised. ''Have fun.''

By five o'clock that evening it was pitch-dark, the blackness of the sky unrelieved by a single star. Sara drew the curtains, put lots of wood in the stove and ate her supper. Then she settled down to work. The radio was playing quietly in the background. The logs shifted in the stove. Some of her grade-nine students had not only read the works they had been assigned, they had actually indulged in some original thought. The sound of the radio dropped from her consciousness.

At eight-thirty she stopped for a coffee, did a few stretching exercises and added some more logs to the fire. At quarter to ten, when the doorbell rang, she still had several essay questions left to mark.

She glanced at her watch, frowning a little. But then her brow cleared. Of course, it was Cornelia, come to gloat over her purchases. Sara hurried to the door and unlocked it.

But it was not Cornelia standing on the doorstep. Cal had rung the bell.

Sara had managed to forget about Cal for the past three hours, and she did not want to be reminded of him. Furthermore, she was wearing her oldest track-suit and no doubt had ink on her face. She said, "Go away, Cal, it's late," and shut the door. Or at least she tried to shut the door. But something was in the way. A boot.

She glowered at it. There was snow on it. She said, "Go play in the snow, Cal—I don't want to see you."

The boot did not move. "I want to come in."

"Well, you can't. I'm going to bed."

Cal said patiently, "Sara, the longer I stand here, the colder your house is going to get. I'm not going to leave. So you might as well invite me in, and we'll close the door and conserve energy."

"We could conserve more energy if you simply left!" she snapped.

His answer was to insert himself in the door and try to close it behind him, a process made more difficult because Sara was still clutching the knob. He reached down and detached her fingers, then shut the door, saying with great sobriety, "The world's supply of fossil fuels is not inexhaustible, you know."

Sara said with dangerous calm, "Would you mind explaining why you're here? It is neither Tuesday nor Thursday. As I'm sure you know."

"I was talking to Cornelia this evening. She said you were sick."

Sara's jaw dropped. "Sick?" she repeated. "I'm not sick!"

"Cornelia said you were."

"Then Cornelia lied," said Sara, a vengeful look in her eye as she remembered Cornelia's innocent questions about Sara's plans for Friday night. "I'm perfectly healthy, thank you for your concern, and good night."

His steel-toed boots planted a foot apart on the mat, Cal stood his ground. "Your sister is one of the most truthful people I know. So why would she lie?"

"I have no idea," Sara replied, thereby becoming less than truthful herself. "Go home, Cal."

"I'm not leaving until we get to the bottom of this."

"I'll call the police."

He gave her a lazy smile that affected her more than she would have cared to admit and drawled, "Go ahead. Although I've been known to pick up policemen and throw them through doorways."

Sara's red hair gleamed under the light. She said childishly, "I wish I could pick you up and throw you out the door!"

"A physical impossibility, I'm afraid. In certain respects the sexes will never be equal."

There was devilment in the gray eyes. "Then we seem to have reached an impasse, haven't we?" Sara said pleasantly. "You can do what you like, Cal Mathieson, but I'm going to bed. I had a busy day at school, and I've been marking exams all evening. So I'm tired."

"Fine," Cal said, just as pleasantly. "I'll sleep on the chesterfield, and we'll continue this discussion in the morning."

Sara was beginning to enjoy herself; this kind of confrontation was far preferable to the icy formality of their lessons together. She said with blatant insincerity, "I do hope you won't be too uncomfortable—the chesterfield's at least a foot too short for you."

"I'll manage," Cal said placidly. He hung his jacket by the door and bent to unlace his boots. After he had lined them up neatly on the mat, he hauled his sweater over his head. His hair ruffled, all the mischief of a much younger Cal in his smile, he said, beginning to unbutton his shirt, "Good night, Sara... unless you want to share the chesterfield with me?"

She had been staring at the strip of tanned flesh at his throat. She backed up a couple of steps, mumbled, "Good night," and heard him say, laughter in his voice, "Don't be frightened if you hear me moving around in the middle of the night—I'll only be stoking up the fire."

"I'll try not to scream," Sara replied, keeping her face straight with an effort. Turning, she went into her bedroom, closed the door and sat down on her bed. She should be furious with Cornelia for interfering and furious with Cal for staying when she had asked him to leave. But she was not furious at all; merely very happy to know that Cal was in the next room and that he cared enough about her to have come here after he had talked to Cornelia. She found herself looking forward to tomorrow morning, something she had not done for a long time. Humming softly, she got ready for bed and fell asleep almost immediately.

SARA WOKE in the middle of the night. The wind had come up a little, so that she could hear the soft swish of snow against her window. She had remembered the moment she had awoken that Cal was in the house. She tiptoed into the living room, switching on the lamp by the table. He was asleep on the chesterfield, which was indeed too short for him, enough so that his feet were dangling over the end and his head was twisted at an uncomfortable angle against the arm. She clutched the back of the chesterfield, swept by a wave of love for him. Then, without stopping to think, she reached over and shook his shoulder. "Cal."

He woke with a start, sat up, grabbed his neck with an exclamation of pain and said, "Sara! Are you okay?"

"No," she said calmly.

"What's wrong?"

He kicked himself free of the covers and stood up. He was wearing only his undershorts; not for the first time Sara decided it was very nice to be in love with a man who made her feel small and fragile when she was neither. "I'm suffering from a terminal attack of guilt," she said.

There had never been anything backward about Cal's wits. "For condemning me to the chesterfield, you mean? We could fix that easily enough." He dropped his bantering manner, resting his hands on the shoulders of her green nightgown. "I want you so much, Sara. The last couple of weeks have been hell, being with you and yet not with you."

There was such naked longing in his eyes and so total an absence of pride that Sara knew now was not the time for explanations: they could come later. "My bed is much more comfortable than the chesterfield," she ventured.

He took her by the hand and led her through the bedroom door, then drew her down to the bed. From the other room a soft light shone on his face. He said quietly, "Come here, Sara."

She went into his arms without hesitation. As they lay down together he held her close, not speaking, his breath ruffling her hair. She was so happy she felt like crying. He said finally, "This is where I belong."

Sara agreed with him wholeheartedly, but was afraid to say so. She held herself very still and heard him ask, "Do you think we belong together?"

How could she say anything but the truth when her cheek was resting against his chest and she could feel his heartbeat as her own? "Yes," she said. "Yes, we belong together."

He said in a low voice, "I can't imagine feeling closer to anyone than I do to you now, just holding you . . . it feels so good."

He was not a man for flowery adjectives. "Tell me I'm not dreaming," said Sara.

"You're not. I told you that making love to you was the most wonderful thing that had ever happened to me."

"Then why have you been so miserable to me since then?" she cried.

"When we're alone together like this and I'm holding you, I know we belong together . . . how could it possibly be otherwise? But we can't spend all our time alone together. The rest of the world exists, Sara, and we're part of it, and out there you're an educated woman, a schoolteacher, and I'm a carpenter who never made it to high school. How can we belong together in that world?''

She sat up so suddenly that her breasts bounced against his arm. ''You know what? You're scared of me!''

Her eyes were wide. He rested his weight on one elbow and said gravely, ''Terrified.''

''Don't laugh at me, Cal! You're scared of what people will think.''

''Sure I am. You think I want people saying you've thrown yourself away on me?''

''You've got a lousy self-image.''

''I'm a glorified carpenter, Sara, that's all.''

''Oh, grow up, Cal,'' she said furiously. ''You're a craftsman. An artisan who makes beautiful furniture. And a year from now I'll guarantee that you'll be able to read any book ever published about furniture, so that you can expand and add new designs. And I'll tell you something else.'' She poked his bare chest with her finger. ''I also guarantee that a year from now you'll be able to write the high school equivalency exams and pass them with flying colors. And then if you want to go to university and get some useless letters after your name, you can!''

He said very deliberately, ''I never know if I love you most of all when you're angry, or laughing, or just about to kiss me. Probably the last of the three.'' And he kissed her firmly on the mouth.

She clutched his shoulder and gasped, ''Love me? You don't love me!''

His eyes were very tender. ''Who says I don't?''

"*I* do! That's why you didn't want to make love to me again."

"For someone with two university degrees, you're not very smart."

She was gaping at him like a stranded fish. He said gently, "Sara my darling, shut your mouth. I love you."

She burst into tears, butted her face into his chest and sobbed, "I love you, too! I started falling in love with you the very first night we met. If we both love each other, why have I been so unhappy the last two weeks?"

"Sweetheart, don't cry! I was scared to tell you I loved you."

"I knew you were afraid of me," she mumbled.

"Scared of myself, not you. After we made love two weeks ago, and you went off to school and I went home, my whole past came crashing down on me. So I could drive the truck. So what? I was still the dumb kid in the back row, the hell-raiser who could set the tavern on its ear on a Saturday night, the carpenter who could make a chair but couldn't write up the bill for it. Yeah, I ran away, Sara. But if it's any consolation to you, I've been miserable, too."

She said bellicosely, "You can't possibly have been as miserable as I've been!"

He laughed, hugging her to him. "Oh Sara, Sara, how you've changed me! Remember how I met you? You were attacking a vicious dog with your bare hands to save a couple of deer, as courageous and crazy an act as I've seen in a long time. You were so beautiful you blinded me. You loved your family. You laughed as if laughter was like the sunshine, free for all to enjoy...but you didn't laugh at me when you found out

I couldn't read a single page in any one of your books. No, you did your best to help me. You meet life head-on, don't you, Sara? As I watched you I almost felt it might be possible for me to do the same. Leave behind all the deceptions I've lived with for so long and step into the sunshine beside you. But then I'd get frightened, because I've hidden so much of myself for so long, and I'd run again . . . I thought you made love to me because you were sorry for me.''

She was still gaping at him. ''I told you once I wasn't sorry for you! I thought we made love because you were grateful.''

''So we were both wrong.'' He traced the faint blue shadows under her eyes. ''Cornelia knew you were unhappy, didn't she? That's why she made a point of coming out to the workshop last night and telling me you were ill. Well, she didn't actually say you were ill, when I think about it. She said she was very worried about you because you weren't yourself. As a friend of yours, would I mind dropping in on you to see if you were okay and keeping you company for a while, it would relieve her mind. And then she looked at me with those big brown eyes of hers and said, 'Don't for heaven's sake tell her I sent you.' ''

''I must have been in worse shape than I thought. Cornelia isn't normally the interfering type.'' Sara smiled at Cal in the semidarkness. ''But I guess I'll forgive her.''

''I'll refinish every stick of furniture she owns for nothing!'' His eyes wandered possessively over Sara's face, as though he were memorizing her features one by one. He suddenly tightened his arms around her, his face full of strain. ''God, Sara, don't ever leave me.''

As if she were taking the most solemn of vows she said, "I won't, I promise," and remembered how all the people who had been significant to him had left him: his parents and Annalise, Jen and finally Dougal. Feeling near to tears again, she managed a joke. "You're perfectly safe right now—I'm going to hold on to you the whole night." And she suited actions to words, wrapping her arms around him.

"That could get you into trouble!" He kissed her slowly and deeply. "I want to make love to you again, Sara . . . now that we know we love each other."

Her answer was to entwine her legs around his and lift her face for a second kiss. It was a slow, gentle loving, deeply personal and intensely felt, for now they could speak of their feelings and allow their bodies to express those feelings; and its aftermath was the kind of happiness that comes only rarely in a lifetime, if at all.

Sara fell asleep first. Cal was lying on his side, facing her. As he watched her sleep, within him, like the germination of a tiny seed, was born the knowledge of his need for her. He had forced himself to be self-sufficient for years, and his solitary life had been enough for him until he had met Sara. Now he was beginning to understand the emergence of love, with all its surging contradictions: vulnerability, protectiveness, joy and fear. Because he loved her he would never be the same again. He carried as part of him the wonder of loving her, but its opposite he also bore, the unspoken terror that he might lose her.

But somehow losing her seemed an impossibility when she was lying in bed with him, her naked body curled against his. The house was enfolded in the si-

lence of the first snowfall. Sara loved him. Within five
minutes Cal, too, was asleep.

SARA WOKE FIRST in the morning. Cal was sprawled
beside her, taking up rather a lot of the bed; king-size
beds must be designed with men like Cal in mind, she
thought, admiring the play of light on the long hollow
of his spine. Reluctant to disturb him, she slid out of
bed, showered and washed her hair, then crawled back
under the blankets. Cal opened one eye. "You smell
nice," he murmured. "What are you trying to do to
me?"

She was lying very close to him. She said innocently, "It would seem whatever it is, I've succeeded."

As was inevitable, they made love again. Midmorn-
ing Cal got up, drove to his house to put wood in the
furnace and came back changed and clean-shaven. He
settled himself on the chesterfield, struggling through
a couple of magazines while Sara marked some more
papers. They had lunch. They went for a walk in the
woods, their steps the first in the pristine snow, and
when they got home decided so much activity necessitated a rest. The rest somehow turned into a tumultuous lovemaking, after which they fell asleep.

Fortunately they were out of bed when Cornelia's car
pulled into the yard about eight o'clock that evening.
Sara went to open the door, Cal close behind her.

Cornelia banged the snow from her boots, stepped
inside, looked from one to the other of them and said,
"Thank goodness—it worked! You're both invited for
dinner tomorrow night."

"You're conniving and underhanded," Sara said
severely.

"Also deceitful," Cal added.

"Desperate straits call for desperate measures," Cornelia said firmly. But she was blushing a little and added quickly, "I'll never do anything like that again. It was too much like playing God! You won't tell Laird, will you? With his Presbyterian principles, he'd be shocked."

"And rightly so," said Sara, spoiling the effect of her words by winking at Cal. "We'd like to go for dinner, wouldn't we?"

"Sounds good to me." He put his arm around Sara's shoulders and said, "Thanks, Cornelia," and they all knew he was thanking her for more than a dinner invitation.

"I won't stay, then," Cornelia said hastily; maybe she had caught sight of the rumpled bed through the open bedroom door. "See you tomorrow."

At Cornelia and Laird's the following evening Sara and Cal tried to put a decent face on their behavior and act as if they were merely good friends; but they found it necessary to touch each other quite frequently and to exchange secret smiles when they thought no one else was looking. Cornelia missed none of this and invited Cal for Christmas. Cal accepted. Sara hugged him and hugged Cornelia and hugged Laird, and she and Cal left when the children went to bed so they could go to bed themselves.

The next few days were as blissfully happy for Sara as the preceding days had been miserable. She and Cal spent all of their free time together, sleeping at her house or his, cooking, shopping, making love, laughing, talking, discovering in the manner of lovers any number of delightful things about each other. Although Cal never mentioned marriage, Sara was not at all concerned. The barriers Cal had erected so many years ago had fallen, and slowly he was stepping out from behind them into a new world. He was learning to trust this new world, to expose himself to it and to enjoy it. She knew he could not be rushed. She had no wish to rush him, for it was joy enough to see his spontaneity and hear his laughter, to be enfolded in his love and to give him love flowing over in return.

They cut a Christmas tree for Cornelia and Laird and helped the children decorate it. On Christmas Eve they all went to church at midnight. The minute they came home Malcolm clamored, "Can I open my presents yet?"

"Tomorrow morning," Laird said patiently. This question had been asked of him several times in the past few days.

"That's ages away!"

"Not if you go to bed and go to sleep."

Not surprisingly, Malcolm was not enthused by this suggestion. "But—"

Cornelia said in an authoritative tone, "Santa Claus won't come until you're asleep, Malcolm."

Fifteen minutes later Malcolm was asleep. When Caitlin had followed suit, Cornelia and Laird started removing gifts from various hiding places in the house and placing them under the spreading boughs of the fir tree in the living room. Then Cornelia switched out all but the tree lights and curled up on the chesterfield beside Laird. "It's so pretty, isn't it?" she murmured a few minutes later. "I'm like Malcolm. I hate to go to bed. But I guess I'd better, it'll be a busy day tomorrow."

Hand in hand Laird and Cornelia went upstairs. Sara had been hoping all evening that she would have a little time alone with Cal. "I'd like you to open one of your presents now," she said, rummaging under the tree for a small flat parcel and handing it to him. The wrapping paper was decorated with chickadees and snow-covered spruce trees, and she had pasted on a premade bow, having little faith in her ability to tie her own.

Cal turned the package over in his hands. "Why now?"

"You'll see."

Carefully he removed the paper without tearing it. There were two framed photographs inside, one of a group of young teenagers, the other an enlargement of one of the girls, a blond girl with blue eyes. Cal said quietly, "Annalise."

"I found out the name of the photographer from the school," Sara said. "One Saturday a month or so ago I went to see him and asked him if he could do an enlargement from the group negative." Cal was silent; he was staring fixedly at the photographs. She added anxiously, "You're not offended?"

"Of course not," he said slowly. "It threw me, that's all, seeing her face after all these years."

"That's why I didn't want you opening the present in front of everyone."

He looked up. "It's funny, I always had difficulty remembering her features, but now that I've seen the photograph I wonder how I could ever have forgotten."

His voice was under control; his hands were not shaking. Had she hoped that Annalise's photograph would penetrate his formidable self-control and allow him to weep for his sister's death? "Cal," she said impulsively, "you've never shed a tear since the fire, have you?"

"No. And it's too late now."

"It's never too late."

His response was to wrap the paper around the photos as carefully as he had unwrapped it. "I'll treasure these, Sara—it was thoughtful of you to go to so much trouble." He glanced over at her with a trace of a smile. "And now we'd better get some sleep. Unfortunately, not together."

They had decided not to share a room at Cornelia's. "We won't get much sleep anyway," Sara said philosophically. "I expect Malcolm will be up at dawn." She put her arms around Cal's waist. "Good night, Cal. I love you."

He gave her one of the slow, deliberate kisses that always turned her knees to water, and said, "Good night, sweetheart. Thank you again for the gift." Then they went to their separate beds.

Malcolm did not wake until the relatively respectable hour of eight o'clock; by nine the whole family was sitting in front of a blazing fire drinking cocoa and eating Cornelia's cinnamon rolls in a sea of torn wrapping paper and crumpled ribbon. Caitlin settled herself in the armchair with her pile of new books. Cal, Laird and Malcolm repaired to the rec room to set up Malcolm's new train set. Cornelia and Sara went to the kitchen, where the turkey was already sizzling in the oven. Sara hugged her sister and said, "I'm so happy, Lia! This is the best Christmas of my whole life."

Cornelia smiled. "And the best for Cal, too, I'd be willing to bet."

"It's lovely having him here as part of the family. I only wish Mum could be here to meet him."

In one of those moments that bind past and present, it seemed as though Maureen Deane could at any

minute walk into the kitchen, prepared to take on a
sixteen-pound turkey and any number of dinner guests,
a drink in one hand, a cigarette in the other, a quip
ready on her lips. Sara even glanced involuntarily over
her shoulder, the echo of her mother's hearty laugh in
her ears.

Cornelia wiped her eyes. "I'm sure she'd be happy
for you, Sara."

Sara nodded her agreement, blew her nose and began peeling potatoes. They all went cross-country
skiing before dinner and, as a consequence, ate far too
much. They sang carols in the evening. Then Cal and
Sara went home to his house, ostensibly to stoke the
furnace, in actuality, to make love. As Cal caressed
Sara's naked breast, he murmured, "You're the best
Christmas gift of all."

She stroked the curve of his ribs. "Did you enjoy
yourself today, Cal?"

His hand stilled. "I felt overwhelmed by it. So much
love, so many family traditions that all of you take for
granted, gifts and food in abundance." He hesitated in
a way that was characteristic of him. "Do you want
children, Sara?"

The answer came from deep within her, without
thought. "Yes."

He was staring absorbedly at the pulse in her throat.
"I don't know anything about children. What if I lost
my temper with them? Or if at fourteen they turned out
like me?"

She took a moment to think out her reply. "I was
watching you today with Caitlin and Malcolm. You
treated them beautifully, as if they were people in their
own right. Which they are, of course. They just happen to be younger than us. Cornelia said to me once

that she had learned more by having children than she had in all her years of nursing. We'd learn and grow with the children, Cal.''

"And I suppose there are no guarantees," he said slowly, and she saw the look in his eyes that came only when he thought of Annalise.

She pulled him to her and held him tightly. "None whatsoever."

It was the closest he had come to talking about the future. When the past had gripped him so strongly and for so long, she could not blame him for fearing the future. She could only give him all her love in the present and trust the days ahead would bring their own solutions.

CHAPTER FOURTEEN

DURING CHRISTMAS BREAK Cal and Sara resumed their lessons, working for a couple of hours every day. They were dealing partly with menus and cookbooks, which seemed appropriate to the season, and partly with technical books about carpentry, which interested Cal far more than Sara. He had started to make her a grandfather clock, working with painstaking slowness but infinite satisfaction, and this satisfaction became her own and helped ease the disappointment she still felt about Bonnie.

The ground was blanketed in snow the evening Sara went to baby-sit for Laird and Cornelia, who were going to a post-Christmas dinner-dance in Halifax. Cal had stayed home to work on the clock, for he and Sara still did not feel comfortable with the idea of sleeping together in Laird's house, in the presence of the children. Sara phoned him about ten-thirty, just before she went to bed. "I miss you," she said.

"I miss you, too. The house seems very quiet without you. But I got the inlay done for the pediment facing. It was tricky, and it took quite a while. I may go out for a walk now. I don't feel like going to bed by myself."

"I decided to take my book to bed, but it doesn't seem like much of a substitute."

He laughed. "I should hope not! So you miss me, Sara...do you love me?"

"Are you forgetting this is a party line?"

"No. The neighbors might as well know now as later."

"Yes, I love you. Passionately, rapturously and forever."

He said seriously, "I love you, too."

He was not as apt to verbalize his feelings as frequently or as easily as she, so that in consequence she valued his utterances of love. "I hope you'll sleep well," she said huskily.

"I will. I'll see you tomorrow morning."

Cal put down the phone. He had never liked it as a means of communication, which was difficult enough without adding the handicaps of plastic mouthpieces and miles of wire. He did not want Sara's disembodied voice; he wanted the living woman, flesh of his flesh and blood of his blood, the keeper of his soul. He should have told her that, he thought unhappily. To put into words the complexity of emotion that she aroused in him was often impossible for him. In bed with her, holding her naked in his arms, he could allow his body to speak for him of adoration and desire. To tell her she was his life's blood, to make his mouth shape the words, was infinitely more difficult.

He piled the logs in the wood stove for the night, put on his boots and parka and went outside. A three-quarter moon cast long, tangled shadows on the snow. The stars were a frail twinkling in the dead black of the sky. If he blinked, Cal thought, they might vanish.

After he had walked along the driveway to the road, he turned left because he did not want to pass Sara's house, now empty of her presence, unlit, deserted. The past few days, amidst his happiness, perhaps fed by it, there had flitted through his mind more than once the thought that something might happen to her. She might die. People did die. Annalise had died. His terror at the prospect of losing Sara was a measure of his love. He understood now, as he had not at fourteen, how one was the companion of the other.

He walked fast, his breath making little clouds in the cold air, his boots squeaking in the frozen snow. The gaunt trees were but another version of the blackness of the sky; the woods were held by the cold as by a vise, pinioned into submission. As he walked he tried to shake off his mood of foreboding, telling himself that this was the first night in two weeks that he and Sara had been apart, that he was bound to miss her, loving her as he did, that he would see her in less than twelve hours and that those twelve hours would not have changed her. Sara was constant. Sara was real. She would not vanish and leave him alone.

He had walked so hard and so fast that he had reached Percy Gillis's driveway, and it was there that he heard the sound his subconscious had been blocking out: a high-pitched, anguished baying that made the hair prickle on the back of his neck, for it was like the tormented wailing of a ghost, the cry of a spirit that could not rest. He thought of Annalise and a chill ran along his spine.

But when the sound came again his common sense reasserted itself. Percy was the dogcatcher. A dog was baying at the moon as its wolf forebears had done for centuries. There were no ghosts. No tormented souls. Only a dog in a cage.

He decided to turn back and was just beginning to retrace his steps when the dog howled again. Others joined in, barking in a frenzied chorus. Cal frowned. There was no reason for them to bark, not at midnight on a cold December night. Had something happened to Percy? Had he fallen in the snow because he was drunk? Had there been a fight?

Reluctantly Cal turned once again. He did not want to walk the long driveway to Percy's tumbledown dwelling, nor did he want to see the dogs in their cages; he had hated zoos ever since as a child on a school expedition to a wildlife park he had seen an arctic fox running in endless, mad circles around its pen. But if Percy had fallen he would freeze to death on a night like this. Hunching his shoulders, Cal strode up the driveway. The snow was smooth and pristine. Percy had not driven in or out for at least forty-eight hours.

Percy's truck was gone and the house in darkness. When the dogs saw Cal coming, they set up a cacophony of yelping and barking, scrabbling at the wire mesh with their paws, racing up and down in the cages, whining in frantic appeal. Cal walked closer. Their water dishes were frozen solid. The food dishes were empty. And Percy had not been here for two days.

Feeling the slow burn of anger, Cal walked to the house and banged on the door as loudly as he could. "Percy!" he yelled. "Percy, wake up!"

There was no answer. Not that he had expected one, for the house had that quality of silence that bespoke desertion. He went round the side of the house to the shed. The door was flimsy, with a rusted padlock. The howling of the dogs urging him on, Cal ran at it sideways, throwing the whole weight of his body against the stained planks. They splintered but did not quite give way. He ran at the door again, and this time it split so that he almost fell into the shed. With his gloved hands he pulled the rotten boards apart, making enough of a gap that he could enter. At fourteen and fifteen he had often fantasized about breaking and entering; at twenty-five he was finally doing it. And he would be perfectly happy to see a police car drive into the yard at this exact moment.

The shed was dark, littered with a miscellany of objects that seemed designed to trip him. Cal banged his shin against a metal trunk, swore, backed up and cracked the back of his skull against a rusty metal hook dangling from the roof. He swore again.

Stooping, he fumbled among the shadows until his eyes had adjusted to the gloom, and he located against the far wall two feed bags, one already split open. There was a battered saucepan on top of it. He dragged the bag across the floor, lifted it over the stoop and pulled it through the snow to the cages. Then he dug into the bag with the saucepan until it was full of dried chow.

The nearest cage contained a German shepherd, who reminded him, edgily, of his first meeting with Sara. Glad that he was wearing a heavy parka and gloves, he unlatched the slatted door, tipped food in the empty bowl and removed the other, putting it on the ground. The dog attacked the chow in great gulps, scarcely chewing it. The animal had probably been able to slake its thirst by eating snow, but there was certainly nothing more substantial to eat in the cage.

There were two other dogs, a bedraggled mongrel that snapped at Cal ungratefully when he filled its dish and a beagle that wriggled obsequiously, cowering at the slightest move of his arm. He fed the beagle, cracked the ice in the water dishes, made a cursory search for an outside tap and then repeated with the front door of the house the procedure he had followed with the shed door. He could have walked back to his house and brought a can of water in the truck; he did not want to. The front door was less amenable than the shed door, but finally one panel ripped open sufficiently for him to insert his hand and unsnap the lock. He flipped on the light switch and walked through to the kitchen, wrinkling his nose at the state it was in. Luckily the house was cold, otherwise the smell would have been a great deal more objectionable.

He found a galvanized pail in the corner and filled it at the sink. Then he went outside and gave the dogs water. The makeshift plywood huts that served as kennels were bare of straw or any other covering that might have conserved warmth. Vengefully Cal went back into the house, where he found some old blankets in one of the bedrooms; these he stuffed into the kennels. The mongrel snapped at him again.

He was replacing the dog chow against the far wall of the shed when he heard the grumble of an engine with muffler trouble and the rattle of loose metal that always accompanied Percy's vehicles. He straightened, his teeth gleaming in a smile that Sara would have deplored. Dodging the metal hook, he crossed the dirt floor of the shed and stepped out on the snow just as the truck shuddered to a halt. Percy climbed out of the driver's seat. Two other men, neither of whom Cal recognized, got out on the far side.

"Hello, Percy," Cal said clearly.

Percy staggered round to face him. He was wearing an old orange boilersuit, a bright blue toque pulled down over his ears. "What the hell are you doin' here?"

The other two men came round the hood of the truck; they were younger than Percy, and bigger, which pleased Cal rather than dismaying him. His body loose and relaxed, he approached the three of them. "I heard the dogs barking and thought you might be in trouble. So I came up to take a look."

"I'm not in no trouble."

"I see that." Cal's voice was knife-sharp. "But the dogs were in trouble. No food or water for the past two days. You're supposed to look after them, Percy."

Percy blustered, "I fed 'em yesterday."

"Yeah? We had snow two days ago and none since. How did you walk to the cages without leaving any footprints?"

One of the younger men snickered. Percy glared at him and snarled, "Okay, okay, so I didn't feed 'em. They didn't die, did they?"

"No, they didn't die. Just as well for you they didn't. Because part of your job as dogcatcher is to look after those dogs. You get paid good money by the county to do so. Are you spending the money on booze, Percy?"

"None o' your goddamn business."

"I'm making it my business. I'm going to be checking here every day or two to see that you're treating those dogs right, and the first time I see anything wrong I'm going to the police to report you for cruelty to animals and to the county office to report you for not doing your job. You got that, Percy?"

"You step on my land and I'll report you for trespassin'."

"No, you won't. Because if you do, I'll tell them why I'm trespassing. And you wouldn't like that, would you?"

"You bastard."

Cal's hands clenched inside his gloves. Then one of the younger men, the one with the checked hunting jacket and the stringy black hair, interjected, "You want we should rough this guy up a little, Perce? That way he won't come round here trespassin'."

Percy ignored him, his face screwed up in unaccustomed thought. "How'd you get in the shed?"

Cal's grin was fiendish. "I kicked the door in."

"You broke the law!" Percy cried, his voice rife with indignation.

"That's right." Cal rocked on the balls of his feet. "You want to make something of it?"

The black-haired man yelped, "He broke in the house too, Percy."

Percy swiveled. "By God, he did!"

"Break and entry," Cal said softly. "Call the police, Percy."

Percy, who could show low cunning but rarely intelligence, shot a hunted look over his shoulder at the back of the truck, which Cal had already surmised was loaded with illegal liquor. "I should call 'em," he said without much conviction. "Yeah, I should. That's a crime, that is. Against the law."

"We don't need no police," said the black-haired man. "Let's clean up on him. There's three of us to one of him—that'll teach him to go pokin' his nose where it ain't wanted. Whaddya say, Ralphie?"

Ralphie, blue jacketed and dour, nodded. Percy looked shifty. "Hold on, Pete...there's more than one way to skin a cat."

The other two men began advancing on Cal, one on either side of him. "C'mon Perce," said Pete. "Let's have a little fun."

Cal felt the old familiar surge of adrenaline, the supernatural sharpness of his senses and the surge of power to his body. "Sure," he said. "Come on, Percy. Three against one, that's your idea of a fair fight."

"Listen, you guys," Percy whined, "you don't wanta tangle with him. It's okay for you, but I gotta live down the road from him. You beat him up, he'll lay for me. Or he'll go to the cops." He shot Cal a venomous glance. "And they'll believe him, not me, 'cause he's the kind the cops listen to."

Cal, remembering his checkered past, smothered a smile. Pete was obviously unconvinced by Percy's logic and spoiling for a fight. He took two steps closer; he stank of cheap rum. "His word against ours. There ain't no witnesses."

"Lay off, Pete," Percy ordered, turning back to the truck. "C'mon, we got work to do. Ralphie, you can fix them doors."

Percy was a very successful bootlegger, and Pete plainly liked a drink. Cal met the close-spaced eyes squarely and saw them waver and drop. "You're lucky," Pete said sulkily. "Damn lucky. We'd have cleaned the floor with you."

Cal, who felt exhilaratingly like a ten-year-old, said pleasantly, "I'd have wiped your face in the snow. It might have improved the look of it."

Pete swung at him, Percy yelled an obscenity and Cal made a couple of passes with his fists. "Get moving, Pete," he mocked. "Or Percy won't sell you any more of that ten-dollar rum."

Pete spat in the snow at Cal's feet, mouthed a couple of words that took Cal back ten years and then stalked over to the truck. Cal suspected he might have a weapon there, a hunting knife or a shotgun. Giving the truck a wide berth, he said, "Remember what I said about the dogs, Percy. Don't you ever neglect them again. Got that?" His smile included all three of the men. "You'd better hurry up and unload, because I might still be tempted to call the police." Then, whistling, he began to walk down the driveway.

He was not feeling quite as carefree as he sounded. He had known men like Pete in the past, men who did not always heed the voice of reason but could explode into rages that wreaked havoc on everything around them. As a teenager he had been like that himself, and he still feared his own potential for destruction. His back felt vulnerable; his ears were pricked for the crunch of boots in the snow. He heard the rumble of argument, Pete's raised voice with Percy's overriding it. The truck door slammed. One of the dogs barked. Then there was only the swish of snow under his feet and the creaking of spruce boughs in the cold.

He had made an enemy tonight, he knew, because he had made a fool of Percy in front of his cohorts and Percy would not easily forgive that. But it had been worth it.

Still whistling, he tramped home.

Sara, the next morning, was not amused by Cal's lighthearted account of the incident. "You were egging them on!" she said, horrified.

"Oh well, I knew I was safe."

"But there were three of them. You wouldn't have stood a chance."

"Two, Sara. Percy couldn't swat a fly. And they'd all been drinking."

She scowled at him. "You wanted a fight, didn't you?"

Shamefaced, he admitted, "I wouldn't have run from one. I sure wanted to get the message across to Percy about those dogs."

"I understand about the dogs. The situation you describe is horrible. What I don't understand is why you hung around trying to pick a fight when you should have come home and phoned the police."

He rested a hand on her shoulder; it was rigid with tension. "Hey, what's wrong?" he said gently. "I'm a big boy, Sara, I've looked after myself for twenty-five years. I've got enough sense that if things had really looked nasty last night, if they'd had guns, for instance—"

"Guns!"

"—I'd have hightailed it out of there. Sara, I wouldn't have told you about it if I'd known you'd get this upset."

She let out her breath in a long sigh. "You mustn't stop telling me things just to protect me. I don't know why I'm so upset... well, that's not the truth. I do know. What would I do if something happened to you, Cal? What if they'd left you lying in the snow last night and I didn't know where you were?"

They had come to the crux of the matter. "That's funny you should say that," Cal said slowly. "Because I've been thinking about you in the same way. What if you had a car accident between Cornelia's and here or if you got cancer like your mother? How would I ever live without you?" He tried to knead the tightness from her muscles. "There aren't any answers, Sara. We love each other, so we're vulnerable. And no matter if you disappeared tomorrow, you'd still have given me the most beautiful moments of my life. No one can take those from me."

"The dark side of love," Sara said thoughtfully. "What we mustn't do is smother each other because of it." She put her arms around him, resting her cheek on his chest, where she could feel the heavy beat of his heart. "Oh Cal, we have so much to learn."

He rubbed his chin in her curls. "Despite all this gloomy talk, I do believe we have a lifetime to learn it in. And do you know something, Sara? I didn't fight last night. Ten years ago I would have, nothing would have stopped me."

"That's right, you didn't. So maybe you don't need to be so afraid of your temper."

"Mind you, by the time Percy arrived I'd had the time to cool down. Literally. It was a cold night. I don't know what I would have done if he'd arrived right after I'd seen the state the dogs were in—I'd probably have gone for him and to hell with the consequences."

She shivered, wishing she could allay Cal's fear of his own violence, yet knowing no one could do that for him. "I need to hold on to you," she said. "Let's go to bed."

So at ten o'clock in the morning, they did.

On the last Sunday in December Sara was sitting on her living room floor taping Revenue Canada's latest directive on the tax situation for small businesses. The directive managed to complicate the simple and failed to simplify the complicated. Sara did not envy Cal. She would have dumped the whole thing on the lap of the nearest accountant, whose business it was to decipher such governmental obscurities. But Cal, she now knew, liked to get to the bottom of things, his mind not satisfied with a surface view or with the easy way out. Trying to keep her voice from becoming a monotone as boring as the material she was reading, from section C, subsection 3, paragraph 2, part b, she ploughed on. Cal was home cooking dinner for her, using recipes he could now read—or so she hoped. He had told her he would omit any ingredients he could not decipher. Barbecued spare ribs without the ribs? Apple pie without cinnamon? Hurriedly she brought her mind back to what she was reading.

The doorbell rang in the middle of section E, subsection 4. Sara stopped the tape recorder and marked her place, noting with relief that she had only two more pages to read and wondering who her rescuer could be. As she glanced at her watch she realized she would have been in the middle of her session with Bonnie at this time a month ago.

She opened the front door. Even though Bonnie had been on her mind, at first sight the woman on the step was a stranger, her head wrapped in a navy wool scarf, her nose red with cold. Then Sara recalled a thin woman with arthritic fingers sitting at a wooden table in a bare little room. "You're Bonnie's mother!" she exclaimed. "Come in, Mrs. Dawson. It's cold, isn't it? Here, let me take your coat."

Marlene Dawson clumped the caked snow from her boots. "You busy?" she asked.

"Not at all," Sara responded. "In fact, there's nothing I'd like better than a cup of tea. You'll join me, won't you?" She hung Marlene's cheap blue bomber jacket on the rack; the jacket was too light to furnish much warmth. "Did you walk?" she said with concern.

"Yeah. It's not so cold if you keep movin'."

According to the weather report, it was twenty below zero with a windchill factor to lower the temperature even further. She remembered the sleazy thin fabric of Marlene's jacket and ushered the woman into the living room to the seat nearest the wood stove. She threw in another log and opened the damper to give more heat. "You must be frozen," she said. "I'll get you a pair of slippers."

The slippers were lamb's wool, one of Cal's Christmas gifts, and much too large for Marlene. She was rubbing her hands together as if they pained her and looking around the room with very much the same expression as Bonnie had worn previously, as though the cozy, unpretentious room was a palace. Quickly Sara went into the kitchen to put the kettle on.

When she came back Marlene was leaning toward the fire. She was wearing a pale blue sweater and navy slacks, both very clean, with her hair ruthlessly pulled back from her face. Sara sat down across from her. "How's Bonnie?" she asked. "I saw her in the cafeteria just before Christmas, but I didn't have much chance to talk to her."

"She's okay. That Danny's a nice kid, though I'm not crazy about them goin' steady and seein' so much of each other. But Bonnie's perked right up since she met him. I got an appointment for her at the doctor's next week, figure she should go on the pill."

Sara blinked at such directness, she who could be just as direct herself. "She's very young."

"I got pregnant when I wasn't much older than her," Marlene said dispassionately. "That's why I got married so young. I don't want that for her." For the first time Marlene's turquoise eyes looked right at Sara. "You mad at her for quittin' her lessons?"

Sara shook her head. "No, I wasn't angry—but I was disappointed. I'd hoped she'd continue all year—

we were making progress. It was slow, but it was there."

"Soon as she met Danny I knew she'd quit."

Sara grimaced. "You were smarter than I was. I'd hoped that having a boyfriend would give her all the more incentive. Do you think she'll come back?"

"Dunno."

Marlene was staring at the fire again. Sara excused herself to make the tea, putting out a few cookies, as well, and then carrying the tray into the living room. She had no idea why Marlene was here and was reluctant to ask, so she chattered on about the unusually cold weather they were having for December and the record apple crop in the fall. Finally, into a pause in the conversation, Marlene said abruptly, "I came here to ask you somethin'."

Sara leaned over and refilled Marlene's cup. "Yes?"

Marlene gazed into the teacup with the intensity of a fortune-teller. "You might not wanna do it, and if you don't, you say so."

"I will, Marlene. What is it?"

There was color in Marlene's sallow face that had nothing to do with the cold. "Will you teach me to read?"

"Yes," Sara said immediately, and was proud of herself for showing none of her surprise.

"You will?" Marlene looked up. "You mean it?"

"I'll do the best I can. And if you want to learn, I'm sure we'll succeed."

"Yeah . . . I wanna learn. I used to look at all that stuff you did with Bonnie, all them scrapbooks and the writin' you did, and wish that it was me goin'. I was mad at her when she quit. Real mad. She had a proper teacher spendin' all that time with her, and she upped and quit. But there's no talkin' to Bonnie when she gets her mind made up. Might just as well talk to that wood stove.''

Sara laughed. ''I know what you mean. But she's young and she may well come round.''

''It's not so easy when you're older . . . you get set in your ways, like. Everett, now, he thinks I'm crazy. Don't understand one bit why I wanted to come down here. He thinks readin' is for people like you, school-teachers and such, and not much good for the rest of us.'' Her mouth quirked. ''You never know. I might even get him interested. That'd be somethin', wouldn't it?''

Remembering Everett's black-browed silences, Sara had to agree. ''Did you go back to school after Bonnie was born, Marlene?''

Marlene shook her head. ''Wasn't done in them days. You had a kid, you stayed home. And Everett was workin' in the woods then, did that for ten years till he got his leg smashed, so it was best I was home with Bonnie and cookin' and the like.'' She shrugged philosophically. ''I got more time now.''

''What happened to his leg?''

''Dozer tipped and landed on him.''

Sara winced. ''So he was never able to work in the woods again?''

''No. It was hard on him. That was winter work, see, which meant he was busy all year round. He's not a man for sittin' and starin' at the four walls.'' Marlene frowned, trying to articulate her thoughts. ''I reckon he felt guilty. He was the man, see, he was the one who was supposed to go out and bring home the money, and after the accident he had to go on unemployment and then welfare. They paid him money to sit around and do nothin'. That's no good for a man like Everett.''

"It's no good for anyone. There's a lot more than money involved... it's the dignity of working and paying your own way and taking responsibility for yourself.'' Sara sighed, wishing she knew the answer to a situation like Everett's, if indeed there was an answer.

She tried to bring her mind back to Marlene, her next question based on her experience with Cal. "What would you like to be able to read most of all, Marlene?''

"The want ads in the newspaper. There might be jobs I could do, housekeepin' or baby-sittin'. But if I can't read the ads, I can't get the job. Same goes for Everett. I could read 'em for him, too.''

"What would be next on the list?''

"I'd like to be able to fill in the welfare forms. I gotta go to a neighbor as it is. She's a real nice woman, but it ain't the same as if I could fill 'em in for myself. Always makes me feel kinda small to ask her.''

"Maybe you could bring one with you next time.''

Marlene looked uncomfortable. "Got one on me now. Hope you don't think I was takin' it for granted that you'd teach me.''

"Of course not.'' Sara glanced at her watch and abandoned Revenue Canada without regret. "If you like we could make a start right now. I'm going out at five, so I could drive you home before that.''

Marlene's expression changed from unease to belligerence. "I'm gonna pay for the lessons.''

Feeling her way, Sara said, "You'd rather do that?''

"Yeah. It was different for Bonnie. She's just a kid. But if you're gonna drive me back and forth and spend your time on me, I can't take that for free."

Something much more important than dollars and cents was being discussed here, Sara knew: pride, and a woman's right to pay her own way. "I do understand," she said.

Marlene pulled a creased white envelope out of the pocket of her slacks and plunked it on the coffee table. "This is for the first lesson."

"Thank you," Sara said. "Why don't we move to the table by the window, if you're warmer now. I'll get some paper and a couple of pencils, and we'll at least get an idea of where we should begin."

If Marlene had pride where money matters were concerned, she had none for her lack of learning. Gripping the pencil between her stiff-jointed fingers, she laboriously printed her name, then went through the alphabet. "I can't write so good," she said to Sara. "But you'll show me how to do it better, won't you? I can make the numbers, you want I should show you?"

Her eagerness tugged at Sara's heart. They worked for another fifteen or twenty minutes on the formation of the letters and numerals, then Sara switched to reading, afraid that Marlene's arthritis must be paining her. Again Marlene threw herself into the work, straining after every word Sara said, her brows knitted with effort.

They stopped at four-thirty. Marlene carefully folded the welfare form and put it back in her pocket. "I can read some of the words on it now," she said. "It ain't so scary when you can read some of 'em. When I used to look at it before, all the letters'd run together and then I'd get in a panic, like. Couldn't have read it if you'd paid me." She looked at Sara in surprise. "I'm tired. Tireder than if I'd cleaned the whole house and baked bread for the week."

Sara smiled. "You were concentrating, Marlene."

"Time sure went fast. Can we do this again next week?"

"Sure. I'll come and get you on Sunday at one."

"I'll practice the letters like you said. And we'll start the want ads, okay?"

"I'll pick up a couple of newspapers through the week."

Marlene would not quit as Bonnie had. In fact Bonnie might even be encouraged to start the lessons again when she saw how hard her mother was working. Full of optimism, Sara drove Marlene home. When she got back to her own place to change, the first thing she did was open the envelope Marlene had left her. It contained a worn one dollar bill and some silver. Sara hated to think what sacrifice the money represented and knew she had no choice whatsoever in taking it.

CHAPTER FIFTEEN

CAL AND SARA spent New Year's Eve at a house party at Cornelia and Laird's. For New Year's Day Cal had made dinner reservations at a country inn eighty or ninety miles away, in the Annapolis Valley. Sara knew the occasion was a milestone for him, another step into the world that the literate take for granted. She had coached him thoroughly on how to deal with the menu, the wine list and the cutlery, and desperately wanted everything to go smoothly for him.

She had purposely bought a new dress, a very feminine dress of softly draped crepe with full sleeves tightly buttoned at the cuff and a plunging neckline that she hoped would distract him from his nervousness about such hurdles as the maitre d' and the tip. He, she knew, had bought a new suit. Cal had suggested they leave early because he wanted to show her the place on South Mountain where he had grown up. So he arrived to pick her up midafternoon.

She had never seen him in a suit before. He looked magnificent. His hair was brushed smooth, and the dark gray fabric fitted his body so perfectly that he looked like a sophisticated stranger whom she might meet in a bar in Montreal. And then his face broke into a grin and he became the Cal she knew, the man who had taught her what it was like to come home.

"For a moment I scarcely knew you," she said breathlessly.

He put his arms around her and kissed her. "Same old Cal," he said. "Recognize the technique?" Then with a gleam in his eye he peered down the dip in her neckline. "What are you trying to do to me?"

"Keep your mind off the waitress."

"She'd have to be Raquel Welch before I'd notice her. Are you ready?"

"I'll put on my lipstick now that you've greeted me," Sara said demurely.

"In that case..." He kissed her again, taking his time.

"We'll never leave if you keep that up."

"Let's not be too late home," he said, sliding his fingers along the borders of her bodice.

"The sooner we go, the sooner we'll be back," she teased. "Cal, stop!"

Although they set off lightheartedly enough, Cal grew more and more silent as they approached his old home. He was not withdrawing intentionally, Sara was sure, and she began to wonder about the wisdom of revisiting the site of so much of his unhappiness and struggle. They turned off the main highway, following the deeply gouged riverbed in the valley. The river was flanked by farms and orchards, the neat rows of trees like hunched black skeletons in the snow. Then they turned left and began to wind up the side of the mountain. The snowbanks grew deeper, their edges fluted by the wind, as a tangle of spruce and fir usurped the orderly orchards. The houses were few and far between and seemed to Sara's eyes to be growing smaller and meaner, as though the sky were pressing down on them. Cal had not said a word since they had begun their ascent.

"How much farther?" she asked.

"A couple of miles."

The road changed from pavement to dirt, with patches of ice. Cal drove more slowly, looking neither to the left nor the right. The pale winter sunlight faded from the sky.

With all her heart Sara wished she was elsewhere, for the top of the mountain with its black-limbed trees and lowering sky was appallingly lonely. Only those who could not afford to purchase the lush meadows in the valley would live here, she thought. Those, and the misfits in society, the men and women who feared or despised day-to-day contact with neighbors. Cal drove past a wooden, boxlike trailer with a plume of smoke rising from its metal chimney; a few minutes later she saw a square unpainted shed, seemingly held upright by the pine trees behind it. More smoke. People lived there.

Then Cal slowed the car to a crawl, his eyes searching through the woods to his right. "It was near that maple," he muttered, more to himself than to her, and pulled over to the edge of the road, shutting off the engine. "I'm going to walk over there," he added. "You don't have to come." Bending forward, he tucked his trouser legs into the tops of his boots and drew up the zippers.

She could only see him in profile. There was no give to his face, no softness. He had retreated behind barriers again, reminding her painfully of those frustrating weeks when she had first known him, when he had been unreachable and cruelly distant. She said with assumed calm, "Would you prefer me to stay here?"

He did not look at her. "I don't care."

She zippered her own boots, which were knee-high and had unsuitably high heels for tramping through the woods. Then she buttoned her coat to her chin, drew on her gloves and got out of the car.

The silence on top of the mountain was a force, a living, brooding presence as real as the snow and the still, dark trees. There was no wind. The cold sucked the breath from Sara's lungs and stabbed at her sinuses. You could die in such cold, she thought.

Cal was striding toward the maple tree. It was long dead, its trunk pockmarked by woodpeckers, its limbs amputated by wind and weather. Sara hurried after him, her leather boots skidding in the snow. She felt frightened, as though in the next few minutes she might lose Cal. He would vanish into the woods and she would discover that her happiness had been a dream, and the home she had found in him an illusion. This place was his home; a place she could not share.

He stopped so abruptly that she almost ran into him. She followed the direction of his gaze.

There was a clearing in the trees, a rectangular patch of smooth white snow, its surface broken only by the heads of weeds. Spruce trees huddled around its perimeter. Sticking out of the snow in the far corner, jagged as a broken tooth, were the crumbled remains of a brick chimney. Some of the bricks were charred black.

Sara wrapped her arms around herself, the cold that bit into her a chill of the spirit rather than the body. Then Cal climbed over the snowbank that the plough had left and began walking toward the chimney.

She could not have borne to have been left alone by the side of the road; only by keeping close to him could she tamp down the panic in her soul. Stepping into the hollows left by his boots, which made her strides ridiculously long, she followed him. He stopped in the middle of the clearing and suddenly seemed to become aware that she was with him. "This was where the house was," he said redundantly.

Sara had never felt so useless in her life. When she could not stand the press of silence on her ears any longer, she said, "It wasn't very big."

"Only one room. The stove was over by the chimney."

What are we doing here? she wanted to cry. *Why are you torturing yourself like this?* "Where did you sleep?" she asked, trying to sound matter-of-fact.

"Over there. Mum and Dad slept here, and Annalise in the far corner." Something shivered in his voice. "Nearest the stove."

She took a couple of steps in the calf-deep snow, putting herself between him and the chimney, a living barrier to ward off unbearable memories. "Don't, Cal!" she said. "Please don't."

"Don't what, Sara?"

In the midst of her distress she was relieved that he still knew her name. "You can't change the past," she said incoherently. "You mustn't hold yourself reponsible for it."

"You could smell the smoke a hundred yards away."

She gripped the sleeve of his overcoat. "It was a terrible tragedy. But Annalise of all people wouldn't want you to scourge yourself with guilt all these years . . . I know she wouldn't."

For the first time since they had begun to climb the mountain Cal met her gaze. "How can you be so sure of that, Sara?" he said bitterly.

"Because of the way you described her to me, gentle and sensitive. Because she loved you."

He flinched. "Did you have to say that?"

"It's the truth." She tugged at his sleeve, her fingertips numb inside her gloves. "Cal, let's leave here, it'll be dark soon."

But he was staring at the corner beside the chimney. "If only I could know she didn't suffer," he whispered. "I used to have nightmares when I was younger. I'd be fighting my way through the smoke, listening to her scream. But I never found her. Never."

And then, suddenly, something in him broke. She saw his face convulse, as if he had been stabbed by knives and heard an agonized, dry sob burst from his throat. She put her arms around him, pulling his head down to her shoulder, and held him with all the strength of her body and the love in her heart. He did not cry easily, he who had never cried before; and his tears froze on the collar of her coat.

Her feet were aching with cold when he finally grew still in her arms, his shoulders no longer shuddering, the dreadful, harsh weeping no longer flaying her. Miraculously she produced exactly the right degree of lightness in her voice. "I don't have a handkerchief or even a tissue, Cal, and my purse is in the car."

"I've got one." He straightened and blew his nose.

Because she was frightened that he might regret his emotion she said quietly, "You've needed to do that for years, Cal."

"I never could."

"Perhaps you had to come back here."

He looked around at the encroaching trees, from which the darkness had stolen all color, then looked down at her. "You're cold. Let's go back to the car."

"Have you been here long enough? Or maybe you want to be alone for a while."

"No. There's nothing more for me here."

They tramped back to the road through the snow. Cal turned on the car heater and in low gear began the descent of the mountain. The valley, spread out in front of them, was like a landscape painted by one of the more depressing Victorians: apple trees crawling in punctilious parallel lines over the slopes, the riverbed snaking through the snow and the spruce trees coarse black brushstrokes in a scene obscured by the gathering of night.

The road was slippery enough that Sara kept silent, allowing Cal to concentrate on the driving. He did not speak until they had crossed the metal bridge over the river. "I couldn't have gone there alone, Sara. Thanks."

"For a while I didn't think you wanted me there."

"No. I was aware of you the whole time." His eyes fastened on the road, he added, "I was brought up that boys don't cry."

"I sometimes think it's time for the male liberation movement," Sara said vigorously. "Men don't cry. Men shouldn't show emotion. Men have to go out to work. Men have to be tough and aggressive and always ready for a fight . . . it's all such nonsense! Why shouldn't you cry when you feel sad?"

"So you don't think the less of me?"

She rested her gloved hand on his thigh. "Oh no, Cal! I think the more of you because you trusted me with your emotions. Maybe when we were holding onto each other up there in the snow we were being more intimate than we've ever been in bed."

Cal frowned. "So loving each other is being real with each other."

"Psychologists call it being authentic. No games, no playacting. We can take off the masks that we wear in public because we trust each other."

"That's an immense freedom," he said, even more slowly.

It was her turn to stop short. "I suppose it is. The freedom to be real. Not very many people want that, do they? They prefer the masks."

"I want it of you, Sara. That was what was so difficult when we first met—I couldn't be real with you. I didn't have the guts to tell you I couldn't read, and I was terrified of you finding out."

"We've laid that ghost to rest, Cal." Her tone was not wholly joking. "Any more skeletons in the closet?"

He checked the traffic before pulling back onto the main highway. "Let's leave the skeletons alone. We've had enough heavy stuff for one evening. This is New Year's Day, after all—a time of beginnings, not of looking backward." His smile was boyish. "I want this to be a romantic dinner. Table by the fire, candlelight, wine, the whole works. A first for us, Sara."

Although she smiled back, Sara was aware of an inner uneasiness. There was another skeleton in the closet—Cal's fear of his own violence—and he was still running from it. Nor would he ask her to marry him until that skeleton, too, was laid to rest. The thought that he might not ask her terrified her, because she wanted to marry him more than anything else on earth.

But Sara had learned patience and something of wisdom since moving to Haliburton. Cal must not be pushed into anything against his own instincts. When he was ready to marry her, he would. She accepted his change of subject, and by the time they reached their destination she was both hungry and in the mood for romance.

The inn was a refurbished Victorian mansion with lofty molded ceilings, velvet drapes and Persian carpets over polished floors. Sara felt as if she should be equipped with a bustle, a high-buttoned neckline and a mind too pure to notice how Cal's striped shirt set off the taut muscles of his throat, and was rather pleased to have none of those attributes.

Their table was by the fire. The candlelight flickered over her cleavage in a most un-Victorian way, and Cal dealt with the menu and the wine list as if to the manor born. When the waitress had delivered their appetizer, Sara leaned over the table and whispered accusingly, "I think you've been fooling me, Cal Mathieson. You've been bringing beautiful women to high-class restaurants for years."

"Don't lean forward like that, it does terrible things to my blood pressure. And I swear you're the first." He raised his wineglass. "I'm doing all right, am I?"

"Stop fishing for compliments."

"I could never have been with a more beautiful woman, Sara."

Solemnly she clicked her glass against his. "Nor I with a more handsome man."

"Would it be considered poor etiquette for me to tear that dress from your body and ravish you in front of the fire?"

She dipped a piece of pickled herring in cream. "I would love it. But you might shock the waitress."

"Not to mention the very stern-looking couple two tables over."

Sara glanced to her right. "Poor things, they're not having nearly such a nice time as we are."

"And I'm quite sure they've never even contemplated doing in bed what I'm going to do to you when we get home."

She giggled and said what she had wanted to say ever since they had stood by the ruins of the old chimney. "Cal, I love you."

"Lust," he complained, "that's all it is. You want me for my body."

"Oh, that too."

His smile was heartbreakingly tender. "I love you, too, Sara. I'll still love you when I'm a crotchety old man of ninety and too old to do anything about it."

"I'll be a little old lady of ninety then. But I still plan to be able to do something about it," she said decidedly.

"Do you, now? Maybe we have to keep in practice, do you think that's the secret?"

She was honest enough to admit that she loved it when he included her in his future. "I think it's worth a try," she said, and impaled a piece of herring on her fork. "Do you want to try a piece of my Solomon Gundy?"

"If that's all I'm being offered."

"Right now it is. I might make you a better offer later."

"Promise?"

"Promise."

"I'll hold you to it," he said.

THREE HOURS LATER they were driving home through the village of Haliburton. "The lights are still on at Cornelia's," Cal said. "If I didn't have more basic urges on my mind, I'd suggest we drop in for a coffee."

"Caffeine keeps you awake."

"Sleep was not the basic urge I was contemplating." He turned down the dirt road to the lake. "Your place or mine?"

"Yours. It feels more like home."

So they swung into Cal's driveway between the close-growing trees. As the house and barn came into sight Cal braked. "There's a light on in the barn," he said, a puzzled note in his voice. "I never leave the light on. Stay here, Sara."

He turned off the engine and opened his door as quietly as he could. From the barn came a loud thud and then the sound of wood splintering. Cal began to run.

Sara had no intention of staying in the car. She ran after him. It sounded as if a bull elephant was running amok in the barn, for the tinkle of broken glass and the clang of metal had added themselves to the noise.

The side door had been broken open. She blinked at Cal's low-voiced epithet, quite sure he did not know she was behind him, and followed him through Peg's office, which did not appear to have been touched, into the workshop.

A bull elephant had not run amok. Percy Gillis had. The chaos was indescribable and the noise deafening, for like a man possessed Percy was laying about him with a metal sledgehammer. Cal's roar of protest came too late. The sledgehammer smashed through the hood of the grandfather clock.

Cal moved so quickly that all Sara saw was a blur. He lifted Percy bodily, holding him three feet above the ground. The sledgehammer was wrenched from Percy's hand, remaining imbedded in the carved mahogany face of the clock. Percy's legs flailed the air. "Put me down!" he squealed, and added a string of curses that made Cal's single outburst pale in comparison.

"That clock was for Sara!" Cal cried in a choked voice, and shook Percy so that his head wobbled on his skinny neck like a throttled chicken's.

The sound of her own name galvanized Sara to action. The man of violence had reappeared, the man Cal himself feared. She feared him, too. She scurried round the band saw; its metal surface had been dinted by the sledgehammer. Cal must not be allowed to hurt Percy in the heat of anger. He would never forgive himself. Worse, he would never marry her. She knew him well enough for that.

Fully prepared to launch herself at him, she braced herself against the workbench, her boots scrunching among the shards of broken glass. Neither man saw her. Their eyes were locked, Cal's in outrage, Percy's in abject terror. "Put me down," Percy shrilled. "If you'd left them dogs alone, not stuck your nose in where it's not wanted, I wouldn't be here."

Cal's face changed. He gave his head a little shake, fury replaced by a gradual, ironic acceptance of a situation that, because it included Percy, also included elements of farce. He lowered Percy to the ground, if not gently, at least with no intent to harm. Gripping Percy's sleeve, he said, "So this is all my fault, is it? You don't believe that any more than I do, Percy."

With his feet on the floor rather than in the air, Percy was bolder. "You made a fool of me in front of Pete and Ralphie. Thought this'd teach you a lesson."

"Well, it's sure taught me—"

Afterward Sara was never sure what made her turn her head. Did the smallest of sounds alert her? The clink of broken glass or the shuffle of a boot in the sawdust on the floor? Whatever the reason, she dragged her gaze away from Percy and Cal to the shadowed corner across from her.

A man in a checked jacket was creeping up behind Cal. He was crouched low, carrying a metal wrecking bar.

She blinked, wondering if she had drunk too much wine. But the man did not go away. He had stringy black hair. His eyes were glued to Cal's back as he began to raise the metal bar. It was curved, ending in two points.

Percy was forgotten. Sara grabbed a hammer from the bench and hurled herself at Cal's attacker. "Don't you do that!" she cried, much as if he had been Malcolm about to throw a rock at an unsuspecting bird.

Then everything happened very fast. The man's head swung round; visibly his close-set eyes switched targets from Cal to herself. He jabbed the bar at her as if it were a spear. Automatically she stepped backward.

Cal elbowed her aside, seized the wrecking bar and flung it to the ground with a bellow of rage. The effect on the black-haired man was dramatic. With the speed of one who has departed fights before, he ducked, spun around and ran for the door to Peg's office.

Cal lunged after him. Then he stopped dead as abruptly as if he had run into a stone wall. The blind rage retreated from his eyes, leaving them rinsed clear and sane and steady. He passed a hand over his forehead, and his shoulders sagged as he let out his breath. The outer door of the barn slammed shut.

Very slowly Cal turned his head to look at Sara. "I didn't do it," he said. "When he went for you, I saw red. But then something happened, and I knew I had to let him go."

She wanted to throw her arms around Cal and hug him. But from the corner of her eye she could see Percy edging toward Peg's office. "You might as well let Percy go, as well," she said.

Cal made a valiant effort to gather his wits. "No, Percy lives here, the other guy's a stranger. Come here, Percy."

"I ain't done nuthin'," Percy whined, rather ludicrously under the circumstances.

"I hate to disagree with you," Cal said with a touch of wintry humor. "Percy, I'm going to do two things. First of all I'm going to get Sara to write out a list of everything you've damaged in here and you're going to sign it. I'll keep the list just in case I ever need it. And secondly, I'm going to get myself a dog, maybe a German shepherd, and train it to keep people like you off my property."

Percy's face was full of self-righteous indignation. "I won't sign no list!"

"Yes, you will. Because if you don't I'll call the police." Cal surveyed the destruction all around him and his mouth tightened. "A policeman won't think this is a joke. You want to see the inside of a jail?"

Percy's jaw dropped, revealing uneven, tobacco-stained teeth. "I'm an old man, they wouldn't touch me."

As if he could not bear to prolong the conversation, Cal propelled Percy over to a pine chair, which was untouched by the sledgehammer. "You sit there while Sara writes the list."

Percy tugged at his cap, his bloodshot eyes narrowing craftily. "I never learned to write my name."

"Won't work, Percy. I've seen you sign welfare cheques." Cal glanced over his shoulder. "Get a move on, Sara, I want him out of here."

Sara got paper and a pen from Peg's office and began laboriously annotating the damage, which was not quite as bad as it looked. Half an hour with a broom would clean up much of the mess. The band saw was dented and two hickory chairs had been reduced to kindling. The battered face of the grandfather clock made her feel sick. Quickly she added the clock to the list and passed it to Cal. "Sign it, Percy," he said in a level voice. "Or I'll call the police."

Cal, who was a very large man, was between Percy and the door. Scowling ferociously, Percy scrawled his name across the bottom of the list and threw it back at Cal, who added pleasantly, "And please don't swear at me. There's a lady present. Sara, you keep this list for now while I walk Percy to the end of the driveway. I just want to make sure he knows the way home."

Sara drew back as Percy shambled past her; he smelled as pungently of rum as the workshop smelled of varnish. Too much rum and too little soap, she thought, wrinkling her nose. Then she bent down and began picking up nails, sorting them into little piles on the counter.

When Cal came back in the barn he said grimly, "I put the fear of God in him. He won't be back."

"It's a good thing we got home when we did. I think he was just getting warmed up."

Cal kicked aside a broken jar and took hold of the sledgehammer, levering it from the ruined face of the clock. "I wish we'd been two minutes earlier, we might have saved this," he said, running his finger over the gouged mahogany as gently as though it were an open wound. "I was making it for you."

One of the rosettes he had carved for the hood was lying in the sawdust on the floor. Sara stooped and picked it up. Cal had put hours of work into the clock already. She could not say facilely, "Make me another one."

"I'll make you another," he said, "for a wedding present."

She nearly dropped the rosette. "Who am I marrying?" she croaked.

"Me."

There was a gap of several feet and a battered band saw between them. She allowed all her love to show in her face and said, "Cal, are you asking me to marry you?"

"Yeah...I meant to do it differently, take you for another candlelit dinner or propose on the lakeshore under a full moon. But I've got to ask you now—and you know why, don't you?"

She smiled. "Because Percy walked out of here in one piece and because you didn't attack the other man. In other words, you kept your temper."

"I lost it when I saw the clock—my gift for you, ruined. But I couldn't hurt Percy. It was as if I saw him as he was, a pathetic small-time bootlegger who's too much of a coward to do anything to your face. And then I even managed to keep my cool when the other guy—his name's Pete, by the way—went for you. If I can do that, I never need to worry about my temper again—because you're the most precious person in the world to me."

"No more skeletons in the closet," Sara said shakily.

"That's right. Sara, I could feel the anger literally drain away. Like water running down a sink."

"Don't you remember what I told you once? That there were all kinds of reasons for you to fight as a kid, but that those reasons don't exist anymore."

"Yeah, I remember. And you were right. At thirteen I was as full of anger as Percy is of rum, and I guess it had to find an outlet. I even know why I was angry—because I always felt cheated. I saw all the nice kids from the good homes, where the parents had jobs and the kids had proper clothes and went skiing in Vermont at Christmas and down south in the March break, and I felt as if that world was totally beyond my reach. It's not beyond my reach now, though. If I want those things I can have them. So the anger's gone, Sara. I don't need to fight anymore."

She sensed that she should not touch him. Not yet. "That's a major victory," she said.

"Part of the reason I've changed is because I'm learning to read. I can't pick up a novel yet and read it from cover to cover. But I can read a map so we can go on a trip, and I can read a menu so we can go out for dinner, and the carpentry books are making more and more sense every time I pick them up. For the first time in my life I feel as though I can fit into society... I'm part of the current in the river, not the rock the river flows around and leaves behind. I've moved out of the darkness and into the light. Sara, I'm not explaining myself very well, and for God's sake don't think I'm asking you just because I'm grateful for all you've done, because that's not the case at all...but will you marry me?"

"Provided you tell me why you're asking."

"Because I love you. Because I can be real with you. Because I can't live without you." His smile was infectious. "Will that do for a start?"

"Oh, that's a very good start."

"There are other reasons. I want us to have children and to bring them up together...does that interest you?"

"Very much."

"And the best way to keep my reading teacher is to have her under my own roof."

"Barefoot and pregnant?" Sara said quizzically.

He laughed. "You're far too strong-minded to fall into that trap, sweetheart. But there is one more reason."

"And what's that?"

"I want to see if we can keep our hands off each other when we're ninety."

"I rather doubt that we'll be able to," she said.

He grabbed a piece of wood for a stick, hunched his shoulders and shuffled over to her like an old man, his hands shaking and his eyes peering at her shortsightedly. "I might have trouble finding you."

"Then I'll have to put myself in your path, won't I?" Sara said, suiting action to the words.

His face was at a level with hers. "Why, I do believe it's my dear wife Sara," he muttered in a cracked voice, and suddenly was kissing her with all a young man's ardor.

She had been waiting for this all day. Into the first pause she muttered, "Oh, Cal, I do love you," and into the second, "We don't have to wait until we're ninety, do we?"

"Since I refuse to make love on a floor covered with nails, sawdust and broken glass, you'll have to wait until we can get from here to the bedroom."

"So why are we standing here talking?"

"Because there's one thing we haven't settled yet."

She looked at him in faint dismay. "Not another skeleton?"

"I asked you a question a couple of minutes ago. You haven't really given me your answer."

"Oh." She smiled at him, her face alight with love. "Yes, Cal, I'll marry you. I can't imagine anything that would give me greater joy."

He took her face in his hands, his gray eyes deeply serious. "I pledge myself to you, Sara, body and soul. For as long as I live."

"And I to you." Her voice not quite steady, she added, "We scarcely need a wedding ceremony."

"Yes, we do. I want the whole world to know I love you—certainly the whole village of Haliburton. Even though, essentially, it comes down to you and me."

"You and me," Sara echoed. "I like the sound of that."

He gave her the smile she was beginning to recognize. "Maybe we should sleep on it. Just to be sure."

"I'm perfectly sure," she said demurely. "But we could head for the bedroom anyway, I suppose."

And eventually they did fall asleep.

For the millions who can't read
Give the Gift of Literacy

One out of five adults in North America
cannot read or write well enough
to fill out a job application
or understand the directions on a bottle of medicine.

**You can change all this by joining the fight
against illiteracy.**

For more information write to:
Contact, Box 81826, Lincoln, Neb. 68501
In the United States, call toll free: 800-228-3225

**The only degree you need
is a degree of caring**

"This ad made possible with the cooperation of the Coalition for Literacy and the Ad Council."
Give the Gift of Literacy Campaign is a project of the book and periodical industry,
in partnership with Telephone Pioneers of America.

LIT—A—1

Harlequin Superromance

COMING NEXT MONTH

#258 PINECONES AND ORCHIDS • Suzanne Ellison
Real Estate Agent Robbin Walker is flabbergasted
when her best friend and neighbor, Safety Inspector
Ted Ballard, starts talking marriage! Robbin had always
dreamed of being swept off her feet with orchids and
fancy dinners . . . not corsages made out of pinecones or
sharing noisy meals with their families at the local pizza
joint! Or is that what real love is all about. . . .?

#259 NOW THERE'S TOMORROW • Cara West
Amber's career as a divorce mediator provides her with
all the real-life drama anyone could crave, so she isn't
interested in the advances of an exciting ex-cop turned
renovator. But when a child is inexplicably left on her
doorstep, Amber decides that a man like Gil Massey
could be very helpful indeed. . . .

#260 WHAT COMES NATURALLY • Margaret Gayle
Finding herself on a canoe trip in the wilds of northern
Ontario without mousse, blow-dryer or makeup is
highly exasperating for Elizabeth Wright. But the worst
part is facing cosmetics rival, Justin Archer. Gradually
the two of them begin to let their hair down—in more
ways that one.

#261 THIS TIME FOR US • Elaine K. Stirling
When Sylvie Castellano volunteers to help
Russ McTaggart with his scale-model designs, she is
doing more than assembling miniature fences. She is
finding the strength through Russ and his work to
piece together her life. . . .

ATTRACTIVE, SPACE SAVING BOOK RACK

Display your most prized novels on this handsome and sturdy book rack. The hand-rubbed walnut finish will blend into your library decor with quiet elegance, providing a practical organizer for your favorite hard-or soft-covered books.

Only $9.95

Approximately 16" x 8" when assembled

Assembles in seconds!

To order, rush your name, address and zip code, along with a check or money order for $10.70* ($9.95 plus 75¢ postage and handling) payable to *Harlequin Reader Service*:

Harlequin Reader Service
Book Rack Offer
901 Fuhrmann Blvd.
P.O. Box 1325
Buffalo, NY 14269-1325

Offer not available in Canada.

*New York residents add appropriate sales tax.

BKR-1R

Take 4 books & a surprise gift FREE

SPECIAL LIMITED-TIME OFFER

Mail to   **Harlequin Reader Service**®

In the U.S.   In Canada
901 Fuhrmann Blvd.   P.O. Box 609
P.O. Box 1394   Fort Erie, Ontario
Buffalo, N.Y. 14240-1394   L2A 5X3

YES!   Please send me 4 free Harlequin American
Romance® novels and my free surprise gift. Then send me 4
brand-new novels every month as they come off the presses. Bill
me at the low price of $2.25 each*—a 10% saving off the retail
price. There is no minimum number of books I must purchase. I
can always return a shipment and cancel at any time. Even if I
never buy another book from Harlequin, the 4 free novels and the
surprise gift are mine to keep forever.   154 BPA BP7S
*Plus 49¢ postage and handling per shipment in Canada.

Name   (PLEASE PRINT)

Address   Apt. No.

City   State/Prov.   Zip/Postal Code

This offer is limited to one order per household and not valid to present
subscribers. Price is subject to change.   DOAR-SUB-1A